Book One of The King's Renegade

ASUNDER

A Vatan Chronicle
by
L. Steinworth

Cover art and design:

Liz Steinworth

www.theartofliz.com

Editors:

Kim Gibson

www.kmgibson.ca

Erica Russikoff

www.ericaedits.com

Map:

Doug Turner

www.aylethbook.com

Dedicated to my mother

The strongest person I know.

AUTHOR'S NOTE

One can view a work of art and arrive at their own conclusions about what the piece's mood and meaning is, but they can't ever truly know the artist's intent. This realization gripped me hard ever since I began painting 'Burden' in 2014. As I layered on a series of brush strokes, I was compelled to tell the story hiding behind the character's hood. And so, I wrote.

VATAN

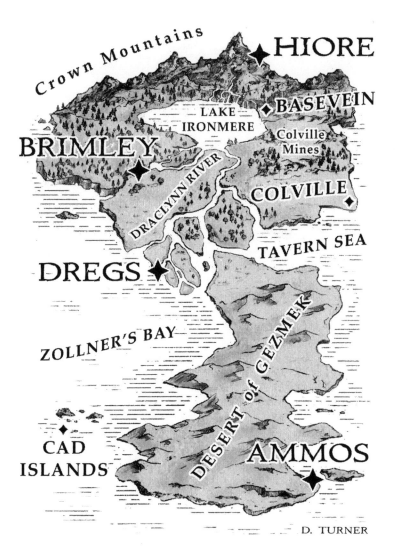

D. TURNER

CONTENTS

THE AMBUSH

CHAPTER ONE

Squirrel beamed as if he'd just found the lost treasure of Gezmek. Understandable, as the merchant's cart passing by carried a mound of colorful Ammosian silks that shimmered like jewels. Each piece was as alluring as the next, and the boy was spellbound.

Alden appreciated Squirrel's fascination—the fabrics were beautiful. Some changed from a radiant gold to a deep lavender. Others reflected leaves or the cloudy sky above, seemingly blending in with the world. But beside the brilliant luster, the silks were also desired for their durability as they were strong like armor.

An eager grin began to spread mischievously across Squirrel's freckled face as the merchants neared. Then he raised his bow.

Damnit...

Squirrel flinched as Alden grabbed him by the scruff. The boy shifted as if he had only been stretching his legs then glanced up with crescent-shaped eyes, pleading innocence. Alden shook his head, knowing all too well the thief's inner desires. With a light shove, he released him. Squirrel scurried beside a nearby boulder, attempting to hide in it's shade.

Alden frowned. Squirrel desperately needed a new cloak, and one which could deflect a blade or his carelessness would be perfect. After years of action and neglect, what he wore now bore holes so large that it did little to conceal the thief.

After this heist, I'll buy him a silk cloak, even it it means forfeiting my own rations again.

Alden surveyed his other companions on the hill. His shadow commander studied the road below like a hawk stalking prey. He wore a fine, black woolen cowl over a long suede jacket. Secured around his chest, arms, and legs was a complete set of thick boiled leather armor. Alden picked at his fraying bracer, wishing he could afford such luxuries. As if sensing the scrutiny, the commander turned to exchange a glance. A flare of hatred sparked between them and Alden rolled his head away.

Higher up the hill sat Trod and Paige.

Trod sat tense and alert. He held a bit of rope tight between his hands, weaving it now and again between his dark ebony fingers. A buzzing bee hovering around his bald head didn't even break his concentration from the road, ready for the ambush to begin at a moment's notice.

Paige, however, watched the bee with interest. When the bug flew away, the pale, orange-haired woman shifted to watch colorful leaves blow off trees, the passing of clouds, and even the ground.

Rumors were that they were lovers, yet Alden could see no true signs of courtship. He suspected similar gossip was said about himself and his partner. *If only.*

Alden turned to look at her. In the setting sun, his partner's short brown hair glowed like a bush caught aflame as it danced wildly in the wind. The lower half was longer and woven into a raggedy braid which rested on her chest. Alden followed the line down to explore her body's fit contour. Strong arms held her as she leaned against the hill. His gaze paused when her tunic fluttered in the settling breeze, showing off a set of toned, leather-covered legs. The glimmer of a hidden dagger winked at him. Then a gust of wind whipped the fabric in a flurry, sending Alden's eyes back to her face. His partner studied the environment around her with a smile. *Kira.*

Kira leaned forward as a pair of riders trotted down the trail. Although they looked to be capable protectors, they led no carriage. Like the silk cart, they weren't the intended victims. The thief eased back down into the grass, letting her legs kick up then sway. She huffed and threw Alden a look of impatience.

Alden shrugged.

Two dimples formed on each side of Kira's full lips as she continued to stare at him playfully. Alden wanted to glance away, disallowing his eyes and heart the pleasure of viewing her, but he couldn't help but smile back. He knew that look. It was the same roguish one she'd given him the day they met, the day fate had allowed him to enter this life.

Movement from around the bend drew their attention. It was a carriage escorted by a troop of well-armed guards. Thin, shining plate armor protected their bodies. Black capes danced proudly with the troop's synchronized steps.

The carriage they protected was just as extravagant. Hand-carved details with finely painted trim outlined its curves. Lavishly embroidered curtains hung in the windows behind a decorative screen. Even the steps leading to the door had a chiseled design.

"Reynold," said Trod in a hushed tone to the shadow commander. He pointed down the road.

Reyn nodded, having already seen it, and crouched with a thirsty grin. "Get ready."

"You must keep your dress pristine, Mayli Drake!" scolded a dry and cracking voice.

Mayli rolled her eyes. "Lidia, our silk is anything but delicate," she said before biting a spicy chocolate cookie. The snap of the crisp treat sent a layer of crumbs down into her lap, dusting the shimmering orange gown with crumbs.

Her lady-in-waiting growled as she brushed Mayli clean of debris. "But your presentation is!" She leaned back and dabbed her hands clean on a handkerchief. "And today is an important time to show it! Now straighten up. Princes have little patience for such indecorous mannerisms, as should you!" Lidia gave an encouraging slap on her thigh.

Mayli obeyed with an irritated moan.

In the absence of conversation, Mayli listened to the slop of mud under the carriage's wheels, the rhythmic marching of boots crunching dried leaves, the clang of scabbards clashing against armor, and the swoosh of capes beating in the wind. To ensure proper provisions had been made before her arrival, her father, King Bakhari, sent guards to work with the local sentries to lock up scoundrels, shoo away beggars, and relocate the homeless out of main streets. A troop even spent two days scouting ahead for possible threats. They found nothing, but Mayli still requested extra men to escort her through northern Vatan.

A guard sat quietly across from her, unconcerned. His shoulders were drooped and his hand rested away from the hilt of his sword. Dark skin melded with the shadow under the protective cover of his helm and white scarf. Beyond it, Mayli saw that his brow was relaxed and eyes soft as he watched out the window.

His name was Kelvan, or possibly Kent. She couldn't quite remember. When they were introduced, it had been brief as if she had just met a horse or been presented a ship—just a tool used to serve a purpose, not a friend to provide good company. He was handsome, like many in the force. Each were strong, fit men with an unquestionable dedication to her and her family. Mayli knew many well and cherished their company. This guard, however, she did not know—yet.

She smiled. "Anything interesting out there?"

The guard blinked, unsure if he was being addressed. Mayli watched with amusement as he looked to Lidia as if the old woman cared to see the world around her. She was too focused on threading through the final laces of a white and decorative corset. Mayli eyed the item, remembering the torturous device would soon be wrapped around her.

Then she smiled impishly and flashed her eyes to the guard. "You'll have to help with that later. Lidia's fingers are growing weak, but I'm sure your strong hands can tighten it nicely around me!" Mayli leaned toward the guard with an inviting gaze.

Lidia ended her fuss with the lace and stared in horror. "Mayli Drake!"

"What?" Mayli cried innocently. "I can't put it on myself! And you complain about your crooked old fingers all the time! Why shouldn't the man help my lady-in-waiting so nobly?"

Sour wrinkles grew around the woman's tight-pursed lips. The glare enhanced the old woman's age, making her appear ancient.

Mayli batted her eyes to her guard, expecting an alluring smirk or bite of interest to her invitation. However, he lacked either, and only shifted uncomfortably as he averted his gaze back out the window. Mayli sighed and leaned back against the wall to do the same. Kendel, she finally decided, bored her.

She wished her previous escort, Charli Damgard, was accompanying her. Mayli was sure that, by now, they would have been deep in conversation about the differences across Vatan's landscape. Charli would go on to explain that, unlike the dry climate of Ammos, the leaves in the north changed in color and then fell off because the trees were preparing for the colder months. Although she knew already, she would listen. There was always something Charli could enlighten her about as he was well-traveled, served in the war, and had explored the Desert of Gezmek.

When the topic of local knowledge became exhausting, Charli and she would philosophize over something silly, like what made the best archer: a cat or a rat. Mayli guessed a cat, but she knew he would—for the sake of challenging her—claim the rat as the victor for reasons she'd fail to consider. Charli always made a point to help expand her knowledge and discuss anything to keep her mind from wandering down a dark path. A charming trait he developed to help her forget the horrors from three years past.

An earthy crack boomed, jarring Mayli from thought. Her guard no longer possessed his calm demeanor and was now ready and alert—one hand tight around the hilt of his sword and the other on the door's handle.

Lidia, however, took a calm breath and put her hands in her lap. "Just a thunderclap, my lady. Storms are frequent here this time of year."

Then, horses whinnied and the carriage began to shake. At first only slightly, but then violently as the rolling thunder grew. Just as Mayli turned her head to the window she saw several boulders charging down the hill. She threw herself away from the window and clung to Lidia. Together, they prepared for impact.

⯇————⯇

Alden leapt onto the overturned carriage. As it teetered, he steadied himself into a crouch and pulled at the door. "Locked," he called.

Kira landed alongside him, taking out a set of small tools. Alden guarded while she picked the lock, but there wasn't much of a fight left. The landslide had gone exactly as Paige and Trod had planned, leaving many guards lost under rocks and logs. Those who had survived were facing a worse fate of battling shadows.

Squirrel stayed on the hill, using a boulder as cover as he exchanged arrows with an archer below. Alden feared the contest between bows would end soon with his friend on the losing side, but Reyn slipped past a flurry of blades and tumbled to introduce his long rapier into the back of the skilled archer. A loud cry echoed off the hills.

"And open," Kira said. With a flick of her wrist, the carriage's door swung wide.

Alden inhaled as the alluring smell of spiced perfume whiffed out. Together they cautiously peered inside. Pillows, blankets, and the drapery hung over everything like a gypsy den. Cookies littered the floor.

A young woman sat rubbing her head. He guessed her to be only a few years younger than himself at the tail end of her teen years, but her thick makeup hid the truth. She had tanned olive skin, which lay mostly hidden behind a white feathered jacket and shimmering orange dress. Wrapped loosely around her black hair was a silk scarf to match the gown.

A guard was crouched beside an older woman, checking for a pulse. Before he could catch a read, he threw his head up, noticing them. He stood and attempted to release his sword from his scabbard. However, from within the confines of the small overturned carriage, he knocked his elbow against the side, failing to draw his blade completely out.

"Lemme help ya with that!" Kira offered kindly, then dove in. Her boot met the guard's chest and sent him against the arched roof with a grunt. Kira gripped the hilt and twisted it free from his scabbard. In one quick motion, she used the man's own blade to split his neck.

Alden winced as the young woman screamed, watching the murder. But no blood escaped the guard. The man coughed from the blow, then blinked.

"Damn Ammosian silk," Kira growled. Before the guard could fight back, she knocked him out.

Now safe, Alden hopped down with a thud, startling his target. She backed away as if she could flee. Alden shook his head. "Sorry, there's no escape," he said, creeping forward.

The woman swiped, forcing Alden to dodge claws to his face. Seizing the opportunity, she hopped up to catch the ledge of the carriage. Before she could pull herself up, Alden snatched her jacket and yanked. Feathers from it exploded into the air as she fell into him.

Alden stared in disbelief at the woman's now exposed shoulder. Upon her shoulder was a tattoo; a falcon with wings spread in the shape of a pulled composite bow with four-pointed stars flanking its sides and head. But because the crest was illustrated with a shield, Alden knew it wasn't just a noble coat of arms of Ammos...

She was royalty.

His breathing stopped, but his heart pounded loud in his ears. Not even the continuous screams from outside the carriage could compete with the warning bells inside his head. He felt her struggling in his arms and realized then that he was squeezing her. Timidly, Alden broke his gaze from the brand and locked eyes with Princess Mayli Drake.

"Nice!" said Kira.

Alden glanced at his partner, expecting her knowing stare, but the thief was busy pocketing a coin purse and stuffing a few cookies in her mouth. Quickly, he shrugged the princess's jacket up to cover her tattoo. "Ki, focus."

"Yeah, yeah..." she said, sliding over.

Mayli squirmed and threw a kick as Kira approached. The thief grabbed her foot before it met her face. She then held her while Alden finished securing the princess's arms back with rope. Once bound, he used the scarf to blind and gag her.

There was a whistle.

"Time to go," Kira said, clamping Alden on his shoulder before leaping to the open door.

Alden gently hoisted Mayli up, dodging kicking feet as Kira helped pull her out. He followed after.

The thick smell of dirt and blood hit his nose. His gut turned, seeing the litter of fallen Ammosian guards. Many were dead or nearing death and Reyn was taking it upon himself to finish off anyone pleading for their lives. Trod worked at freeing the tethered horses from the carriage, trying to calm them while Paige watched down the path. Squirrel, now freed from his post up on the hill, floated around each body, blissfully gathering loot. He found a small sack and emptied its contents into his hand. He squealed with joy.

"Coin?" Kira asked, hopping to the ground.

"Better!" Squirrel raised his hand in victory. "Chocolate-covered coffee beans!"

"More energy is the last thing you need, Squirrel!"

The boy popped a handful into his mouth and chewed proudly. Kira furrowed her brow. Squirrel slowed his munching, looked away, and gulped forcefully.

When Kira glanced his way, Alden pulled his hood tight to ensure it still concealed his face. He felt sick, heart reeling at the revelation of whom he had just attacked. He clenched his fists till the knuckles turned white.

Why her?

"Get your asses going, before someone else comes along!" Reyn snapped as he used his boot to shove the last crying guard off his rapier. He whipped his blade and blood sprayed across the ground in a slick red line, pointing the way. Some landed on Alden's cheek, dripping down like a warm tear. Alden glared, wishing he could paint the same stroke of crimson across the shadow commander's face. Reyn gave Alden a cocky sneer before marching up the hill.

Kira attempted to follow, but the Princess of Ammos fought back like a wild horse—kicking and tugging with all her might. As the thief wrestled to break her, Alden came to his partner's side and tried to gently lead Mayli. Still, she stubbornly twisted and struggled, making the uphill climb difficult.

With an annoyed moan, Reyn slid down the slope, dirt flaring up in his wake. He shoved Alden into Kira, breaking their grip on their prisoner. Without hesitation, the shadow commander punched Princess Mayli squarely in the jaw. The unexpected blow sent the blindfolded woman to the ground. She lay unconscious.

"She's supposed to be unhurt!" Alden growled, crouching to check on the princess.

Reyn scoffed. "Well, then, keep her under control." He gestured towards where he'd hit her. "That's on you."

Alden fumed, fighting the urge to finally slit Reyn's throat. *Killing him would be justifiable*, he thought touching his knife, but Reyn saw the act and smirked. Keeping his composure, Alden pushed his feelings aside and gently scooped Mayli up.

Together, they faded into the forest above. Paige took the lead, navigating the woods effortlessly, only taking a few short moments to touch a tree, study the wind, or read the landscape. Eventually, she stopped at the mouth of a small cave where a set of precariously placed rocks loomed above the entrance. Once everyone was inside, Trod tugged at a rope. A loud snap echoed through the corridor as boulders fell, sealing them inside the dark tunnel.

Paige lit a torch and started surveying the walls. While they waited for her to get her bearings, Alden set the princess carefully on the ground. He lightly pulled her hair away. With a pointed button nose, long black lashes and tanned skin, the Princess of Ammos was as beautiful as rumors had told. He frowned, seeing a deep red bruise peeking out from under her gag. Alden knew how hard Reyn liked to punch, and the man had no reservations when it came to women.

"Was that *really* necessary?" Alden snarled as he stood to face Reyn.

The shadow commander cocked his head.

Alden gestured toward the unconscious woman to illustrate his complaint.

Reyn huffed with annoyance. "There's a reason you aren't usually on these missions," he said under his breath, glaring at Kira. He snarled. "We're not in the business of chivalry. If you don't have the guts to use force next time, use this." Reyn shoved a vial into Alden's chest and brushed past.

"What brew is that?" Kira asked.

"Still don't recognize it?" Reyn scanned Kira up and down. "No, perhaps not... It tends to make one forget..." he said, winking.

Kira covered her mouth in disgust and Alden pulled Kira behind him.

Reyn smiled between them. "Just have her breathe it in. Will do the same thing I did to the girl—just not as fun."

"And you only give this to me now? Could have been helpful in the carriage!"

Reyn displayed teeth that shone an even brighter shade of yellow in the torchlight. "I was curious to see what you were capable of. Not much, as it turns out."

Alden narrowed his eyes at Reyn, but the shadow commander straightened up, unthreatened.

"The way has been found," said a chalky voice.

They all looked to Trod. Beside him was Paige, pointing quietly.

Reyn brushed past Alden, nearly knocking the vial from his grasp. He pocketed it, then lifted the princess back into his arms with tender care.

Alden followed his party as they traveled down seemingly endless halls. Each turn was like a labyrinth, but Paige led them confidently. She touched the walls and surveyed the floor as if it told secrets only she could hear.

After hours, an eerie breeze blew over him. It was warm and smelled of sweet hill blossoms. Stepping around the corner revealed the forest and sky. The beautiful auburn sunset shone through the canopy of swaying trees. Their tall trunks danced around the mouth of the pit, tossing leaves into the cave as if welcoming its visitors.

A decaying corpse of a young deer lay on the ground. From its broken leg Alden assumed that it had fallen into the mine. Trod walked over to investigate. He took out some dried weeds and flowers bound tightly in a string. He placed it on the deer's skull, mumbled a few words Alden couldn't understand, and then retrieved the bundle.

"Get this place in order. Pierz will be here at dawn!" Reyn commanded, kicking the bones aside, earning a scowl from Trod. He ignored the look and rolled out a blanket in the middle of the pit.

Alden brought Mayli to a gnarly tangle of roots protruding from the cave wall. Sweat beaded on his brow as Kira kept a watchful eye on how he tied the princess. Nervous, he roughly added an extra knot and met Kira's gaze. She frowned and continued helping prepare a fire.

After a while, the smell of thyme and cooked meat began to bloom. Squirrel bounced impatiently on his knees for it to finish cooking, occasionally popping one of his chocolate-covered coffee beans in his mouth. Finally, Reyn helped himself to a bowl and a roasted rabbit leg. This invited Squirrel to do the same, followed by the rest.

Alden waited to be last. When he reached for his serving, he found only a few chunks of meat and a couple potatoes floating in a thin broth. Alden took a labored mouthful and chewed slowly. Each bite felt like a chore, as his concern for the princess ruined his usually substantial hunger.

Swallowing his last bite, grief struck him. *Mayli would be starved, and a warm meal might have helped her trust me.*

Alden rolled his head to look at Reyn. "Who's our client?"

Reyn's stringy, black hair drooped in front of his beady eyes as he leaned forward. He pointed his hulk of rabbit at Alden. "That's none of your concern," he said with a discussion-ending tone. He then ripped into the meat with a ravenous bite.

"Do you know who the woman is?"

Reyn spat out some gristle at Alden's feet. "It's irrelevant! She could be a farmer's daughter, my sister, or a queen. All we do is what Pierz says. This time, it's kidnapping. Last week, we secured a bribe then robbed the same client. Who it is, or for what reason, doesn't matter. It's no different from any other job, Alden. It's just how we make a living. So, until we hear back from Pierz, just sit tight!" Reyn sat up and threw his unfinished leg of rabbit into the fire. "It's going to be a long night, and we need to be well rested for tomorrow. Take shifts. Alden and Kira, you first."

Alden took a breath, concluding Reyn didn't know the young woman they kidnapped was Princess Mayli, or did and still didn't care. He wouldn't put it past him. The man didn't need a reason to kill, steal, or fight. He'd do it solely for the thrill, making him the perfect shadow commander for the Shadowen Thieves Guild. It took many years of unquestionable dedication for Reyn to have achieved rank just under their leader, Pierz.

Reyn flung himself into his bedroll and settled in as the others finished their meals. Paige and Trod were next to retire and lay side-by-side in a far-off corner, whispering quietly.

Before Squirrel retreated, he extended his hand. Alden looked at the clenched fist questionably. Squirrel bobbed it and grinned cheerfully, instructing him to accept his offering. As Alden opened his palm, the boy released a handful of chocolate-covered coffee beans. Alden smiled back, thanking him. He'd be needing the energy.

THE DECISION

CHAPTER THREE

Mayli shifted uncomfortably. Her face burned with pain from where someone had struck her. Never before had she personally been so greatly disrespected. She'd be sure to have her father strike down every last fool who dared touch her, especially the two who had apprehended her in the carriage. They had killed Lidia. Killed her guard, whose name she wished she had made a point to remember. *Ken? He died trying to defend me. Would Charli have fallen just the same?*

Mayli shivered, wishing her captives had the decency to provide her a blanket, a pillow…or anything. She shifted again but roots jabbed at her no matter which way she turned. Dirt crumbled and fell inside her dress and down her back. The more she moved, the more she found herself becoming covered in filth. Finally, feeling as though she was now part of the wall, she gave up.

Hushed voices murmured nearby. Curious, Mayli moved her head around in an attempt to peek beyond the blindfold. Through a crack, she could make out a pair of malevolent shadows silhouetted by the fire's faint glow.

Alden took out the bottle Reyn had given him. It held a clear liquid with oily orbs clinging to the surface. Closing his eyes, he rolled it in his hands, feeling the contours of the glass. He squeezed the bulbous bottom and absently played with the rope choking its neck as he debated using the drug on Kira. Alden had to trust that Reyn saved more elegant bottles for richer, deadlier poisons or their antidotes. From the simple design, this *had* to be just a sleep potion.

Reyn implied he had used this poison on Kira before...

Alden eyed the mound behind him where the shadow commander snored.

That bastard.

With a snarl, Alden looked back to the fire.

Kira was staring.

He froze.

She eyed what he held warily. "You're not talking much."

Ashamed, he pocketed the bottle. "Nothing to discuss."

"Uh-huh. Then what has ya so upset?"

"I'm not upset," Alden countered calmly.

Kira raised a brow.

He picked up a branch to poke the fire. Coals growled and hissed in response. He overturned a log, allowing the unburned tip access to the low flame. It crackled back as if to thank him, then the den grew brighter.

Kira leaned forward, resting her arms on her knees, and gave Alden a long, hard stare. One long enough for him to break his absent gaze from the hungry fire and finally look at her. When he did, she nodded toward their prisoner. "What about her?"

He resisted the urge to look at Mayli. His heart pounded knowing how well Kira could observe tells. "Just another job," Alden lied. He tried to sound uninterested, as if Reyn's words had made an impact.

"Yeah. But this is a good one," she said with gleeful confidence, looking at the woman and then back at him.

"It's the worst yet," he grumbled, tossing the stick into the diminishing fire and sulked further in his hood.

"Worse than in the Cads?"

"Maybe."

Alden leaned forward with the bottle clenched in his hand, but upon seeing him get up, Kira quickly stood and strapped the canvas bag across her back. "I'll get more wood," she offered sweetly, signaling him down with a wave of her hand.

Alden nodded and sat back in relief. Although he knew Kira well, he still watched in awe as she scaled the cliff face. She used roots as if she were a deckhand climbing a rope to tend sails, and nimbly hoisted herself upon ledges. As she skirted around, dirt fell and rocks loosened, threatening to break free from the thin web of roots holding them in place. After reaching the top, Kira smiled down at him. He smiled back, heart breaking. She waved, then disappeared into the forest. He listened to the crackling of leaves until the sounds became distant, and then, she was gone.

He stared longingly. *Bye, Kira.*

Seizing the opportunity, he moved like a fox—swift and silent —creeping up beside Princess Mayli. She lifted her head and let out a worried whimper. Alden checked back around the den to ensure the thieves still slumbered. He took another glance up to where Kira had vanished, relieved he didn't need to use the vial on his beloved friend to flee.

Alden gripped the bottle firmly and popped off its cork. Resisting the urge to smell the liquid first, he dampened a corner of his cloak and lifted it to the princess's nose. She jerked back and squirmed. Alden reacted quickly by pressing his cloak tight to her face. After a short moment, she quieted. His heart throbbed with worry, fearing Reyn had set him up, but Alden relaxed, seeing her chest still rising with breath as she slept. He pocketed the knockout drug.

"Alden?" asked a groggy, inquisitive voice.

Alden's back tingled with fear. He slipped his hand into his cloak and gripped his dagger. He turned on his heel and began to draw the blade, but as the inquisitor came into view a falling rock struck the lad's head. Squirrel crumbled to the floor, groaning as he lost consciousness. Dirt rolled down the cave wall from where Kira had climbed.

Must have been shaken loose when Kira climbed up. Lucky!

Alden squatted beside his friend and touched his head where the rock hit. He felt blood wetting his short hair and parted it to find a shallow cut and an egg-shaped lump developing. *He'll be fine. Besides, Kira will help when she returns.*

Absconding with his burden, Alden fled. He guessed which corners could lead him out, but only seemed to find himself deeper within the mines of Colville. Overwhelmed after hours wandering, he set the princess down.

Alden leaned against the rough stone wall to catch his breath. He looked down. Although he couldn't see, he knew the thinning soles of his boots needed mending. The little pay from the guild recently made waiting for his allowance taxing.

Luckily, Prince Briar Densen of Brimley was the captain of the guard in Dregs now, and paid him for passing along information about the Shadowen Thieves Guild. Unfortunately, it had been nearly a month since his last visit and he was down to just a few coppers. Enough to buy him a good cup of Brim tea and a mediocre meal.

Irritated by sharp rocks poking his back, Alden shoved off, bumping into the adjacent wall with his hands. He stroked the smooth surface of stone while he contemplated his plan. *The princess would hate it if she knew she was receiving help from a Densen.*

After a moment, he looked up.

Smooth? He smirked. *So, this is what the pathfinder was feeling for.*

He scooped Mayli over his shoulder. With one arm wrapped around the woman's legs, he let his other hand guide him along soft corners like a map until he was led up an inclined slope. At the end, he spotted a ladder that was bathed in the cool midnight light.

Alden took a step but the old wood snapped. He set Mayli down. The princess moaned, rolling her head. Cautiously, he stepped away and tested the ladder again. It creaked, complaining about his light weight, but held.

"Princess," he said calmly, announcing his presence.

Mayli lifted her head toward a gruff, disembodied voice. Everything was a haze and her ears rung along with a pounding headache. As she tried to move she felt restricted. Faint recollections of a carriage ride tempted her memory. *There was Lidia. A guard... Blood.* She flinched as a finger touched her cheek then worked its way to pull her blindfold off. She blinked to gain focus, then her eyes grew wide. *Thieves!*

The man quickly stood and looked away. "You need to climb. The ladder won't hold us both at once."

She glanced at the crumbled wood beside the man's scuffed boots. She followed the long brown cloak up to his face. The thief turned his head slightly, silhouetting his deep frown upon his stubbled chin in the night sky. A glint of white reflected in his eye from under his dark hood. Mayli swallowed.

The thief squatted beside her. The heavy scent of smoke and his musty sweat hit her as he leaned in. Mayli squinted her eyes shut and backed into the dirt wall as far as she could. The man advanced, wrapping his hands around her body. She squealed and jerked her knee into his gut.

"Uff…" grunted the man, backing off slightly.

As Mayli prepared to buck again, her feet were pressed down and a knife appeared before her face. She froze.

"Stop fighting me," the thief warned. "I'm just gonna tie your waist, then cut your hands free."

Staring at the black blade, Mayli nodded ardently.

Leaning in once more, the thief threaded the rope behind her back and tied a complicated knot securely around her waist. Then he gripped her arm before pressing the blade between her wrists. As each thread was severed, Mayli felt lighter. She gazed up at the open sky eagerly. Once freed, she reached up to her gag and pulled it off.

Before she could speak, the man interjected, "Best pretend that's still around your mouth. I don't want to argue with you."

She spat at his feet.

He stepped away, leash in hand, then gestured at the ladder.

Mayli cursed under her breath as she began her ascent. After one step, it cracked. Realizing just how brittle the wood was, she climbed more delicately, careful not to break any more wavering planks. Once she reached the open field above, she took off running.

Freedom!

She yelped as her stomach wrenched and she fell to the ground. The snap of wood burst from the cave as the thief hurried up the ladder. Mayli struggled on the ground, clawing desperately at the knot. He walked slowly toward her, coiling the rope in his hands.

"Help!" she called out desperately.

"I'm trying to help…"

Ignoring him, she scurried away.

"Of course. Why would you trust me…" groaned the man. He pulled once more, causing her to slip and fall mid-step. As she rolled to get up, he knelt beside her and snatched her arms. She gasped, tasting dirt as her head bore into the grass. He quickly tied the rope around her wrists and stuffed the scarf back into her mouth. A tickling piece of grass remained.

As she sobbed, the man groaned. "Until you can listen to reason, it is going to be this way," he said gently while moving to a respectful distance, rope in hand. "You can trust that I won't hurt you. I promise."

Mayli rolled to sit up, choking slightly as she took in a quavering breath. Once steady, she tilted her head towards him—glaring. Her body ached and her wrists burned from where she was bound. Her chin throbbed painfully as if someone had hit her. *Liar.*

After a moment, a cool breeze passed over the overgrown field and he turned his face away, as if ashamed.

She hobbled to stand.

"Ready?" he asked.

Mayli cursed but her words were lost behind the gag. He nodded and started down the trail. When she refused to follow he tugged, forcing her along.

Soon, they reached a thicket as dense as a castle wall. Mayli blinked as he stepped in and held back branches like a door. She scoffed at his chivalry and looked back to the open moonlit field. The grass waved in the wind, beckoning her to come run through it. Taking a breath deprived of fresh air, she said goodbye to her chance at freedom, then turned to cross the threshold, joining the thief among the shadows.

Under the canopy of trees, the moon failed to shine through, cloaking them in a world of darkness. While the man managed to dodge most obstacles, Mayli was blind to them and much less graceful. Clueless to a crack in the earth, she stepped into it. The thief, noticing the fall, turned to catch her. Mayli shrugged the man away. She fell, landing in a pile of sticks and needles. They jabbed everywhere her silk dress didn't cover. The man reached down but Mayli got up on her own and continued forth.

Mayli held back whimpers of pain. Her light, jeweled sandals provided little protection against the rocks, twigs, and debris that gouged at her exposed feet. Branches bit and tore at her, stealing away threads and feathers from her jacket like beggars demanding coin. She cried, feeling as though her dignity, too, was being stripped away.

After what seemed like a full turn of an hourglass, the woods finally cleared. Beyond it was a finely groomed cornfield that seemed to go on for a countless span of miles. As they traveled within the cover of the field, Mayli saw small homes along the road. She tugged like a stubborn mule at each passing building, desperate to fight her fate. The thief fought back, just as dedicated to his unknown goal. Exhausted from the fight, she once again fell limp in surrender, crying.

Mayli thought back to the voyage from Ammos to Colville the previous day. *That* was supposed to be the worst thing about her trip to Hiore. She despised being stuck on a ship, never being able to keep her balance from feeling ill. Lidia, her lady-in-waiting, would bring her a special brew of tea made to ease the sickness. Although it helped, she loathed the drink for several reasons. First, it was bitter; second, it originated from Brimley...

Mayli shook her head, trying to cast away a bad memory, but as she let go of one horror, another echoed in her mind: the carriage and poor Lidia.

"Bastard!" she yelled, but all she managed past the gag was a muffled growl.

The thief looked back at her and stopped. She dropped to her knees to regain her breath and relax her tired legs. He stood over her, watchful and alert, still poised and confident. She rolled her eyes and then looked to the dirt on her dress, feeling less so. After a short rest, he reached down and stood her up.

"Won't be much farther," he assured.

She turned up her nose and walked forward. She led the way for another mile until he directed her down a farm's access road lined by swaying rows of browning grain. At its end, surrounded by post-and-rail fencing, rested a millhouse that hugged a bend in the creek. Piles of rocks acted as garden fences and terraced walls of similar stonework held up the building's foundation. A large turning wheel groaned after completing each loop as it dipped back into the black water. Attached to the mill was an overhang that shaded a tired horse from moonlight.

Good, let's steal it so I can finally rest my feet. She wiggled her toes, relieving a pebble and easing a growing blister. Instead, the thief ushered her onto the porch. She blinked, as the thief politely knock.

Nothing stirred.

Slowly, she turned her head to look up at the hooded man. He glanced down for a moment, then pounded on the door.

"Dean!" he called, careful so his voice didn't carry over neighboring fields.

Again, they waited. When there was still no reply, he stepped back from under the canopy. He snatched a stone from off the wall and rolled it in his fingers. With a calculated aim, he tossed it up. The stone struck a window's shutter with a loud thunk. Finally, his persistence was rewarded by a candle's glow.

The shutter swung open and a head peered out the window. The millworker, who she guessed to be Dean, looked from the thief to her. His face twisted in disgust, then he and the light disappeared back inside.

Mayli exchanged another glance with the thief.

A moment later, the candle's glow reappeared behind the front door. There was a slick sound of metal scraping. Something clicked. A chain rattled. Finally, the door creaked open.

The old man, dressed in a dull blue nightgown, ushered them inside and quickly relocked the door behind them. He shifted to his right to tuck the drapes closed. He muttered curses as he found another window to cover. With the room now private, the miller jerked a serious look at the thief. His brows drew a deep line between his eyes. Mayli suspected the crevasse would split his head in two like an axe to a log if he tried glaring any harder.

"Why are *you* here?" the man snarled.

The thief ignored the miller's question and only looked around casually, as if admiring the humble decor.

"Who's here, love?" said a sweet voice.

Mayli looked up to see a large, round, sleepy-eyed woman appear at the top of the stairs. Upon seeing guests, she bobbed down and joined them in the open kitchen. She grabbed Dean's hand, leading the candle to the thief's hooded face, illuminating it.

Dark eyes twinkled in the dancing flame, revealing flecks of warm brown.

"Oh!" she gasped, throwing her heavy arms around him. The thief stiffened but then gently embraced her. A smile escaped his lips. The wife pulled back, holding his face. "You're so thin..."

"Answer me!" Dean's frown now matched his brow as he glared harder. He folded his arms.

"Uh." The thief pulled away from the wife's affectionate hands and looked at Mayli.

The woman gasped "Why...she's all tied up!" She hurried over and began releasing the gag.

Mayli's abductor inched forward, but Dean grabbed his shoulder, halting his approach. He shrugged him off and tried again. This time, the wife threw him a menacing look, warning him to stay back. At that, he obeyed.

"I'm Mary. What's your name, dear?" she asked in a soft, motherly tone as the scarf fell away from Mayli's mouth.

She lowered her head and exercised her jaw before replying. "Ma...Mayli." She decided to keep the introduction simple as friends of thieves didn't deserve the respect of formalities.

The woman shot her head back at the hooded man in both disgust and disbelief. Her chest expanded like a fluffed-up hen, and her face began to redden. He scowled back and nodded toward the cog room. She exited the kitchen with Dean, exchanging hushed words. The thief led Mayli to the railing and tied her to it. He gave it a firm tug before following the couple into the next room, slamming the door and leaving her alone.

Mayli tested the knot and tried to move her fingers to free herself. Hopeless. She looked around. The mill house was a small and quaint home, nothing extravagant. There was no table, only a counter space that hung over three stools. Tall cupboards surrounded the kitchen, doors open, exposing stacks of dishes and mismatched cups—some wood, some clay or even metal. She could have sworn one was gold, but decided it was likely copper. Sacks of wheat waiting to be milled filled every nook and cranny. Flour coated most surfaces like a light dusting of fresh desert snow.

Most everything in the home seemed to strictly serve the mill: scales, scoops, sifters, and gears sat on shelves. A broom accompanied by a pan and bucket rested in the corner. The walls bore little decoration, not even a painting, but one piece down the hall mounted proudly above the fireplace caught her eye—a shield. Half was painted in a dusty shade of blue, the other was left raw to shine silver. Illustrated on it was a black tree growing from a diamond-shaped seed. A pyramid of three raindrops was etched into the blue, revealing silver. The other side had the inverse of color and three stars. Thick scars cut across the metal, and a tight cluster of arrows were lodged deep inside, telling of its bloody past.

"The Brim War…"

The door swung back open and the thief emerged with clenched fists. He was snarling like a rabid dog. Mayli stepped out of his way as he strode into the kitchen nook and flung open a cupboard door. Irritably, he started throwing its contents on the polished wood-slab counter behind him.

Dean and Mary entered slowly, staring at her. She wanted to plead for their help but felt she'd find no sympathy among them.

The couple's alliance with the fallen kingdom proved that they, along with her abductor, were indeed enemies.

After the thief had successfully torn apart the pantry and left the kitchen a dismal mess, Mayli could see a staircase leading down. She leaned over to get a better look, but there was only darkness. She trembled, knowing that was likely her next destination.

The thief pulled out a quill and ink set as well as a piece of parchment from a pouch on his belt. He looked around as if searching for the right words and then began to write. After finishing, he folded the letter into thirds. He snatched the candle from Dean's hand. The miller took in a maddened breath.

The thief tipped the candle, making the flame hiss and let wax pool on the letter. With careful pressure, he stamped it with the pommel of his dagger. As it cooled, he gave the miller his instructions: "Since you won't let us stay another day, deliver this as fast as you can, but say *nothing* about our visit to anyone! *Just* the letter."

Dean sneered at the paper.

"Dammit, you don't have a choice!"

"Ah, fuck you!" Dean pointed his finger close to the thief's face, then whipped it toward Mayli. "And her too!"

"Dean Wilkus!" Mary hissed.

Dean looked to his wife and his gaze calmed, but only for a moment before raising his voice once more. "It's no thanks to her we're all living in shambles!"

Mayli jumped back from the accusation. "What?! No! Thank the Densens for Brimley's destruction!"

The thief looked to her, lips turning down before taking a steadied breath. Facing Dean he pleaded in a relaxed and enticing tone while offering the letter once more. "Look, none of us are to blame…"

"Hah!" Dean scoffed.

Mayli also huffed loudly, earning an irritated look from the thief before he rolled his eyes back to the miller.

The two men stared, each reluctant to break gaze. The hooded man raised his chin and straightened his posture, his hand resting casually on the hilt of his dagger. Dean grumbled and snatched the letter. "Fine." He then scowled unjustly at Mayli, who returned the look.

The thief positioned himself between them to break their contest and began to untie her. "Don't mind him," he said quietly.

Mayli blinked at the man who abducted her. "Don't mind him?"

He walked her to the staircase beyond the cupboards. Terrified of what fate awaited her in the darkness, Mayli held back. She gave one last look to the couple. Dean continued to glare between the both of them. Mary held her hands clasped in front of her chest with a worried brow. The thief stared off into the darkness, waiting patiently. With no other choice, Mayli gripped the railing and descended into the unknown.

Once at the bottom, the thief used the flame of his candle and lit a torch on the wall, revealing a room full of lavish contraband. Piles of expensive Ammosian silks were folded neatly in a stack in the corner. A suit of thin but strong armor from the mountains of Hiore was crammed awkwardly in a chest. Well-framed paintings and miscellaneous artworks leaned against a wall beside a tower of crates. Rare wines and exotic jarred food sat waiting on shelves, surrounded by a mess of jewels, gold, and treasures. There was a bookcase full of tomes and scrolls, some even with ancient texts from Gezmek.

Using crates and silks, the thief began to construct a makeshift bed. After he had completed one, Mayli was relieved to watch him craft another on the opposite side of the room for himself. She sat on hers, glad it was made with more blankets than his own.

Dean entered with a tray of food. He stopped short at the

sight of what had been done with his precious smuggled goods. "I see you've made yourself at home."

"Aren't I?" The thief leaned back in his bed and played with a jeweled trinket he found nearby.

Dean set the tray down. "Look, I'll prepare Fawn now and leave before sunrise. I should reach Dregs in four days."

"Four?" The thief stopped his fidgeting and looked at the miller. "I can't wait a week!"

"She acts like an old mare now. Can't push her like I used to before the war. Besides, I'll also need some things to deliver… That is, if you've left anything intact!" Dean snatched the treasure from the thief, who only smirked in amusement. The miller continued to explain as he set it back down on the shelf, "It would be suspicious to others if I arrived unexpectedly and empty-handed at a time like this."

After consideration, the thief nodded, disappointment still lining his face. Dean grabbed the chest of armor and a small bag before he returned upstairs. The muffled sound of shifting items could be heard above after he closed the secret door.

The thief leaned into the corner and brought his foot up on the bed, crossing an arm over his knee. His fingers played with his knife absently while he watched the lambent torch. "Eat," he said.

Two plates of dried meat and bread, though crude in appearance, sat seductively on the crate. Beside each was a wooden mug of water. Mayli's stomach grumbled. It had been half a day since she had last eaten, and the empty feeling was unique. *This must be what real hunger is.* She picked up the meat and bit.

As she chewed, Mayli quickly questioned whether it was really just leather. She wouldn't put it past Dean the way he scowled at her. She'd never had anything so bland. Even on board ships the food was never this dull. It was tough, dry, and held only a dusty, smoked flavor. Though the food was bad, the salt caused her tongue to salivate and her empty stomach cried out in demand for more. Before she knew it, nothing was left.

Needing to wet her mouth, Mayli took her cup and drank desperately. Feeling a rough texture, she pulled it back. Etched into the mug was a falcon, with wings spread, surrounded by three, four-pointed stars.

Ammos?

It surprised her that these people owned something pertaining to her home after the war. *Likely stolen.* She looked up to notice the other mug had a similar etching, only it was carved like the shield in the room above. The tree and seed of Brimley. She chuckled at the idea of serving coordinating dishes. *Probably Mary's doing.*

Mayli placed her empty mug back on the tray and bravely faced the hooded man. "Well, thief, what is your plan now that you've captured your very own princess?" she said, stiff-toned and valiant, trying to ignore the weapon he brandished.

He tilted his head down and his hood cast a threatening shadow over his face. Still, light found angles of his cheek and a glimmer of a sardonic smile. Mayli took a step back. "Explain to me what is happening!" she demanded with a small dog-like yap.

He tapped the tip of his knife, thinking. Then looked up to truly gaze upon her eyes—or so she thought. His face was still shadowed with mystery. Only the thin peppering of stubble on his chin continued to reveal itself. He drew the knife away from his finger and shrugged. "I'm…not entirely sure," he admitted.

"How can you not be? *You* kidnapped me!" She threw her hands up in the air.

The thief sighed. "I did what I was ordered to do: ambush the carriage and take the woman to the mines. *You* just happened to be that woman. Pierz or Reyn didn't mention it was gonna be the damn Princess of Ammos." He gestured toward her right arm with his knife.

Mayli looked down and self-consciously put her hand to the

tattoo hiding beneath the feathered jacket. Feeling as though she was giving a formal bow, she quickly folded her arms.

"Mayli—" The man continued in a more civil tone, "—I may be a renegade, but I am no traitor."

Mayli stared at the liar. "But you're from Brimley..." Though it was just a guess from the shield and mug, the way he tensed his body confirmed her statement to be true. People from the fallen kingdom were all considered traitors, liars, and outcasts because of the war. It was not something anyone, even a thief, would be likely to admit.

He shook his head with a half-amused chuckle, then stood suddenly. "If you have finished eating, I'll need to tie your hands again."

"Absolutely not!" she protested in her defiant royal tone.

"I can't have you trying to stab me while I sleep."

"I would never do such a thing! I am not a murderer!"

He paused for a moment, then spoke softly, "You would kill if you were trying to survive or protect someone you love. That doesn't make you a murderer..."

She folded her arms.

"Please?" he begged, motioning her to turn and collected the frayed rope off the floor.

Mayli turned, knowing she had no real choice. She sulked as her abductor once again took hold of her arms. He tied the rope gently, yet the knot held firm. After being released, she walked to her bed and plopped onto it with a pout.

She rolled around in an attempt to get comfortable, but her skin itched from the fine coating of scratches from the trials in the forest. Dirt clung to her sweat-beaded body like sap, and twigs had threaded their way into her clothes and hair. After finding the least painful position—face kissing the wall and knees hugged in—she settled down. Still, Mayli felt helpless as she lay bound on a heap of stolen Ammosian silks, in a hidden cellar of her enemies, far from home with a mysterious man.

Hearing him approach, Mayli's heart raced. To her horror, he reached over her, his smell wafting over her once more. She tensed and squeezed her eyes as if she could shut everything away. Her skin crawled at an unexpected touch, but soon she relaxed at the familiar feel of smooth silks being dropped over her. She released her breath only after hearing him walk away.

Alden snuffed out the torch and navigated back to his own pile of crates and silks by candlelight. He blew out the remaining flame, leaving the room dark and smoky. Making no attempt to get comfortable, he laid down. The day's events had overwhelmed him—angered him. Alden looked toward the princess but was unable to see anything beyond the expired torch's glowing tip. He twisted back to stare at what he remembered to be a stone-arched ceiling. Shutting his eyes, he clapped his hands onto his face, then slid them up under his hood and clenched his hair. With an exasperated moan, he quietly cursed.

DECEIT

CHAPTER FOUR

"*W*here is she?"

Kira pried an eye open to see dark silhouettes stalking through the camp. They kicked things out of their way while inspecting the sleeping thieves. A shadow stopped, looked down, and then thrust a boot into the side of Reyn. Kira grinned.

"OIE! I'll skin you!" Reyn exclaimed, jolting awake.

The man knocked Reyn's sleepy punches aside and gripped his collar to hold him up. "Where is the girl, Reynold!"

"Pierz?"

The guild leader shoved him to the dirt.

Reyn scrambled to his feet. "The girl? Why, Alden tied her to the roots over th…"

Pierz followed Reyn's extended—and now drooping—arm to see shreds of rope and a few white feathers. He frowned, then ticked his finger around as he counted his troop.

"Where's Alden?"

"Kira was on first watch with him!" Reyn twirled to point at her bedroll. It lay empty. His greasy hair swung around as he spotted her crumpled on the dirt floor. "Kira? What the fuck are you doing over there?"

Kira took a deep breath and stood on wobbly legs, using the wall to keep balance. "...I'm not sure," she lied, rubbing her forehead.

"You're not *sure?*" growled Pierz, stepping closer.

Kira looked at herself as if trying to comprehend why she had been on the floor. Her heart raced.

"Kira, where is Alden and the girl?"

She searched for a man she knew wasn't there. Kira shook her head with an open mouth, hoping her performance was as convincing as the bruise she had given herself to appear that Alden had fought her.

Reyn stomped over and slapped her back to the ground. "Useless bitch!"

Pierz gazed around the camp and pulled his face mask off. "Will someone please explain how you all let a simple shadow seeker slip away with my asset?"

The rest of the thieves—now awake—sat quietly, having no answer.

Squirrel rolled next to Kira and looked up at her as she wiped her lip, eyes concerned. Kira snapped her head toward Reyn who continued to loom above her. "He must have used that damn vial you gave him!"

"Fuck!" Pierz yelled, kicking Reyn's bedding into the campfire as he began to circle the pit, flexing his hands.

Nobody dared move.

Eventually, Reyn foolishly pried. "Who was she?"

Pierz stopped his pacing and dirt crunched as he spun to face Reyn. He cocked his head to the side like a dog. "What...?"

Reyn flinched as if he had just been slapped himself. Kira hid a pleased grin as the man slumped in regret for questioning their leader which, regardless of the query, was unwise.

"Sorry, sir, it's just, if she was, uh, someone important, we might figure out where he took her. Alden was prodding for information. I didn't think anything of it at the time. Just thought he was being annoying…"

Pierz stared at his shadow commander until the man looked away, which didn't take long. After a collected breath, Pierz moved on. "This was supposed to heighten our reputation…not ruin it. We need to find her immediately," he said, addressing the group, holding the gaze with each of his thieves. Pierz paused on Kira. "You knew Alden best. Tell me. Where could he be taking her?"

Kira gulped. "I've never seen him leave Colville outside of guild missions," she lied, hoping no one kept an eye on Alden as closely as she. "But I doubt he'd go back there with our control over the city."

Reyn pointed an accusatory finger at her. "You have to know something! He's your underling, your responsibility! You're the one who wanted him on this mission; this lands on your shoulders!"

"Maybe if you hadn't been cutting his pay and pocketing it for yourself, he wouldn't have needed to steal from us!" she snapped back.

Pierz gave Reyn a sidelong glance. Then the corners of his lips formed a wry smile as if he had just decided on a satisfactory punishment. When Reyn's face drained of color in understanding, Pierz looked back at her. "Who does Alden know that he could sell her to?"

"Not sure, but there are always those in the Cad Islands willing to pay a high price for fine-looking people, especially nobles. And that's not an unfamiliar place for any of us." Kira opened her arms, presenting the group.

Pierz nodded, but still, his brow furrowed. "He must know someone."

Kira hesitated, watching her leader judge her bruised face. *How bad is it? Hopefully it looks as bad as it feels.* She shrugged. "He was pretty reclusive. But I kept a good watch. There was his land-lord, Mr. Grey; an old woman named Pat he bought art supplies from; he would visit *The Albatross* when it docked; and there wa…"

"*The Albatross*? Prince Briar's ship?" interrupted Pierz.

Reyn stepped forward out of rage. "You never thought to tell me about his meetings with royalty before?"

"Royalty? Ha. Sometimes I forget the guard captain's true title." Kira scratched her head, as if retrieving the memory had just caused an itch. She threw a rude gaze at Reyn. "And no. I never saw who he met with, didn't care. It is a huge ship. Could have been anybody he was seeing!"

"Likely whores," Reyn teased.

Kira rolled her eyes.

Pierz stroked his short goatee in thought. "Briar's uncle, King Olivar Colte of Dregs… Rumor has it someone has been selling women to him," he said with disgust, allowing them to imagine the king's reasoning.

Kira saw Reyn smirk. *Bastard.*

"If Alden has been meeting with Briar Densen, or anyone on that ship, he could be assisting with that. That or he could be working for his cousin, Colin. I can see how the promise of a king's payout would be justifiable to him to risk turning on us." He looked solely at Reyn and the assassin's smile subsided. After he lowered his head in shame, Pierz looked back to her. "Kira, take Squirrel and Trod to Dregs and confirm who Alden was seeing on *The Albatross*. See what you can learn about Olivar's harem too. Reyn, Paige, and the three of you—" Pierz pointed with his knife, separating half of his men that he had brought with him, "—start tracking his trail. The rest of you come with me; we'll scout out the harbor. We are meeting with our client in a fortnight at Thielen's Lodge in the Cad Islands. We best find her by then."

Everyone bowed their heads and placed their arms across

their chest to grip their shoulder. Footsteps neared until Kira saw Pierz's fine boots in front of her. He lightly lifted her chin to look at him. She fought the urge to glance away as he examined her more closely. Her beating heart relaxed as Pierz flattened his mouth into a sorrowing frown. He patted her shoulder, then tugged his face mask over his nose before stepping away.

Kira released a breath, proud she'd kept up the act. She watched with satisfaction as Reyn grabbed his bedroll from the fire pit and brushed off soot. He inspected where the warm coals had chewed away at the bag's lining and had burned the feathered stuffing, causing it to stink. Discarding the burned bedding, Reyn snatched Alden's abandoned roll instead. He squished it, admiring the thick down cushion. With a grin, he stored it away. Reyn then slipped his hand into his pocket and retrieved a decorative vial. His smirk grew wider as he twirled it between his fingers. Kira paled, wondering which of his cruel toxins that one was as he coated his blade with it.

Alden, I hope you'll be all right...

Reyn snapped his attention to Kira and marched over. She took a step back, looking at the blade in fear, but he grabbed her arm, pulling her in close. "Guess your boy didn't love you after all." Kira tried to jerk away as he stroked her bruised face, adding to the pain, and leaned closer. "Don't worry...I'll never leave you."

Kira tugged her arm free and pushed past him to collect her things. Her back tingled in fear at the thought of things returning to how they were before Alden had relieved her of Reyn's abuse.

As Kira stuffed her pack, she noticed Trod and Paige looking longingly toward each other. As they readied to leave, the two finally met up. They said little but expressed everything as they held hands, saying their goodbyes.

"Get over yourselves!" called Reyn.

Trod glowered at Reyn, but Paige pulled away, concluding their farewell. She joined the shadow commander and began searching the ground for signs of Alden's escape. Kira cringed as Paige led the group down a tunnel, pointing out a white feather.

Trod continued to stare at his friend until she turned back and smiled before disappearing behind a bend. As he stepped forward, Kira caught his shoulder, holding him back.

"It won't be long," she said.

He pulled away, readjusted his tunic, and swung his bag over his back.

Squirrel joined them and stared at Kira. She turned away and started her climb up the cave wall to the forest above.

*M*ayli woke to a knock. She wanted to believe it was either her younger brother Jair demanding lessons in archery, Charli offering a massage, or even her father talking about his plans for her to marry the Prince of Hiore. Mayli would have even settled for Lidia barking the day's tasks and that she put on a constricting dress. But none were going to happen. Her body ached as an awful reminder that such comforts were gone. Lidia was dead, there was no guard to protect her, and she was far from home.

A torch roared to life and Mayli opened her eyes. Across the room, the thief reached for the door and pulled it open.

The plump wife emerged, breaking the still silence with a clatter of rattling dishes. Fragrant charred and meaty smells overwhelmed the small room as Mary carried in an appetizing tray of bacon, eggs, and toast. Two mugs of light-colored liquid sloshed with her swaying hips. The thief reached up and stole his immediately. He sipped it with a rambunctious smile. Mary winked and set the tray on a stack of crates, lips upturned when she spotted the thief's untouched plate from the night before.

The woman turned and greeted Mayli with a similar pitiful expression. She could only imagine what horror she looked like, with hair curling out of line, makeup smeared, and a frightened countenance. Nothing like how a princess should look. Mayli attempted a stern and proud look and sat up with a poised chin.

Mary sat on the bed. "There, there, deary," Mary cooed as she began working her fat fingers around the knot that bound Mayli's wrists, taking the time to be gentle. Once the knot was free she handed Mayli the other mug of tea. Like before, it had her family's crest.

Mayli managed a smile as she took it, happy to be cared for by such a kind and cheerful person in this moment of utter darkness. Then she smelled the aroma rising from the mug.

"Brim tea!" Mary announced proudly.

Mayli frowned, but the woman smiled wide at her reaction and lifted the mug, encouraging her to try it. Its light tan shade was unique, so Mayli politely took a small and curious sip. To her surprise, it was sweet and creamy. An earthy lavender undertone danced in her mouth, and she looked at the woman pleasingly. "Oh, this is actually good!"

"Natives make it best, my dear. Secrets passed on through the generations, just like your culture with archery. I'm sure you've only been served our tea as a bitter remedy," the woman assumed, shaking her head as if offended. "I'm afraid it has become a lost art."

Mayli took another sip. She shifted her eyes, noticing the hooded man watching. He drank his tea and grinned behind the Brimleyn mug.

What a creep.

After breakfast, the man swung on a pack Mary put together for him and looked at Mayli. "Ready?"

Mayli freely stepped forward, relieved to have survived the night and feeling slightly more relaxed after Mary's tender care, but the thief didn't move. Mayli followed his gaze to what he held. With a groan, she turned around, forfeiting her arms to her abductor yet again. After he had finished tying her up, he wrapped her scarf tightly around her head and again into her mouth.

"Sorry, I don't trust you."

Mayli scoffed at the irony.

The two ascended into the dark, candle-lit kitchen. A faint red hue peeked shyly through the blinds, and Mayli slumped at the realization that they had only slept a few hours. A door creaked open above them. Mary came down the stairs, shaking a dark blue linen cloak. She approached Mayli and wrapped it around her, pulling the hood over her head and clasping a silver buckle.

"Take care, my dear," she said, patting Mayli's cheek. Stepping back, Mary raised her hand to her right arm, covered her shoulder and bowed formally.

Mayli blinked in wonder.

Mary's mouth opened to say something more, but the thief cleared his throat. The miller's wife frowned and gestured for Mayli to follow as the man left.

Mayli stepped out on the stoop beside the thief. A light and airy ghost-like fog rolled across the farmland, leaving the grass wet with dew. The lawn twinkled as the sun began to reveal itself and the wind picked up. The rustling of trees drew her attention upward. Their vibrant green leaves were just starting to turn, painting the landscape a colorful combination of bright yellow, orange, and a touch of red. Feeling the bite of autumn, Mayli shivered, pulling the blue cloak further around her. Despite its color representing her enemy, she was grateful for its warmth.

As the thief began his walk, his hood turned toward the mill. With just his chin poking out, Mayli noticed him mouth "Thank you" to Mary. She saw the woman nod back to him warmly but could see the worry in her eyes. Mayli eyed the long road west and took a deep breath, preparing herself to face whatever dangers the miller's wife feared they might endure.

After dodging travelers and townsfolk for hours, Mayli spotted a scouting party paused on the path. A watchful archer protected the party's rear while an orange-haired woman checked a map. Two guards flanked the sides of a single rider cloaked in a rich violet cape and shining armor. *A Hiorean knight!*

A tight grip snagged her arm and she was once again pulled into the thicket. The thief crouched close beside her. As he put his finger to his lips to hush her, Mayli jerked her knee up into his crotch.

He cried out in pain, then bit his lip to silence his wail, wincing hard. He coughed as he leaned into her, trying to recover.

She shrugged him off and threw herself to the nearest tree. Using a broken branch, she scraped her face along it. "HELP!" she yelled as the gag came free.

The thief reached up and clamped his hand over her mouth, but it was too late; hoofbeats were approaching. He threw his head to look.

She followed his gaze. The scouts were approaching quickly, the horseman even faster.

The thief tried to lead her into the woods. "May, we gotta go!"

She shook her head ferociously. "If that were true you'd let me go with the Hioreans!"

"They are sh—"

An arrow hissed between them.

"Unhand her!" shouted the knight as he rode to the rescue, cape flying heroically behind him.

"*Please...*" the thief said and then—to her shock—lightly grabbed her right shoulder where her tattoo hid.

"How dare you touch me there!" Mayli pulled back and

twirled her body around, smashing her elbow to his face. He grunted in pain as he staggered backward.

Another arrow sang in the air before lodging into a tree dangerously close beside her. *Repulsive aim!*

The thief looked from her, to the arrow, and then back down the path, weighing his chances. Backing away, he gave one final and odd, disheartened look, then fled into the forest.

Now free, Mayli ran from the bush to greet the Hiorean knight. His horse reared in surprise and the rider struggled to stay on, cursing the animal. Giving up, he quickly dismounted and shoved the horse away.

"Help! I, ah… I'm Mayli Drake, Princess of Ammos!" she gasped eagerly.

The man raised his eyebrows, then flattened them out again. "Yes. We've been looking for you, Princess."

She smiled and turned to show her bound hands to him. He eyed them momentarily, then pulled her in close. He smelt of oil and rancid milk. She leaned away, trying her best not to gag. The man tugged back and began to pinch and pull at the knot. The rope burned her skin as he worked to release her.

"Who are you?" Mayli questioned while trying not to breathe.

The knight paused and looked north toward the Crown Mountains. "Sir Cole." He pulled the last loop free and rested his hands to his rapier.

Mayli waited, expecting him to bow, but there was no formality. Or he had and she'd missed it—Hioreans were known for their arrogance and their bows were often minimal.

"What were his intentions?" he asked.

"I don't know!" Mayli shook her head and turned to face Sir Cole, rubbing her wrists. "None of it makes any sense! A group of thieves kidnapped me… He was one of them! He didn't say much, but he knew a millworker named Dean! He sent him to deliver a message to someone in Dregs!"

"Dregs? What was the message?"

"Well, I didn't get to read it."

"Was he leading you this way?" the man pointed west.

Mayli nodded.

"Curious…" he said, stroking his beard. As his party caught up, he motioned for a scout to come near. In a hushed tone, he issued instructions into his ear. The man then mounted the horse and galloped away.

Mayli frowned, wishing she could have ridden instead.

"Come, we'll take you where you need to be." The knight began to walk, motioning her along.

She gladly followed.

Alden trailed the patrol of imposters from a safe but watchful distance within the forest. Reyn, a gruff-looking man, and a female archer surrounded Mayli in tight formation. Paige led the party. When they took a break to allow Mayli to catch her breath, Alden crept closer. Once they were within earshot, he hunkered down behind a bush.

"You should have let me ride the horse," moaned Mayli.

"He's fetching reinforcements. You will have a ride soon enough, Princess," Reyn said.

At least I won't have to kill him, but I'll need to act now before he shows up with more comrades. He sucked in a wavering breath. *Comrades? They are thieves. Murderers. Crooks. At least one is a rapist.* Alden closed his eyes and calmed his body and mind, freeing himself from guilt. After a steady exhale, he flung three small daggers.

Two missed while one pierced the archer, catching in her throat. She attempted to scream but her voice was lost. The woman dropped her bow, cupping her hands to her neck. As she pulled out the blade, she fell to the ground.

Alden shifted his foot back and a twig snapped, drawing their attention. The thieves readied their stances and surveyed the brush, trying to pinpoint where the sneak-attack had come from. As Paige spotted the rustling of leaves around him, Alden sprung from hiding.

She hopped back and he took another step in. Their daggers clashed. Without as much as a grunt, Paige kicked him in the chest. As he stumbled back, she sliced at his extended sword arm, drawing blood. He returned the attack, cutting her fingers. The woman's nostrils flared, and she swiped furiously.

The other Shadowen began to circle with his sword outreached.

Paige lashed out again. As she dove, Alden used his flanking to his advantage and grabbed her arm. Using her forward momentum, he then threw the small woman into her ally, just as he had practiced with Kira. The thieves toppled over top each other and Alden pounced at the opportunity.

As quick as he was, Paige had already recovered. Her tiny frame allowed her the grace to tumble out of the way before he could strike.

Changing targets, Alden redirected his focus to the thief who was still recovering on the ground. On instinct, he grabbed the man's hair to pull his head back, pressing his dagger into the man's neck.

Mayli screamed. Alden looked up, fearing Reyn was hurting her, but she was staring in horror. At him. Killing. He glanced at the amount of the blood that he had just spilled with his knife. Alden felt sick as well, listening to the gurgling noises his ex-comrade made. He didn't remember his name but recalled helping him flee from a battle once. They had celebrated their escape over drinks. Alden gently rested the body down.

"Let me go!" Mayli cried as Reyn pulled her closer in.

"You're staying put, bitch!"

Mayli stared in disbelief. "Did you just…?"

She spat into his face.

Reyn grunted, bringing his arm up to wipe his eyes. The princess stomped on Reyn's foot causing him to curse and lose his grip, allowing her to slip past his smooth, stolen armor. As Mayli fled, she tripped over the downed archer. Alden watched her scramble only for a moment longer before Paige's knife flashed in his face. He leaned back.

"Paige, go after the girl!" commanded Reyn. He lifted his rapier to Alden. "He's mine."

Paige swiped at Alden forcing him back. She disengaged, then sprinted into the forest after Mayli. Alden attempted to follow, but Reyn blocked his path. Without the luxury of time to duel, he tossed his last few throwing knives in quick succession. Uninterested in confirming his death, or taking Reyn up on his challenge, Alden chased after the women.

After a short pursuit, Alden heard a scream followed by a deathly sounding thud. He halted, fearful it had been Mayli.

Slowly rounding a bush, Alden's heart pounded, expecting the worst.

To his relief, the princess stood before a creek, highlighted in a lone beam of sunlight fading through the trees. Her black hair danced with her scarf in rays of light as a breeze swirled a few golden leaves around her. She held the dead archer's large bow and her pull hand was frozen in the air, arrow loosed.

Following her trembling gaze, Alden found Paige—dead. She was lying in the mud with an arrow protruding from her heart. Alden blinked at the accuracy. "Woah."

"You!" Mayli shrieked. She drew another arrow from the stolen quiver and notched it, redirecting her aim at him.

Alden raised his hands high in submission. "Mayli..." His eyes locked on her arm, impressed, but not surprised by the Ammosian's ability to pull back and hold such a heavy bow.

A moment passed. With the aim still on him, Mayli shifted her eyes back down at the woman she had killed. She began to shake, causing the bow and arrow to rattle together like a horse's trot. "Hiore…they…"

"They weren't from Hiore," Alden corrected.

She looked up at him with wide eyes and the rattling stopped.

"Just Shadowen thieves. That—" He gestured toward the impostor. "—was Paige."

"Thieves?" She looked down and began to shake once more.

Alden kept his hands up but inched forward in her moment of bewilderment. He reached out and gently touched the quivering bow. To his relief, Mayli relaxed the pull. As she did, he stole the weapon from her.

She hopped away. "You're one of them, too! How am I any better off with you?"

"I'm trying to get you home…"

"Really? By tying me up?" she snapped.

Alden pursed his lips and looked away. Catching sight of Paige, he walked over to squat beside her body. From the arrow shaft, blood still oozed out, blending in with her thin, red hair. He hadn't known her well. She never spoke and the only company she kept was Trod's. Alden had heard that Trod once beat someone sense-less at the accusation that they had purposely shoved Paige at the market. Alden could also never forget the rumors about the punishment he gave to anyone who mocked her, looked at her inappropriately, or catcalled her. Although Alden admired Trod's protective nature, the vengeance that would follow Paige's death worried him. Regardless, Alden searched her body and pocketed her coin purse, day rations, hunting knife, and a map.

"We need to go. Reyn could still be lurking," Alden murmured.

"Reyn?"

"The man you spat on," Alden said with an approving grin.

"That…was not his name." Mayli took a worried step back.

Alden shrugged and looked her in the eye. "Don't expect a thief to be honest."

"Like you?"

"Look." He pointed at Paige. "Her clothes are stolen. That uniform doesn't even fit. It's made for a man twice her size. And there are puncture holes with dried blood." He plucked at the fabric and put his finger in one. "They are from the ambush."

Mayli leaned in to examine then quickly frowned with a nod.

Alden nodded back and stood.

"Ready?" he asked with added warmth to his voice.

She groaned, forfeiting her hands. Alden looked at them. They were black with dirt and red from rope burns. He peered up. The bruise on her face and slightly swollen lip had grown dark. He gave a faint, apologetic smile. She cocked her head as he turned to walk along the bubbling creek, leaving her unbound.

THE CABIN

CHAPTER SIX

*M*ayli paused, seeing the stream disappear over the edge of a small cliff. A light gurgle reflected off the canopy of trees that hung overhead. Cold, fine mist tickled her face. Mayli inched forward. Her heart beat nervously as she observed the small waterfall spilling into a beach-lined creek below.

The thief stepped beside her and peered down, unafraid. Taking only a moment to plot his course, he climbed over the ledge. Before continuing, he turned and extended a hand up to her.

"I can do it on my own," she said with a raised chin. She leapt past him. He followed, carefully checking his footing. She heard him slip once and chuckled at his lack of dexterity. Feeling more confident, Mayli hopped to the bottom. As she landed, her foot slipped from her wet sandal. She spun her arms, attempting to catch balance but fell into the shallows regardless. Feathers from her jacket floated downstream as if they were too embarrassed to be with her any longer.

Mayli sat defeated in the cool water. She closed her eyes,

holding back tears, waiting for the laughter and mockery to follow. Her brother Jair would have, maybe even Charli, but to her surprise, the thief was silent. Footsteps approached and Mayli looked up to see his hand held out once more. Ashamed, she finally accepted.

He lifted her to standing but walked away before she could offer thanks. Mayli sighed and ripped off her beaten and useless sandals, tossing them aside. She squinted blissfully at the comforting feel of sand squishing between her toes, as if she were home in Ammos.

Her eyes fluttered open in surprise, feeling a tap on her arm. The man presented a small clump of brown clay or maybe a rock —she wasn't quite sure. From its bumpy texture, it was difficult to make out exactly what it could be. She leaned in for a closer look.

"Is that food?"

He turned the bar over, examining it. Without lifting his head, he glanced up and offered a doubtful grin. "Yeah?"

Mayli raised a single brow, giving the man an unconvinced stare. He shrugged and tossed it over, forcing her to take it. Now holding the bar, she examined it more thoroughly. Bits of oats and nuts were caked within a grit-like flour. Mayli sneered but her stomach growled. Taking her chances, she bit into the unknown.

Her nose scrunched as she attempted to eat. Notes of dirt and nuts coated her mouth. A moment later she decided starving would be a more pleasing experience and spat out a crumbly mess as she coughed.

"No...it's not," she declared, shoving the rest back into the man's chest as she walked by.

Mayli cupped her hand into the stream below and sipped delicately, rinsing out the foul taste. Once refreshed, Mayli dipped her hand back into the cold water. She hummed softly as the current twisted around her wrists, soothing her rope burns.

She suddenly pulled away after noticing a stranger staring back. *Her.*

Her jacket's once pure-white feathers were now tinted with mud and sweat, matching her tanned skin. Many were frayed or missing. Leaves and bits of debris had turned her hair and scarf into a snarled, twig-like abomination. *A bird might swoop down at any moment, seeking residence.* She attempted to brush her fingers through but met a grievous amount of resistance. She shuddered at the task of straightening her hair out without help from Lidia.

After freeing her hand, she traced down her face, following the pattern of cuts and scrapes. She stopped at the development of a deep lavender bruise growing over her jaw from when one of the thieves—most likely Cole, or whatever his name was—had hit her.

The thief skipped the scone across the water, shattering her reflection. "Let's go," he said, continuing down the beach.

Mayli sighed in relief, seeing a quaint shack upon the river's bend. After traveling miles along the riverbank, her muscles had become a dull throb, her hip ached, and she could feel several thick blisters on her feet she refused to look at. Before she could keep going, the thief pulled her under the cover of a pine tree. His eyes darted around, as if absorbing every odd detail.

Chairs, crates, tools, carts, rugs, furniture, and a collection of unidentifiable items surrounded the home with no particular manner of organization. Glassless windows revealed the same accumulation of things hidden beyond tattered drapes. Tall grass and weeds swarmed everything on the lawn, including an axe, which protruded out from an unseen stump.

Still hesitant, the thief motioned for her to wait, then approached with caution. He crept around mounds of junk, then vanished behind some crates. Mayli blinked as he reappeared in a completely unexpected spot. After searching the perimeter, he approached the shack's entrance.

The thief tried the door, but it refused to budge. She saw him take out a set of tools from his belt and work the keyhole. After a minute, he dropped his arms and cocked his head. He tried the door again. Nothing. Using his shoulder, he gave the door a forceful shove.

As it swung in, Mayli heard the clatter of things falling from within. A plume of dust billowed into the yard as the old and lonesome cabin welcomed its visitor with a cloud-like hug. The man coughed, waving his hand in an attempt to part the dust. He cringed as something inside continued to crash and a wagon wheel rolled out.

At that, Mayli stepped onto the lawn and joined him at his side, peering in. "Real sneaky, thief."

He gave her a snarky smile and brushed past.

Distracted by his humiliation, he plowed right into a mess of net-like and dirt-coated cobwebs drifting from the ceiling. One particularly long strand would have blanketed his hair if it weren't for his hood. Noticing, he desperately clawed it away. Mayli watched as another glided down. Before it touched his face, he let out several hurried puffs of air, blowing it away.

Mayli laughed openly, amused by the thief's fear of webs. He frowned down at her. She chuckled again and strode in, unafraid.

Mayli gaped at the scene. The hoarder's possessions were piled high in ways that clearly shouldn't have held. Furniture disappeared behind mounds of rubbish. Stacks of building materials served as shelves for woodworking tools and other random items like a ladder, sled, and bird feeder. Pots and pans filled racks hanging from the ceiling, yet more lay scattered among the debris.

Seeing the upper half of a stone chimney, the man wove around the cluttered living room and pulled at a drawerless dresser that stood in the way. Beyond it was the fireplace where a cooking rod lay among ashes of wood once burned. He set the bar back into place and began collecting an assortment of wooden scraps for a fire.

Curious about what she could find among the hoarder's collection, Mayli picked through a pile. She tried on a wide-rimmed sun hat which flopped over her face. She peered up, catching her reflection in a pot, giggled then flew it across the room disappearing behind a mound of clutter. Digging further, Mayli found a piece of wood with a glimmer of blue paint. She took a closer look. Turning it over, she realized it was a carved figurine. He had a fat belly, a thin goatee, and long blue cloak made of linen. He wore a crown. On his shoulder was a black tree outlined in a shield. *The King of Brimley*. Mayli quickly tossed it into the fire just as the thief got the flames to ignite.

Curious, the thief grabbed a fire iron and turned her tribute over.

"Cleansing Vatan of lying murderers," she said stepping closer.

He frowned and gripped the iron firmly, knuckles turning white.

Mayli stood by his side. "You must believe Colin is guilty, if you are helping me."

He got up, causing her to jerk back nervously. He eyed her for a moment, then turned his back on the fire and entered into the adjacent room. "I'm helping because *you* are innocent, Mayli."

"So, you agree he's a murderer," Mayli said, standing.

"I didn't say that," he called back.

She walked to the open door, watching the thief shift through a dresser. "But he is."

He shoved the drawer closed so hard the dresser slammed against the wall behind. Dust floated from the ceiling. "Maybe, now switch into these," he said, tossing a heap of clothes.

Mayli fumbled and caught only one. She held it out. The shirt's bottom half was stripped of its black dye from years bathing in sunlight and was now a warm charcoal-gray. Its neck was frayed from lost thread, and its arms bore holes at each sleeve's end. She sneered at the ugly tunic.

"See if these fit too," he said dryly, adding a heap of leather to the pile she finished collecting off the floor. Then he squeezed uncomfortably past, causing her to nearly drop the stack again.

She watched the thief sit, crossing his worn, mud-coated boots. A feather tickled her cheek. She looked down at her destroyed jacket, grimacing. Even her strong silk dress had become a rag. Mayli frowned at the "new" clothes waiting for her approval. With a sniffle, she set the bundle down on the bed.

As Mayli undressed, she peeked behind, curious if the thief would steal a glance. His head was turned away, resting on his fist as he kept watch over the fire.

"Hmm," she hummed, rolling the faded tunic up and tossing it over her head. It draped down to her knees and hung slightly lower in the back. Mayli grabbed a long leather belt and cinched it around her waist, accentuating her slender form. She dug through the pile and found a pair of tall mismatched stockings. They hugged her aching feet as she pulled them on. Feeling comfortable once more, Mayli wrapped her orange silk scarf around her neck, then draped the woolen blue cloak from Mary around her to complete the commoners' look.

She stepped into the open room, feeling the rough fabric rub against her skin. She scratched her belly and loosened the belt. "It's itchy."

"Sorry I can't offer you any Ammosian silks, Princess," the thief said without a glance her way. He turned over a log and continued to poke at the fire, creating a clearing around the inflamed figurine as if trying to save it from its fate.

"Let it burn already." Mayli snatched the iron rod from him and collapsed the logs over top the carved Brimleyn royal. Now satisfied, she offered it back to the thief.

He ignored her and instead stood. Giving her no time to

move aside, he brushed past and walked to the table. With a sweep of his arm, he cleared away the pile of junk that hid it. Mayli cringed at the loud clatter. He picked a pot off the floor and wiped it once with his cloak.

Mayli grimaced, imagining the dirt still coating the surface and what grime he added from his cloak. *Is he really going to use that to cook?* As she opened her mouth, the man splashed some water in. She watched with interest as he then gave it a final and thorough wipe-down.

Bringing it up into a beam of light, he checked it, then sat it down on the table. He took out a sack from his pack and poured long seeds into the pot.

"So, what is that?"

He hesitated, then replied, "Wild rice."

"Rice. Good, so you aren't trying to kill me with another rancid scone," she said playfully to help ease the tension.

The thief just poured water over the grains. He then hooked the pot over the flame and stirred it with a wooden ladle. For a moment, he stared at the fire, then ran his fingers through his hair, brushing off his hood. Firelight reflected off of the thief's short, greasy, brown bangs, and shadows drew hard angled lines across his features. He caught a glimpse of her stare and did a double take to catch her eye. She offered a light apologetic smile, but it wasn't returned.

Mayli took position beside him. He stepped back as she stole the spoon from him and began mimicking the chore of stirring as she had seen him do. He continued to stand beside her. She looked up, meeting his squinting face. "What?"

He closed his eyes while his brows shot up, shaking his head. "Nothing," he said, raising his hands. The thief slipped past without touching her and continued to prepare their meal.

The aroma from the pot held a comforting sweet and earthy scent. Mayli lifted the lid one last time. The rice had grown and split, revealing a soft inner shell. The man leaned over her shoulder to see into the pot. Looking to her, he nodded. She smiled. He finally did too.

Raising his hand, the man presented the only chair in the cabin which had all its legs and a thatched seat. She gladly sat and watched as he scooped rice into a chipped bowl. He stripped pieces of the miller's dried pork into it, then added bread.

He slid the bowl across the table and Mayli caught it before it fell off the table and into her lap. She frowned watching him go outside with his meal. Looking at the food, her lips fell further. It really wasn't appetizing. Dry meat, hard bread, and bland rice. She craved soft meat bathed in a spicy and buttery curry or a flavorful skewer of roasted vegetables. Thinking about Ammosian dishes invoked the odd sensation of hunger once more.

Using the bread as a scoop, Mayli collected some rice and bit in. She cocked her head as the flavor was unique and unexpected. Unlike the white grains she was accustomed to, these held a pleasant nutty undertone. Still, the pork was the same leather-like strip of meat from the night before: tough and salty. It was an odd pairing, but at least it settled her stomach.

Long after she finished, Mayli peeked out the window. Despite it being nearly a half-turn since they cooked, the man had hardly touched his meal. He sat against a cart, hands holding up his face. His hood was up once more, hiding his features, but she saw his chest tremble as it raised, then fell.

Mayli spun away from the window and leaned against the wall, clenching her hands. Her lips wavered between smiling and frowning, unsure what to feel after seeing him cry.

UNCERTAIN ALLIANCES

CHAPTER SEVEN

*A*fter passing by yet another seemingly endless row of corn, Squirrel ran to the farm's edge and yanked a golden cob off. He trotted back with a champion's smile.

Kira, for once, said nothing. She'd advised against stealing a cob for miles, but the boy's curiosity and rebellion couldn't be tamed. *Sometimes lessons needed to be learned.* She eyed the idiotic boy without empathy as he tore open the husk's many layers. He was too eager to break into the cob to notice her stare. Finally, once the kernels were exposed, he chomped into it.

She smiled with great pleasure as Squirrel's face soured. He spat the nuggets out—flavors Kira knew to be dull and earthy. She watched in amusement as the boy tossed the inedible vegetable back into the field.

"Needs a boil," Trod informed, and then retrieved the cob.

"No, this is field corn," Kira explained.

"All corn comes from fields." He sniffed it.

"True…but this corn is for animals."

Trod pocketed it for himself. "We are animals."

Kira looked to Squirrel as he continued to spit on the ground like a drooling dog. She chuckled. "Indeed..."

The boy looked up at her with concerned eyes and a pitiful expression. "I've got hair in my teeth now! Why is it hairy?" He drilled a finger into the gaps in his teeth to liberate the corn silk left behind. He spat again. "Why didn't you tell me it wasn't good, Kira?"

"I remember quite clearly I told ya not to go looking for snacks in those fields." She pointed over the landscape.

"I thought you didn't want me to steal...I didn't think, eh... ah..." He twisted his tongue over a thread lodged seemingly deep between his teeth. Locating it, he pressed his fingernail to his teeth and shimmied it free. "I didn't think it would be so nasty." He spat.

"What do I care if you steal? That's Alden's problem."

At the mention of his name, they fell silent.

After a while, Kira turned around and looked at Squirrel, who tripped in response. He had been staring at her since the mention of Alden and she was about done with it.

"You all right, Squirrel?"

"Oh yeah!" he replied in his usual chipper tone, trying to play off the tumble. "And how about you? How's your bruise?"

Kira touched her face, feeling the lump she gave herself arise. "Fine." Kira continued down the road, looking at something off in the distance, hoping to draw Squirrel's attention away from her. Squirrel followed her gaze, expecting something of importance. He scanned and judged everything with great intrigue. She couldn't help but snicker at his gullibility.

"That must have hurt," he said, finding his focus back on her. "I know being hit sure threw me by surprise! The back of my head won't stop throbbing. Alden's got a quick hook punch...I didn't even see it coming. Did you teach him that?"

That tone... Does he know what I did? She gave him a sidelong glance from behind her hood. "Yeah. Sorry I couldn't have been there sooner."

"It's fine. Sorry I wasn't there for you!"

"Thanks."

Finally, they walked in silence again and without his constant stare.

"So!" Squirrel said loudly, causing her to flinch. "You really think he's working for the King of Dregs?" he said, picking up his pace to meet Kira at her side.

Kira paused at his approach and glared down at him. He blinked innocently. She sighed, continuing her walk. "I suppose it's possible."

"Well, sure, lots of things are. But do *you* think he is?"

"Alden is…" She shook her head. "Too honorable. It would surprise me if he was trafficking women for that slob. Besides, I doubt those rumors are true. Kings aren't like that."

Squirrel nodded in agreement, then cocked his head. "Honorable? So, Alden is trying to save her?"

Kira sucked in her lips. She took an extra step forward to keep her face concealed. "Dunno, maybe we'll find out in Dregs."

"Right! 'Cause that guard prince guy he talks with!"

Kira let the silence answer back. A moment passed before he spoke up again.

"Kira?"

"What?!" she snapped.

"I hope he's okay…" Squirrel said in a soft tone Trod couldn't hear.

Surprised by his sincerity, she slowed to look at him. He held his head low and walked without his typical bounce. Squirrel peered up with a sad smile, then looked back down at the road. Kira contemplated the idea that Squirrel wasn't trying to get her to admit to her lies, and that this was his way of saying that he, too, was on Alden's side.

Kira recalled how Squirrel had always admired Alden. The

boy had, after all, joined the Shadowen Thieves Guild because of him. The orphan was much like Alden in a sense, losing their families and homes during the Brim War and having no one to turn to. Squirrel had been surviving off measly scraps in a nearby alley off Taylor Avenue, the same that hugged the teahouse where Alden lived, The Five Leaves. She often saw the boy begging for coin, food, or even a pair of shoes for his blackened feet that were blistered from the worn cobblestone streets.

Squirrel was a tough kid who wasn't afraid to split a couple noses, and he wouldn't cower if threatened. Kira admired that. She had seen one ruthless fight leave him nursing a sprained wrist and a swollen face, but compared to how he'd left the couple of thugs, Squirrel looked as healthy as a noble.

When Kira pointed Squirrel out to Alden, he pitied the child. To her surprise, he offered a hot cup of tea and a healthy-looking sandwich, one he hardly allowed himself to eat.

Kira warned of what troubles could arise if he continued to intervene, but Alden didn't care. Whatever his reason was for not wanting him to suffer, the man made sure the boy was fed despite what little allowance Kira knew he earned from the guild—no thanks to Reyn.

As Kira expected, Squirrel waited for Alden each day at the teahouse like a lost puppy. Despite Alden's plea for him to stop, Squirrel insisted to carry his bag up to his room or deliver his tea. Desperate to live up to his hero's expectations, the boy began to copy Alden's moves, dressing similarly, and even adopting his habits like hiding out in high-up places, keeping his blade in tip-top condition, reading, and even drawing—which Alden started to teach him. Kira laughed at her friend's discomfort when Squirrel attempted to mimic his same cool, gruff, and lonely voice. Because of Squirrel's adolescence, his own cracked, betraying the act.

Like Alden, his landlord, Mr. Grey, felt pity for Squirrel and offered the boy an apprenticeship in the tea shop in exchange for a room. He learned fast and did a fine job being quick to serve the thirsty locals. But when Squirrel had been caught stealing silver from patrons, it ended his career with Mr. Grey. Instead of being ashamed, Squirrel was proud that was his first time being caught as he'd been at it for months.

Happy to show off all that he had collected up until then, Squirrel dumped a chest out onto his floor. Out came bags of coins, an expensive Hiorean dagger, jewelry, and even a barrage of useless trinkets such as buttons, a knight's cheer-flag, a small patch of chainmail, Kira's favorite corset, a studded belt, three mugs, Alden's bottle of Dune Ale, and for whatever reason, an old sock, complete with a hole in the toe. Kira was impressed, but Alden only shook his head in further disappointment.

It surprised both her and Squirrel that Alden didn't like the idea of taking other people's possessions when he himself was working in a thieves guild. Alden explained that he felt there was something morally wrong taking from the innocent and to avoid such needlessness whenever possible. When Kira raised her eye at him, he stressed the word *innocent*. Granted, anyone they attacked could be found guilty of something one way or another —nobody was pure from evil deeds.

He's been a bad influence, Kira joked to herself. However, his noble influences were exactly the kind she wanted, as she was tired of the cruel life. She thought once she had escaped it, but like the turning of seasons, the shadows sucked her back into the cold.

Up ahead lights from Basevein reflected into Lake Ironmere. Above it loomed Mount Hiore, where many waterfalls draped down like silk. As they entered the town, captivating aromas wafted into the street to greet them. Cooked beef and spiced apple pies tickled her nose, coaxing her to come dine. *A great idea.* Kira thumbed towards the restaurant but Trod kept walking south.

An ensemble of a cello and a melancholy singer drew her

attention as they passed by an inn. The lonely tune reminded her of Alden and Kira craned her neck, wishing she could stay to listen, but Trod still continued forth. With a tired groan, she let memories carry her mindlessly down the road.

Though it had been Alden who invited Squirrel into their lives, it was Kira who offered the boy the option to join the guild. She had realized that there was no stopping the kid's kleptomania, so becoming a Shadowen would be perfect.

Alden was furious and argued that he was too young to be corrupted by the darkness the guild offered. Squirrel begged otherwise, explaining that the streets were just as cruel, if not a worse place to be. Kira agreed. Reluctantly, Alden accepted their logic.

Kira introduced Squirrel to the guild leader, Pierz. Blind to the boy's age, he agreed that if Squirrel could withstand a series of challenges, he would be accepted. Pierz taxed his talents, quizzed his wits, and pushed his strength to questionable limits. When the boy proved promising, Squirrel was then offered the chance to try out an assortment of weapons, such as axes, swords, knives, and maces. When those seemed too grueling for the boy, Pierz offered a bow.

Squirrel and the long-ranged weapon were a perfect pair. With the bow and arrow, he had said he felt as if he were in two places at once. It gave him a sense of speed and power his fast-paced mind otherwise couldn't find. After withstanding the tests, he was a welcomed addition to the Shadowen Thieves Guild as a ranger.

Although he was loyal to Alden, Kira, and the guild, his youth was occasionally problematic, as the teen still had childlike desires. Temptation proved too much to control at times, earning him countless troubles. Once he had his eyes on a gold-tipped Ammosian bow. The black-stained and dual-wood design with a fluff of black fur to silence the string was sought out by the most avid collectors, and Squirrel had to have one.

Unfortunately for Squirrel, Ammosian archers were trained to see the slightest shifts of movement from far-off distances and react quickly to them. In awe of their skill, Squirrel had explained he hadn't even reached the bow before a rapid succession of arrows had pinned his cloak to the wall. As punishment, he was thrown in the stocks.

"See where unchecked desires gets ya?" Alden had said as he casually leaned against the stocks. He looked around, nonchalant, avoiding Squirrel's puppy-like eyes. A group of girls approached with a basket of spoiled eggs. He winked to them and held out a finger for them to wait. They giggled eagerly.

"Alden! Help me!" Squirrel had begged in fear, rattling the locked jaws as the gang approached.

Kira eyed the scheming girls as they lightly tossed the shelled bombs between each other, laughing, careful not to let it burst before the shackled boy could have a taste.

Alden pushed away, spun, and leaned down, looking Squirrel in the eyes. He gave him a firm, unforgiving glare. "No."

The boy pleaded once more, brokenhearted.

"You'll live." Kira ruffled the kid's hair, squeezing out another stressful whine from him.

Alden straightened, and together he and Kira walked away. She had seen Alden close his eyes as if resisting the urge to turn back after they heard the first egg hit. Though they could have easily picked the lock to free him or fended off the troop of girls, Alden had said he wanted his young friend to learn a valuable lesson.

After a few days covered in an assortment of eggs and vegetables, Squirrel was freed by the guards. When they went to collect him, Alden had brought a long, narrow wooden box. It had a simple illustration of white and orange feathers painted along its sides. Kira had a hunch, but was still excited to see what it held.

"What's that?" Squirrel asked, eyeing the box with suspicion as he flicked lettuce off his shoulder.

"A present," Alden said, patting the box.

"For Kira?" Squirrel drawled.

Kira stuck out her tongue in response. It irritated her that Squirrel insisted on prodding that they were lovers when the two —aside from the kin-like bond—kept a very professional line between them. What Squirrel didn't know was that she and Alden actually had once shared a moment of love, however brief. She blushed.

Alden chuckled. "No. Not for Kira. It's for you." He offered the box.

Squirrel cocked his head. *"Why?"*

Alden pulled it back and looked at the box, twisting his mouth to the side as if trying to find a good answer. "I don't know." He shrugged. "You really don't deserve it, but I know being stuck in the stocks and being judged and shamed wasn't ideal. Those girls weren't kind to you, either. Don't worry, not all are like that." He smirked at Kira. She had bit her lip as if to stop her cheeks from growing hotter. "Anyway, it's mostly because I don't want to see you in there again. So…" Alden presented the box back to Squirrel and smiled cheekily.

Squirrel darted his eyes from the box to his friend's face several times before reaching out to open the lid. Inside—to his amazement—was a finely crafted longbow of dual-wood design stained a light walnut to enhance the grain's natural beauty. He gawked at a custom detail carved and painted blue into the bow's grip: a flying squirrel with an arrow across each of its wing-like flaps.

The now wide-eyed boy reached inside with awe. He hesitated and looked back at Alden, who nodded in consent. Squirrel gasped as he lifted the beautiful weapon free from its box as if he had just been gifted the power to rule over all of Vatan. His fingers traced over his newly created emblem and every other minute detail, drawing in gasping breaths.

Squirrel looked around guiltily and hugged the bow in. "You *stole* this?"

"No, Squirrel, I didn't steal that," Alden said with irritation. "I had it custom made for you. I *bought* it. Ya know, with our savings from the guild...coin that *you* let disappear gambling on Noble's Dice almost as fast as you lost that stupid plumed hat you stole last week."

"I didn't lose that! I've...only misplaced it!"

"Good! It looked ridiculous!" she said.

"You said it suited me!"

"And it did," she mocked with a wink.

Squirrel flashed his tongue, then with wide eyes, stared back at the bow in amazement. Alden handed the empty box to Kira and tossed the boy a sinew. In a flash, Squirrel set the bow's tip into his boot. Grunting softly, he managed to twist then hook the string around the nock. Once strung, he carefully pulled back, straining at its resistance.

Alden shrugged. "I didn't know your pull strength, but I told the fletcher your age and described your build. He decided to make it a little heavier so you have something to grow into. Should last you a long while."

"It's perfect!" he said, and carefully relaxed the pull.

"Should be. It's crafted by an Ammosian," Alden said proudly.

"Alden..." Squirrel looked down at the precious gift with newfound admiration. "You're right, I don't deserve this!" he said, offering the bow back.

Alden kept his hands slack at his side. "It's yours. Who else would want a squirrel etched into their bow?" He smirked.

"We will stay here," Trod announced, pulling Kira from her memory—her heart now tender after reminiscing about Alden's generosity and kindness. She hoped none would succeed in ruining his mission rescuing the princess.

Kira looked up. An old and worn-down building that sagged to one side. A few ancient-looking women—who looked as though they might have been part of the decrepit shack them-selves—sat on the deck, discussing how the change in weather was turning over for the new season.

Above them stood a sign that hung crooked over the door. "WAYPOINT" it read. The inn's walls were bowed, and its paint had flaked off at the bottom where snow seemed to rest in the winter. Several layers of color were exposed across the decaying boards, revealing the many makeovers it had seen. The Waypoint's door hung open, letting a flood of light spill into the street.

Trod led the group inside and approached the innkeeper to discuss accommodations. Kira and Squirrel took a seat at a corner table. The bench seat rocked under their weight, and the tabletop wobbled as the boy leaned into it. The two worked together to shift it around but the floor was bowed like waves across a stormy sea.

On the opposite side of the room a mother nursed her child. The father cut into some white meat and helped feed his preoc-cupied wife. In the room's center was a burly man in fine yet dirty clothes, who finished off a mug of ale, froth sticking to his large fur-like mustache. His three companions raised their glasses to summon the barkeep who replenished their drinks. Kira was drawn to order one herself but knew it was best to avoid such temptations, as Alden did.

Trod returned with a key. In his other hand, he gripped three mugs of ale, which she frowned at, having already made her responsible decision.

"Food is coming," he said, sliding the drinks to them.

Taking the ale, Squirrel poured a healthy lot into his throat, much of it spilling down his chin that grew a few proud whiskers. He clanked the mug onto the table, wiped his lips, and turned to Trod. "I'm starved! What's for supper?"

"Didn't ask."

He shifted back to look at Kira with wide, childish eyes. "I hope it's venison! Or goose soup with wild rice!" he rubbed his palms together and squinted as if imagining the food in front of him.

"Brimleyn dishes?" Kira rotated her mug around, trying to resist sipping it out of habit. Some froth spilled down its side and curled up on her finger. Kira lifted her hand to her mouth and sucked it off. She frowned in regret. After sampling the nutty flavor, she only wanted more.

"Yes! I miss home. I'm so bored of Colville's obsession with leafy greens," whined Squirrel.

"Hey, salads are good," said Kira.

"What is venison?" asked Trod.

"Deer! Ya know, those hooved beasts with bones sticking out from their head." Squirrel put his hands up to his head, mimicking antlers. "Yeah?"

"So, a goat?"

"No..." Squirrel looked around the inn, then pointed above the fireplace. "That!"

An impressive head of a ten-pointed buck hung proudly on the stone wall. Its face was shadowed hauntingly from the fire's light dancing below. Glass eyes twinkled, giving life to its fierce scowl.

Trod sat back.

"That's the same animal in the cave you did that weird thing to," Kira informed.

"I'm not sure it is wise to eat such a powerful and majestic beast," said Trod, eyes still locked with the mount's.

Kira and Squirrel exchanged looks, then burst into laughter.

Trod furrowed his brow at them. "Is it not?"

"No, Trod. Deer are very docile, timid animals. Far from powerful and majestic." Kira continued to giggle at the idea.

"Its horns, are they not made to express power?" Trod glanced back at the mount.

Kira looked too. The head was muscular and strong, and its

antlers towered around the beast elegantly. "Those are antlers, and yes they do."

"Like a crown."

Kira chuckled. "Sure, like a crown."

"See, majestic," he said with all seriousness, taking a sip of ale, thus concluding his discussion.

"Delicious, you mean!" Squirrel licked his lips while he watched the innkeeper arrive with a tray of food.

As if the cook had overheard their conversation, three bowls of hearty venison stew, complete with plump potatoes and carrots embraced by a thick gravy-like sauce, was set before them. Kira and Squirrel dove into their meals while Trod stared at his with discontent. He picked up his spoon and ate around the chunks of meat.

Noticing his reluctance to try the venison, Squirrel pointed at it. "Ya gonna eat that?"

"It isn't right to," Trod declared.

"Uh-huh. May I?" Squirrel looked at him with wide hunger-stricken eyes.

"See that it doesn't go to waste," Trod said and leaned away. He looked back at the head above the fireplace, sadness in his eyes. Waving his empty mug, Trod caught the barkeep's attention. After the ale was once again brimming, Trod lifted his cob of corn, requesting it to be cooked. The barkeep eyed the bite-mark, then Trod, who remained expressionless. The man shrugged and walked away to prepare it.

As they finished their meals, Squirrel wiped his fingers on his tunic and then looked to Kira. "Who do you think she is?"

Kira looked around but saw that the new mother had left. Even the troop of burly men had retired for the night. "Who?"

"That girl that Alden took! That *noblewoman...*" he said quietly, looking around the parlor as if people were still in the room.

Kira shook her head and turned to stare out the window, wishing his curiosity would end.

"She was tan. Like me. Though not as dark as many Ammosians." Trod lifted his forearm and tapped his dark skin. "She had the beauty and grace of golden sand. I suspect she's the princess."

Kira clenched her jaw while Squirrel dropped his. She turned away and looked back out the window. Clouds were beginning to blanket the sky, and she could feel them looming over her head as well.

"Wait, so Alden knew?" Squirrel arched a brow. "Why would he care? He's Brimleyn."

"I don't know," she lied without looking back.

"*You* don't know? He's your boyfriend. You know what he'll do even before he does."

"I can't know everything! And he's *not* my boyfriend."

Trod and Squirrel exchanged unconvinced looks.

Kira blew a hot sigh out her nose, snatched the key off the table and pointed at him with it. "I can only gather what I am able to observe; he's never opened up to me! He's turned on us and the guild, and we'll find him." Kira pushed away from the table and stormed down the hall.

"A jealous woman," she heard Trod say before slipping into her room.

BRIMLEY

CHAPTER EIGHT

ayli's arm hung off the bed. Her mouth drooped slightly open and her painted makeup was nearly all faded, exposing the girl underneath. She shivered as a chill swept the room.

Alden untied his woolen cloak and draped it gently over her. Rubbing his arms, he started toward the front door, tiptoeing over the wood planks that were splitting at the seams. Finally outside, he sat in the grass near a broken handcart where he had eaten the night before.

After a while the clouds parted, revealing the sun just above the treeline. Alden smiled at the unfamiliar sensation of sunlight on his skin. He folded his hands behind his head and leaned back into the cart, letting the rays kiss his face…

A voice stirred Alden from his nap.

Mayli stood over him, sun beaming from behind and forcing him to squint. A golden haze surrounded the princess and the edges around her glowed as if she were outlined in a white lace.

Her black hair danced in the wind while songbirds sang mid-morning tunes.

If it weren't for her scowl, she'd look beautiful in this moment... But then again, when didn't she? He smiled.

She crossed her arms.

Is she angry or cold? Probably both.

"I'm hungry," she repeated testily, and then hunkered into her cloak and shivered after the autumn breeze touched her.

Yep. Both.

Alden eyed the sun, noting the distance it had passed in the sky. He guessed that he had slept for no more than a few hours. It was needed, as the last few nights had proved difficult. He had kept himself awake, unable to stop dwelling on the past and what he could make of the future. *If there is such a thing.*

Alden pushed off the cart in an attempt to stand, but it rolled back. He began to stumble but found himself steadied. Then he noticed Mayli at his side, holding him up.

"Thanks…" he said, pulling away awkwardly as he stood.

She folded her arms again. "Shouldn't thieves be dexterous?"

"Did you say you were hungry?"

She bobbed her head enthusiastically with a furrowed brow.

"Then save your tongue for that," he warned with a sarcastic tone, walking back inside with a smile.

Alden opened his pack and retrieved two large sticky buns from a box. They were encased in a gooey caramelized sauce and decorated with roasted pecans. Mayli's eyes grew as wide at the buns. Alden handed one to her. She reached, but he lifted it away, teasing her. The princess snatched it from his hand and threw out her tongue. As it slipped back in her mouth, so did the roll.

"This is delicious!" she gasped with a full mouth.

Alden smiled at her playfulness as he took his bun. "She likes to bake," he said before trying it. The sweet dough kissed his tongue and he squinted in bliss.

"Makes sense for a miller's wife." After licking her finger, she looked up at him. "Are Mary and Dean your parents?"

Alden just smiled with his full mouth.

He was just about to take his second bite when he realized she had already inhaled her bun. Bits of caramel remained on her cheek, and he grinned. *She's clueless.* He waited until he had finished with his own before he tapped his cheek, then winked. Mayli gasped and shielded her head away while she wiped it clean on her sleeve. Alden allowed himself a soft laugh, which only further embarrassed the princess.

She leaned back in her chair and huffed. "What are we doing here?"

His smile vanished. "Nothing. We're leaving." He stood up from the table and began packing.

"What? Already?"

"You want to go home, don't you?" he said, stuffing his bag. He then walked into the bedroom, fetching his cloak off the floor. When he came back out, he opened his mouth to speak.

"I'm ready," Mayli said eagerly before he could ask. She stood by the door.

Alden drew a crooked and amused grin across his face, then flicked his hood up.

As they walked towards the beach, Mayli pointed. "Look at that." She walked to a pile of rubbish and pulled away years of overgrown weeds and vines.

Alden joined the princess as she unveiled an abandoned birch bark canoe. The corner of her mouth began to twist into a smile, triggering his to do the same. He rolled the boat right-side up, then tugged and pulled until they reached the lips of the sandy shore.

"Will it hold?" Mayli put a hand on the gunwale and shook it, creating light ripples in the water.

Alden bent to investigate. There were a few scuffs and dents, places where moss was beginning to grow, but there didn't seem to be any intrusive holes or tears. He picked at its edging. The spruce gum seal had protected the vessel well over its lost years. Alden pushed the canoe fully into the river and stepped one foot in, testing its buoyancy. It swayed under his weight, but no water revealed any leaks. "Should, but I dunno how far we can get without a paddle."

"I'll check!" she said, dashing off to explore.

Alden blinked as branches shook, leaves fell, and after digging within the pile of trash, the princess withdrew an oar. Mayli raised it above her head as if she had just won an arduous victory. She strode over and handed it to him with a smug expression. He took it, amused, and presented the canoe to her like a carriage. Mayli gave him a mock curtsy before climbing in. She sat in the front and leaned against his pack as he set it down. Alden took seat in the back, then pushed off into the river, grinning.

After hours of silent travel along the Draclynn River, the land began to look familiar. He swallowed as they came around the last bend.

An Ammosian warship, with peeling orange and white paint, sat on the riverbank. Down its middle was a gaping tear where planks of wood were cracked and twisted like stretch marks. The ship's bow had been smashed in by a fallen tower that led to Brimley Castle perched on a small bluff.

"No..." gasped Mayli.

"May!"

Before Alden could grab the princess, Mayli leapt into the river. Her body flailed, getting tangled in her long cloak. The fabric wrapped around her, absorbing water with dying thirst. She began to sink as if her boots were trying to find the riverbed.

Alden scrambled forward, sending the canoe into a wobbling tantrum. He hunkered down before he, too, fell in. Seeing the last of the princess's hand dip underwater, Alden reached desperately to grab it. He took Mayli's wrist and lifted her to the side of the boat, then reeled her in to lay over him.

Mayli coughed up water then gasped for air. Alden patted her back to help but she flinched at his touch. Realizing she was on him, the princess pushed herself off and glared. He searched her eyes, mouth splitting open in bewilderment. She shook her head at him, then scooted away.

Mayli sat in a puddle, unmoving. For a moment, they drifted in silence as the current carried them along. Before they neared the ship, Alden took the oar and paddled hard, fighting his way across the stronger current. After he plowed the boat into a sandy beach, he stepped out into the river, uncaring as water flowed freely into his frayed boots. He walked past her and gripped the canoe's bow to pull the boat ashore, offering her a dry landing.

Alden moseyed toward the castle and leaned against the sandstone cliff at its base. With a sigh, he drew his knife. Freshly dried blood lingered from his last fight. His last kill... Using his wet cloak, he rubbed it clean, however a deep reddish sheen still reflected back. *No matter how often or well I clean this murderous thing, I'll never wash away the rich history stained deep within.*

Sheathing the dagger, he looked up to see the princess still in the canoe, shivering.

"Hey..." he called, startling himself with a frog-like voice.

She didn't respond.

Alden cleared his throat and tried again. "Look, you don't need to worry... Nobody is here. The town is burnt, its people gone. The castle has long been abandoned. It's in distress but will provide us shelter until help arrives."

Still nothing.

He took a step forward. "May. I understand the pain that this place causes you..."

"Liar!" Mayli snapped, jerking her head to face him. "Your

mother wasn't murdered here!" She attempted to glare, but her face softened upon seeing his.

He narrowed his wet eyes. "Princess, your war destroyed so many more lives!"

"*My* war?" she interrupted.

"Yes. Now c'mon." He gestured at the graying clouds, turning away. "It's gonna rain soon." After a few steps Alden looked back, realizing she wasn't following. "Mayli!" he barked, his voice carrying sharply. She flinched and stomped after him.

He dragged his feet as he climbed the rubble. He heard Mayli slip on some loose boards and curse in pain. He continued, holding back his instinct to offer a hand. *Let her suffer up this as I have,* he thought, leaping up a ledge. He heard a crunch under him and looked down to see scattered bones breaking under his weight. Alden swallowed as the hollowed eyes of a skull peered back at him. He took a breath and climbed more carefully until he found a gap in the broken wall to slip inside.

As they walked down the noble hallway within Brimley Castle, the sight gripped him. It was every scoundrel's dream to scavenge a castle, and they had taken full advantage. Other than the heavy furniture, little else was left to be found. There were, however, the occasional pieces of crockery, books, or iron candlesticks that lay scattered, things that held no real worth.

"Looters find no value in ugly paintings of false kings, I suppose," Mayli said, noting a large and beautiful painting displaying the crowning of King Liam.

Alden halted and Mayli walked by. As she did, she shifted the lone piece to hang crooked. His hands grew into fists. His breathing slowed, drawing in deep breaths, and he recessed into his hood. He bit his tongue, holding back a list of things he wanted to yell. Alden imagined that if he were a dog, all hair would be on its end—teeth snarling.

Mayli disappeared around the corner. He followed her down a staircase which the led to the large foyer. It was just as he remembered it: Carved wood lined the walls and thick beams loomed overhead. The extension was an attempt to woo those who came in, fooling them that the building hadn't once been an old stone barn. Alden pulled open the large doors to peek outside. Along the long path leading to the broken gatehouse were overturned carts, a catapult—which hadn't even made it to the battlefield—and weeds which grew tall. There was even a young sapling growing in the middle of the road.

Alden stepped back in as he heard Mayli's footsteps echo on tile. He followed her into the grand hall where faded blue banners hung low from the arch-beamed ceiling. In the back was an impressive window where long sheets of blue, black, white, and even some accenting hints of green and yellow stained glass illustrated Brimley's coat of arms—a large oak tree sprouting roots from a seed with three four-pointed stars to the right and three falling raindrops to the left. The cool colors danced upon the floor from the sunlight, mimicking ripples in the water. As fresh air filled the room the fabrics blew. Specks of dust twinkled down like snow.

"Oh! It's lovely in here!" Mayli exclaimed.

Alden smiled, but noticing the flare of sarcasm in her voice, took a better look around. Besides the tapestries of hunting scenes and painted portraits of past kings, another form of artwork decorated the hall. Scratched, inked, and painted along the worn stone and aged oak walls were insulting profanities mocking the kingdom's demise. Drawings of ships and crude illustrations from the battle were scribbled anywhere one could have found space. One even depicted the Brimley crest but with the tree cut down. "Murderer," "queen-killer," "brim-nosed cowards," "liars," and "frauds" were just some of the hurtful slander Alden read before he could look no more.

A ghostly wind blew, raising the hairs on the back of his neck. The airy howl mimicked the banter that once filled the hall as Alden walked by lines of tables. Benches and chairs were tipped and scattered, telling of the panic that grew the night the castle was attacked.

He paused at a raised deck, where a table sat unparalleled from the rest. Elaborately carved legs stuck out from a stained white cloth covering the table. Upon it was a decrepit hog and dishes littering the place setting. Silverware and gold goblets were curiously missing.

Alden picked up a flower from a wilted bouquet. He twisted the lily in his hands. Its brittle petal crumbled away as it spun. At the sight of it decaying in his hands, he gently set it down.

Moving on, Alden searched a fallen tea cart blocking the doorway into the service hall. He sighed when he found nothing of worth. After he cleared their path, Mayli entered into the hall-way. He followed behind until she led them into the servant's quarters.

A long, benched table offered the only place of gathering for the many workers the castle once had. At the end was a fireplace accompanied by a few logs. In the corner stood a curtained-off seat and chamber pot along with a wooden tub without a water supply. Free from privacy, rows of simple bunk beds lined the dormitory. At the foot of each, a chest lay open, exposing what few belongings the servants had possessed.

Alden pulled a boot from a chest and put it up to his own. Finding it too small, he tossed it and sat on the bed with an exhausted sigh.

Seeing that the chests held clothes, Mayli opened one as well. Inside were a few long shirts, slacks and some other garments. They were men's clothes, but she cared more about being dry once again than appearances. Mayli hung her cloak to drip-dry on the wall partition and stepped behind it, stripping her wet rags. Once dressed in a gray tunic and black slacks, she grabbed a quilt off a bed for herself and drew open the heavy, musty curtains.

Outside was a quaint courtyard where a fountain—filled with green algae—collected a light sprinkle of rain. She looked up to see a dark cloud looming in the distance. A flash of light illuminated the sky and the trees shook in the wind as if scared. Just as she forgot she had seen the lightning, a gentle rolling thunder followed.

Mayli turned away from the window to see the thief now slouched against a bedpost, rubbing a cloth over his blade absently. His head was bowed, hidden under the shadow and safety of his hood, but she could see his down-turned and wavering lips like the night before.

"Who did you lose?"

He paused mid-swipe, as if the question had turned him to stone. Mayli thought a whole minute had passed before the statue finally moved and lifted his knife to the ceiling. He twisted it in his fingers, letting the black blade shine purple in the late sun creeping through the window. He stared up at it as if it held a secret. Just when Mayli accepted that he wouldn't answer, he finally brought the blade to his lap and said softly, "Myself."

He glanced up at her, but she shied away to look back out the window. Droplets began to roll down the glass panes as if his sadness caused the castle to cry.

"Since my mother's death, I've felt as though I've fallen into an ocean's fog, lost and unable to control which direction life pulled me. No one seems to care, seems to notice. So, I cling to glimmers of light that shine through the haze, hoping someday I'd be free from the darkness."

When she turned back, the thief was staring, eyes pained yet hopeful. "You will," he promised.

She smiled lightly, then her stomach rumbled loudly. She bit her lip and clenched her belly in embarrassment.

The thief chuckled, then sheathed his dagger. "Let's get to the kitchen."

It was the next door down the hall. Pots, pans, tools, and trays hung from iron rings above each workstation. Dried leafy spices were draped like small decorative flags along the walls and across walkways. An impressive fireplace protruded from the wall that had once been a beating heart to serve and feed the hungry castle, but now it was dormant—starved of life.

The thief placed the bow on a large cutting island and relieved himself of his bracers. Rubbing his arms, he toured the kitchen. Mayli watched as he found a jar and popped the lid open. He sniffed, grinned, and took a cluster of small black leaves from it, adding them to a pouch he kept on his belt. He set the rest aside. As he began collecting other leftover dried goods to prepare their next meal, a door creaked open.

THE LETTER

CHAPTER NINE

The roots of a fallen tree hold firm as darkness pulls at the golden sand.

Briar read the letter, again and again, trying to make sense of the single line in the sun's dimming rays. Giving up, he folded and tucked the parchment in a front-facing pouch on his sword belt and buckled it closed. He glanced casually around the bridge, looking for the man who passed the message along, but Sir Dean was no longer in view, along with the illegal goods he *didn't* see.

Any other guard, despite his commands, would have questioned Dean and harassed him for the Brimleyn crest tattooed upon his shoulder. However, Dean had been good friends with Briar's father, the late Prince Jamus Densen of Brimley. Together they nobly fought to protect their homeland in the war three years past. Though it was risky, Briar honored Dean for his bravery and let him slip by in trade for one of Mary's sticky buns.

Briar bit into the caramel treat, moaning pleasantly. *Captain of the Guard has its perks at least.* As he chewed the sweet baked dough, the sight of a rough yet beautiful woman stiffened his jaw. Leaning casually against a lamppost on the other side of the stone bridge, she was bathed in lamplight. The woman ran a hand through her short hair and flashed her eyes at him as if wanting to be seen. It worked.

She smiled.

He smiled back.

As he enjoyed the idea of a woman looking upon him, the sticky bun surprisingly didn't seem as sweet anymore. Briar's lips twisted up as if he could taste the sweeter thing before him. The corset-like tunic she wore had her bosom yearning to get out. *I could help with that*, he thought with a widening grin. Imagining the ties being loosened down to her waist, Briar's attention was caught by lines of belts and straps accenting her body. There were many pouches, ropes, and knives. *A thief?*

Briar subconsciously touched the pouch that held Alden's letter and his smile vanished. Leading his horse, William, away, Briar pulled from the checkpoint. A rider to his left started to follow, but with a shake of his head and a low whistle, Briar commanded his lieutenant to stay. He looked to where the woman had been, but she was now gone.

Feeling the presence of eyes on his back, Briar gave William a squeeze and trotted back to his office. He tied the black stallion to a rail and retreated inside. After locking the door and closing all the window coverings, he lit a candle. Taking out the letter once more, Briar studied the riddle.

"The roots of a fallen tree hold firm...Brimley, okay..." He held his square and beardless chin, nodding in thought.

Briar took a seat at his cluttered desk and focused on the words. *Golden sand...?* He flipped an hourglass over to watch the grains drip as if it were the clue. With a groan, he shook his head, forcing himself to think harder. When he steadied it, he noticed a raven's note in the morning's mail. He pulled it out from between a few papers and read.

Princess Mayli Drake of Ammos—kidnapped in Colville. Last seen with white feathers jacket, orange silk scarf and dress. Suspects include but are not limited to: King Colin Densen, emissaries of Brimley, thieves, and enemies of Ammos or Hiore.

He bolted from his seat, knocking it to the floor. Surveying the room, Briar noted the things he needed to pack, then dashed around to collect them all. He wrapped up a week's worth of rations, a healer's kit, a northwestern map, rope, and other tools. As he stuffed everything into a set of large leather saddlebags, a knock came to the door.

"Captain, it's Thomas."

"One moment," Briar called back to his lieutenant. He set the bundle down, jogged to his desk to unlock a small hidden drawer. Taking one last look at Alden's letter, he locked it inside the secret compartment. He picked his chair off the floor, then welcomed his lieutenant inside along with a cold and rainy draft.

The tall man ducked as he entered. Once through, he placed his hand over his shoulder, greeting Briar with formality. "We've finished at the city gate for the night. After you left we only came across the usual."

"Relay the usual."

"Huh? Well, uh, a farmer tried bringing in bags of fruit instead of corn, which we confiscated." He grinned as he tossed a pear to Briar. "Then there was a quarrel between rival merchants about competing goods or some nonsensical thing. After that, there were a few thieves causing trouble. Nothing outlandish."

Briar rolled the pear in his hands. "Tell me about the thieves."

"It was a young boy and one of those bald-headed desert folk, sir. It seemed the older one tried to control the kid's sticky fingers, but it only created more of a commotion."

"Boy and a nomad… No pretty woman with unique hair?"

"Uh, no sir."

"Keep a look out while I'm gone. She was eyeing me in the crowd earlier. Something about her didn't feel right."

"Perhaps she thought you dashing."

"Ha! Woman don't choose me thanks to my name and title. Even most whores keep away."

Thomas frowned and looked to the stuffed saddlebag. "You leaving somewhere?"

Briar grabbed a few last items and packed them. Throwing on a long, black cloak, he smiled up at Thomas. "Yep. Take over for me. I'll be out for a week or so... Hard to say when I'll be back."

"You're leaving tonight? You want me to arrange a party to aid you?"

"No!" Briar replied quicker than intended. He recollected himself, tugging his jerkin down. "No, we are already spread too thin looking for the princess. It will just be myself. I have a friend I need to see."

"I understand, sir. I'll fetch Emory from the stable and lead you to the city gate."

"That would be nice," Briar said as he bit into the pear. "Mmm, but first, get me more of this delicious 'corn' to go!"

CHAPTER TEN

"*I* was afraid you weren't going to show," said a dark, steel-cutting voice.

Alden jumped around the center island to defend the princess, but Reyn already had Mayli wrapped in a chokehold.

Reyn whipped his rapier against Alden's hand, drawing blood. "Eh, eh! Leave it."

Alden took his hand away from his dagger, knowing the danger Mayli was now in. He watched helplessly as she squirmed and clawed at the man's bracers, eager to break free. She tried to stomp on his feet but Reyn coiled his grip tighter around the princess's neck and shook her.

"Not gonna work this time, Princess," he hissed.

Mayli's hazel eyes looked up at Alden, pleading for help. His heart sank, knowing he couldn't, not with Reyn in the position he was in. Her eyelids fluttered while she gasped for breath.

"Let her go, Reyn!" Alden growled, fingers twitching.

To Alden's surprise, Reyn obeyed, shoving the princess to him. Alden stepped forward out of reflex. As he caught her, limp and now unconscious body, he felt the needle-like touch of

Reyn's rapier sting his neck. He froze and eyed the shiny and thin steel. Alden hugged Mayli protectively as he felt a drip of blood escape him.

Reyn threw rope at him. "Tie her up," he commanded with as much pride and dominance as if announcing, "Checkmate."

Fearing he had no option but to submit, Alden followed the order. The tip of Reyn's sword traced along Alden's neck and face as a taunt. Alden's heart raced and breath trembled, but the cuts weren't deep. Once Mayli was bound, the shadow commander nodded for him to set her aside. Alden gently guided her down against a nearby cupboard. He stood with ice in his eyes to face Reyn.

"Great, now I can escort you back to Pierz," he said, tossing another rope.

Alden let it hit him and fall to the floor. "We are not going back to the guild."

"Maybe not by your own free will, no, but you *are* coming back with me." Reyn pointed his rapier at the rope and lifted it slightly.

Alden continued to ignore it.

Reyn huffed. "Come now, give up. Kira told us all about you and your secret outings on *The Albatross*."

Alden's mouth fell open involuntarily. *"Kira?"*

"Oh, please. All this time you though Kira was your sweetheart? Ha! Fool."

"She certainly isn't yours!" Alden barked back.

"Well, heh, not sure that's true. We had a bit of fun just before the mission. Got plans for afterward now too now that you'll be out of the picture."

"Bullshit. Kira would never choose to lay with you! Not after everything we did to free her from your control." Alden took an angered step forward, uncaring as Reyn's rapier slipped under his leather armor and dug into his shoulder.

Reyn shrugged. "What can I say? She missed me. She practically begged for me to take her back." He shoved his blade forward, forcing Alden to wince and take a step back. "Unimpressed with you, I'm sure."

Alden fumed, then his face sunk. *Reyn knew I met with Briar because of Kira, which means she had been following me... Her kindness had been an act all along.*

"So, since you couldn't get any action with Kira, you thought to try and get a taste of royalty instead?" Reyn prodded with a lick of his lips. His eyes traced down to Mayli. "I don't blame you." He touched his rapier to the hem of Mayli's tunic, lifting it.

"No!" Alden yelled in disgust as he shifted towards Mayli, drawing Reyn's attention back to him.

"Come on, Alden!" He bent his knees slightly and threw his hand up in exasperation. "What good is capturing a princess if you aren't gaining anything from her?"

"There is everything to gain for her safety!"

"Safety?" Reyn snorted. He ticked his gloved finger in understanding, then began walking casually. "I forgot you were one of those brim-nosed snot refugees who believed your prince was innocent!"

"King."

"What?"

"Liam is dead," Alden corrected stiffly. "Colin is now rightfully king."

Reyn tilted his head down with an exaggerated smile. He scoffed, then brought his hand up to a long, lacy cobweb and rubbed it in his fingers. "Great kingdom he's got." Reyn stood taller. "So, how about this: you give me your cut of what *King* Colin is gonna pay for her, and I won't kill you. Deal?" He offered an open palm covered in spider silk.

Alden leaned away, disgusted. "Piss off."

"C'mon, it's a fair trade."

"You don't make deals, at least none you intend to keep."

"Alden, you are smart but you're a rogue, a thief, a criminal..."

Your king is no better than us. He'll likely murder you after he's done finishing her off like he did her mother. Might as well let me save you the effort."

Alden drew his dagger with heightened speed and lunged forward.

Reyn brought his rapier around and knocked the blade away. "Ah! A deal you'll accept?"

"Fuck you." Alden took a step in then thrust his knee up.

Reyn dodged the attack. He swung his sword. Alden ducked as it sang overhead. With Reyn's arm extended, Alden popped into the opening and swiped his blade across the man's face.

Reyn jumped back, laughing madly as if the cut had tickled. He touched his fingers to the blood, grinning more. Excited, Reyn pushed forward, slashing his long rapier recklessly in the air. Alden hopped back again and again, dodging the constant swing. Losing space, he butted up against a cabinet, rattling dishes. As a silver line flashed near his face, Alden raised his arms to block.

The cut stung as Reyn ripped across his exposed arms, once, then twice. Fearing the next attack wouldn't be so kind, Alden rolled along the cupboards. A dull twang sounded where he had been and where Reyn's sword now stabbed the wood.

Alden scurried to an opening but Reyn was already upon him. He kicked forward, shoving his attacker away to catch a break from the fury. As Alden brought his leg back, he misstepped and he fell to the ground. Before Reyn could capitalize, Alden tumbled under the kitchen's center worktable and peered out at his old commander. He stood grinning with his hands resting calmly on his hips.

"You're just as much a coward as your prince, brim-nose," Reyn teased.

Alden snarled and a bead of sweat crept into his eyes. He wiped his face against his bloodied arm, wetting it further. He licked his lip as another drip fell, tasting iron. Alden attempted to draw in a deep breath, but it was hard labored. *C'mon...think clearly!* He gave his head a shake, wishing he had slept better the previous nights.

Against the cabinets, Alden saw Mayli roll her head as she was gaining consciousness. She was bound. Helpless. Innocent. Haunting visions of things Reyn would do to Mayli stabbed him harder than any wounds he'd received.

With a determined growl, Alden rolled to his feet. He circled the man who threatened their lives. Reyn countered his movement. Besides his bleeding cheek, which he seemed to wear with pride, Reyn was nearly unhurt. His lengthy sword made him untouchable. But not for long.

Alden threw his blade and the cabinet behind Reyn rattled as the knife stuck to it.

He cackled. "Oh, are you getting sloppy already? Fascinating." He stroked his beard, then grinned. "You gave up your precious black dagger. Ready to give up on her now too?"

"Try me!" Alden taunted, drawing Paige's hunting knife.

<hr />

Mayli blinked awake at the clang of steel ringing in her ears. Gaining focus, she saw a black knife protruding from the cabinet a few feet away. *That could have killed me!*

A flash of movement caught her eye and she saw two men fighting. The thief and the other, Cole or...Reyn. The man seemed to use his sword like a stick, toying with the thief as if he were a dog. He had the upper hand with the rapier's long blade, and the thief accumulated many small cuts along his arms. Mayli could see the damage was draining him, and he was now heaving long, exhausted breaths. She swallowed at the realization that wasn't going to last much longer, and she would soon be facing Reyn alone.

Mayli focused on the rope binding her wrists, thankful she

was bound in front this time, and began to gnaw frantically to break free. Her jaw began to cramp and fibers were stuck in-between her teeth. After a few more moments helplessly chomping, she stopped, realizing how foolish she was.

Mayli looked back at the knife and grinned. She scrambled over and positioned the black steel in-between her wrists and the rope. Carefully, she cut herself free, the sharp blade making quick work of her binds. Mayli plucked the weapon from the wall and rubbed her wrists as she surveyed the room. Finally, she spotted it: the bow and quiver the thief had liberated from her after she had killed Paige. And it was just a few yards away.

Alden cried in agony as a knife slipped through his leather armor and sank into his side. He buckled, dropping his last weapon.

Reyn gripped Alden's hair and lifted his head, which he hadn't realized had drooped. The commander then pressed his hand firm around Alden's neck, making him gag. Black eyes pierced him as sharply as the man's blade. Alden blinked as his vision doubled and the room began to twist.

Reyn's two faces formed an exceptionally long smile. "A special blend of toxins, just for you," he said, presenting his poison-laced rapier. "I saved the vial for just the right occasion, since I had to crawl for hours through the most miserable, rat-infested cave and wait for this damn flower to bloom before I could collect its poison."

"Fitting place for vermin like you..." Alden managed to sneer.

"Shut up!" Reyn leaned in with his dagger. Alden felt his side wetten with more blood. "But seeing you like this made it all worth it! Every nick you took, every slice I gave slowed your reflexes—dulled your perception." He sighed with disappointment. "I have an antidote so you won't die—yet. I can't wait to see what Pierz's punishment will be. Besides, there's a show for you to watch with me and the princess."

"Don't you fucking touch her!" Alden squirmed, fighting the pain.

"I'm not the one messing up plans to try to rescue some royal, you piece of shit!" Reyn yelled, squeezing Alden's neck.

Alden gasped for the air he just lost, but none came. Swirls of colors began to dance in his mind and he began to feel light.

Reyn tried to push the dagger in farther, but the blade was stuck between layers of thick leather. Frustrated, he pulled it out. The commander brought it up to Alden's face and wiped his blood across his cheek, giving him a matching red line to Reyn's own wound. He opened his mouth to speak but paused, seeing Alden's pompous smile as he looked beyond.

"What do you have to be happy for? Drug working that quick?"

Alden gave a slow approving nod.

Reyn shifted to follow Alden's gaze just as an arrow whizzed past. It stuck in a cabinet behind them.

"You Ammosian bitch!" Reyn yelled.

Mayli squealed and fumbled to draw. Her quiver crashed to the floor, spilling arrows everywhere. She quickly bent to grab one.

Reyn raised his arm to toss his dagger but halted. An arrow stuck through his skull. The shadow commander stumbled back, colliding into the cabinet. Stacks of plates came shattering around him as he fell to the floor, surrounding his corpse in broken porcelain.

Unable to hold himself up, Alden slid down the stone wall. As he lay on the floor, he put his hand on his wound. Blood leaked slowly between his trembling fingers. His heart raced and head throbbed as the poison consumed him.

"May…"

Mayli stared at the dead man past her bow. Bright blood pooled around him. Unnerved, Mayli dropped the weapon and dashed out the kitchen. She flew down the hall, the servant's quarters, and around a corner, her footsteps echoed around her, beating as fast as her heart. She reached the great hall and clung to the nearest chair. As she panted, she looked around the abandoned dining hall, reading words scribed by her allies. Only one stood out to her: murderer.

As she cried, a voice woke in hear head, recalling the thief's words regarding the matter. "You would kill if you were trying to survive or protect someone you love. That doesn't make you a murderer."

Her eyes fell back to the rope burn around her wrists and thought hard about her adventure. Despite him being a thief, he was patient and—dare she say—chivalrous. More than once he extended his hand to help. He cooked for her, offering more to her than even himself. He slept at a distance and had even given his cloak for extra warmth while he shivered outside. She remembered the look of horror on his face when she had made a break for the Shadowens along the path.

Mayli then recalled the words Reyn had spoken while he had the man pinned in the kitchen; the thief was trying to *save* her. Finally, realization struck. *This knife wasn't a coincidence; he threw it to me!* In a panic, Mayli pushed off the chair and fled back into the kitchen.

"May…" the thief whimpered without looking up.

Mayli began flinging cupboard doors open. Most everything inside was old and moldy, but she ultimately found the right cabinet—one housing a collection of jars filled with an assortment of fine spices, seeds, and leaves. She grabbed a few packed with a red powder and set them out on the center worktable.

After sampling each, she selected one that had a familiar bite to it.

Mayli hurried beside the thief.

His head rolled from one side to the other. "May. I'm sorry…" he moaned. "I didn—"

"It's fine," she interrupted, unbuckling the straps to remove his leather chest plate. Using the knife, she tore open his tunic until the wound at his side was exposed. She hesitated as his blood spilled to the floor. Regaining focus, she poured the jar's contents on the cut.

He yelped and jerked forward, gripping her arm as if to ward off an attack.

Mayli winched, but his fierce strength only lasted a second. His hand fell away and Mayli continued to press the powder in, easing him back. "It will be okay…"

"What is that?" he hissed, peering up at her with one narrowed eye.

"Cayenne."

He sighed. "Poison…"

"No, the spice will help stop the bleed—"

"…sword was poisoned." He took a deep and pained breath. "Reyn has…"

"OH! Uh… I'll get some water!" Mayli exclaimed as she stood, unsure if there was more she could do or how much that could help. She didn't know how to treat poisons. In her haste, she stumbled over something behind her. She paused to stare at Reyn's body.

Two. I've killed two people.

Mayli observed the aftermath of the violence that had taken place moments before. Furniture had shifted, blood was smeared everywhere, and shards of porcelain decorated a corpse like flower petals at a wake.

She shook her head and ran to fetch her waterskin. Mayli

returned to her patient and offered it to him. He didn't move. She shook the bottle, trying to capture his attention. "Here!"

The man's fingers twitched. His head lulled as he lost consciousness. She whined, then knelt behind him, raising his body against hers to hold him up. He was warm and lay heavy against her. Mayli bit the cork and pulled. It released with a loud pop at which he opened his eyes.

Still alive. Good.

She held his head as she set the flask to his lips. Lifting the waterskin slowly, Mayli forced him to drink. She continued to pour until it spilled from his mouth. She set it aside and lowered his head into her lap.

As the man became incredibly weak, Mayli's heart pounded. His breaths were shallow and sweat beaded on his forehead as his body temperature continued to rise. She stripped a piece of cloth from his tunic, dampened it, and then placed it on his forehead. Subconsciously, she found herself petting his face and running her fingers through his hair like a mother cat licking a stillborn to wake. After a nerve-wracking passage of time, his breathing steadied and she felt his pulse become more regular.

"May..." he softly begged, as if she alone could bring him to life.

"I'm here," she assured, stroking his face again. With eyes still shut with pain, he smiled faintly. A warm tear rolled down his cheek and kissed her thumb. When it hit, a wave of emotions flooded her. Unable to handle it all, she leaned forward and buried her face into her hands. Fear, hate, pride, resentment, sorrow, grief, worry, and something else she couldn't quite place...

Her body contracted as she drew in labored and soggy breaths. Then she felt a gentle touch. Fingers wove between her own as the man brought their hands down to his chest. She squeezed—unsure who was comforting whom—but in that moment, she welcomed the bond with her rogue.

LOCKED UP

CHAPTER ELEVEN

$\mathcal{K}$ira stood awkwardly in the dark street as few guards passed by. She held her breath and made an effort to look around innocently—which she was, but the habit still remained. They ignored her and continued into the lookout tower. It was tall, octagonal, made of stone, and topped with beautifully crafted ramparts designed to look like a draclynn's wolf-like head. Torchlight revealed tips of pointed hats that peered out from over the edge as guards periodically scanned the city. Kira imagined they could see every inch of the Dreggan shoreline from there. Long banners blanketed the stone walls—one yellow, one black.

A guard in a long black tabard exited the tower. Kira stepped forward and their eyes met. Before she could ask where to find Briar, the guard turned and left as if pretending he had not seen her. She threw her hands up in exasperation. *The one time I'm glad to find a guard, he runs.*

Kira continued to the tower, but the cry of a metal sign called to her as the ocean breeze swept over the island. She tilted her head. Cloaked under the tower's shadow from the moon was a quaint and lonely wooden shack, splintered and sun-bleached. Through the attic's dark window, she spied the canopy of a formal bed and a banner of Brimley's royal crest of hanging beside it. She looked at the squeaking sign, which hung above the building's door. It displayed a snake coiled around a shield. The guard captain.

"Why can't Dregs just use words?" Kira hopped onto the old porch and took one last look around to ensure she had indeed escaped Squirrel and Trod. When no shadows moved, she knocked.

Silence.

She tried again, but only the sign's irritating whine answered back. Kira then tested the door—locked. *But not for long.* With a flick of her wrist and a twist of her fingers, she manipulated her tools to invite herself in.

"Hello?"

Slim streaks of light from a torch outside lined the room from the slatted window covering. The musty and damp scent of horse tack wafted out from an open chest, which held a few bridles and blankets. To the right was a desk littered with a mess of papers, that fluttered in the breeze she let in. Kira closed the door and wandered in. Around the corner was a hallway lined with three private cells protected by iron bars and stone walls. At the end was a staircase. She followed it up to his empty living quarters.

Kira slowly walked back down to his office. She lit a lantern on the wall, hoping to use it as a beacon. She sat down at his cluttered desk to wait. There were at least five empty ink bottles, one full one, a spill of wax, a fork, a horseshoe, and ten gold—which she pocketed. Notes on deliveries, schedules, and other mundane guard tasks were littered on the desk. As she paged through, she noticed the letter about the kidnapping.

"News spreads fast…"

As she scooted back in the chair, she noticed an unusual lip in the desk's siding. Kira bent to investigate. At the discovery of a small hidden drawer, the corners of her mouth twisted up into a proud grin. She reached underneath and found the keyhole. Unable to resist the urge, she retrieved her lock-picking set once more.

The device wasn't simple; it had a somewhat complicated system of gears that likely challenged most thieves, but Kira wasn't most, and opened it with ease. Inside were more letters. Kira recognized Alden's refined writing and lifted it to read:

The roots of a fallen tree hold firm as darkness pulls at the golden sand.

Kira set it down and withdrew an article on Arkello Densen, the recent self-proclaimed king of Vatan who supposedly escaped Gezmek. According to him, the city still thrived underground and he was the grandson of King Edune, the old King of Vatan. Kira rolled her eyes and set the folder down. Digging through the drawer, she found a few letters from Briar to his older cousin, Colin, discussing the matter and suspicions of his involvement in Queen Margaret's murder. A few other letters discussed the thieves guild. *If found in the wrong hands, these would ruin their chance of ever coming back to power. They are so dense.* Kira gathered a few up and tossed the papers over the logs.

Kira struck a spark and the fire took quickly, happy to help erase the evidence of their secret messages. She watched the paper curl and char while wax dripped like blue blood. Kira smiled at a deed well done.

The door opened. Kira spun, excited to finally talk with her prince. But at the sight of a surprisingly tall, dark-haired man, her heart froze. He wore a black tabard with thin yellow accents. Kira hoped the last words had been chewed away by the flame by the time the guard approached.

"Who are you and what are you doing here?"

"Ah, I'm Kira Harlow. Here to see Prince Briar, Captain of the Guard, sir!" she replied as politely as she could with a dip of her head. She thought too late to lift her arm to her shoulder to bow, so instead smiled awkwardly.

The guard stepped forward and rested a hand on his belt casually, but it was within an inch of his sword. "You're the woman that was eyeing him from the bridge earlier?"

"Yes."

The guard eyed the fireplace. "Why?"

"Ah, that's between us." She looked too but the letters were all gone and the pine was beginning to take flame, heating the small room, with the scent of sap wafting in.

"I'm his lieutenant, Thomas. Anything you need to talk to him about, you can discuss with me."

Kira collapsed into a large tufted leather chair beside the stacked stone fireplace and folded her arms. "It's personal…"

"He's going to be out for a few days. Maybe a week, he said."

"A week?" she gasped.

"Yes, so you can tell me or kindly leave and come back after his return."

Kira twisted her lips in thought. She trusted only those who Alden did, and although Thomas looked like a responsible lieutenant, she wasn't sure he was on Alden's list—few were. So, option one was out. Option two meant she'd get caught up with Trod and Squirrel. It had been hard enough slipping away from Trod's watchful eye on the bridge. Luckily, she had tricked Squirrel into stealing from a noble and created enough of a commotion to flee. Kira smirked to reveal her cat-like fangs to the tall man.

She chose option three.

Kira lunged and Thomas drew his blade with impressive speed. She smiled. *Briar is smart to have this man as his lieutenant. But let's see how quick he really is.* As Thomas opened up, Kira rolled in and slashed his coin purse from his belt. With an amused grin, she hopped back with it in her palm.

The lieutenant lurched forward in anticipation to chase, but she didn't run. He grunted, then adjusted his footing as Kira stood unmoving. Eyeing her, he slapped his sword against her wrist.

Kira obediently dropped the bag, spilling a few silver and gold coins onto the wood floor with a clang. Kira sent her arms wide. "Arrest me!" she cheered, closing her eyes and shaking her hair as she raised her chin proudly. *The lieutenant captured a Shadowen thief!*

Thomas blinked. "Ah…"

"Go on, I stole from you! I assaulted a lieutenant. Lock me up!" She brought her hands forward to await shackles.

"You…didn't even run…"

She groaned. "Is that what is required to get locked up around here? Must I, or can we skip that? I really don't enjoy it." Kira brought her ankle up and leaned in to stretch. She released it, then slumped her shoulders, mocking exhaustion.

Thomas pointed down the hall. "You just want me to lock you up?"

"Yes! Until Briar is back, please. But not here." She ticked a finger toward the holding cells. *Squirrel and Trod could easily free me from there.* "Throw me in the castle dungeon."

"You haven't committed any crimes harsh enough for there."

"Oh, hah, I'm sure I have! I'm a Shadow; I've killed men and women, sabotaged merchants, stolen from nobles, spied on royalty, my own guild leader…you name it!"

"But…ah…" His brow wrinkled in waves of worry as he looked around.

"Must I kill someone now?" Kira drew her blade.

"No! No, don't!"

Kira rested her hands on her hips, tapping her foot impatiently.

The lieutenant scratched his chin, losing his finger within his beard as if to find his thoughts. Having found it, he nodded. "Fine. I'll lock you up if you insist."

"Thanks!" Kira squinted her eyes as if he had just given a heartfelt gift.

"Uh, huh." Thomas stepped towards the door.

"Wait!" Kira called after him. She handed him her blade, then grabbed a pair of manacles that hung by the door and clamped them on herself.

"I don't have the key for that!"

"That's fine! I can pick it!"

"Oh, ah, okay then…"

Kira smiled and followed the lieutenant out. Thankfully, he was unnerved enough to hold her by the arm, issuing her along as if she were a true captive. She played along. They walked down the cobble street lit by damp reflections from lamps. It was starting to mist and Kira could taste the salt in the air and feel the bite of night. She hoped the dungeon would be warm but knew better.

They arrived at the gate house before two well-armed guards. One kept a collection of crumbs in his beard as if saving them for a mid-shift snack, whereas the other stood at attention, her face stone like the walls she protected.

"I've, uh, caught the thief Prince Briar raised concerns about."

The guards raised their poleaxes and the gate opened, welcoming them inside the beautifully gardened bailey. Thomas led her around the curtain wall until they found a guarded door leading towards the castle. The guards stepped aside to allow them passage. Kira jogged forward to be closer to Thomas as she noticed their hungry eyes.

He led her to her cell and stopped as he creaked it open. "You sure?"

Kira handed him the manacles she'd picked along the way. "You betcha!" she said, taking a hesitant step in.

Thomas eyed the shackles and raised his brow up at her. "As you wish," he said, shutting the wrought iron door. He locked it, took another set of chains from nearby and secured them around the bars as well.

Kira grinned, amused. *Smart man indeed.*

Thomas nodded with his lips pressed flat, as if still not convinced that could hold her. He was right. He stepped away to leave.

Kira turned. "And you'll tell Briar the moment he's back, right?"

"Personal matters, yep," he said with a half turn of his head.

Kira looked around and smiled. *It isn't so bad here.* The air was stale, smelling of piss and mold. There was a bench and a thin bedding of damp hay on a cold stone floor. A few dim torches lit the hall, and there was even a waste bucket. Best of all, she was alone. She'd been in much worse conditions...

"Oh, Alden..." Kira moaned as she plopped onto the bench and kicked at some small rocks.

She worried if she was doing the right thing; whether Alden and Briar would trust her. By turning herself in, Kira hoped it would be enough to convince them of her dedication. She sighed. Alden likely wouldn't, despite everything they'd been through. Her thoughts took her back to her first meeting...

Reyn had just finished with her, leaving her in a heap, pants missing and body trembling. Her head spun wildly from whatever disturbing drug he'd administered, but she was able to pull herself from the wet gutter. She followed the wood siding out of the alley. Losing the wall at the corner, Kira fell.

She pushed from the ground but hardly moved. She was sure she had been crying. Suddenly, strong arms lifted her. Kira tensed in fear, but a kind voice spoke.

Alden's.

Fading in and out, she remembered his worried smile hiding under a hood, sympathetic eyes peering into her own. Next thing Kira remembered was that she was at The Five Leaves, drinking the best brew of Brim Tea she'd ever had as the sweet flavor helped ease her worries as well as her vertigo. She was now decent, wearing baggy pants meant for a man. Likely his.

When Alden descended down the stairs, dressed in daggers, leather armor and dark clothes, she had cowered. But he kept his distance, nodded a hello and left without a word.

When Kira tried to pay for the calming drink, Mr. Grey, the shop owner, refused. He explained it had already been paid for, as well as dinner and room above. Kira couldn't understand. People never helped others in need without earning something in return. Suddenly, she feared the stranger's intentions and promptly fled.

Curiosity dug at her for the next few days until she finally returned to the tea shop, but only outside to watch. The Five Leaves had a few patrons. Those who did visit left with happy faces. However, one face never smiled, but seeing it always made hers light up.

Without ever looking around, Alden stepped into the street and walked in the shadows cast by building overhangs. Kira easily followed.

As she stalked, Alden proved himself to be of kind heart. She watched him offer a coin to a sad-looking child, lost in the street. The girl took it with a happy squeal and Kira saw a sliver of a smile emerge from Alden's tight lips. He patted her shoulder and continued towards the harbor. Kira had scoffed. That child hadn't needed handouts—she had clean clothes and buckled shoes. Still, his generosity was something. Once at the docks, Kira learned of his even stranger behavior: spying.

Back then, his methods of gathering information were reckless. He had mastered the art of alerting dogs, knocking over ceramics, or being caught slipping out of shadows. His clumsiness had rewarded him with countless fights, but he was lucky enough to escape without being completely bruised and beaten because of basic combat training.

Kira had enjoyed studying the curious ways he orchestrated

situations. Instead of patiently waiting for the right opportunity to arise, he had rushed in using brute force to try to succeed in his goals. Oftentimes he'd act so obviously inefficient that she couldn't help but laugh out loud, clamping her mouth shut so as not to be caught.

After weeks stalking him—to find relief from her own troubles with Reyn—Kira began to predict Alden's next moves. *He'll look ahead but not behind to double check he wasn't followed. He's going to reach for his dagger...now—yep. And without waiting, he's going to spring into action when the first guard shows his face... There he goes. Now he's clueless about the other three about to flank him because he didn't check his back...*

Knowing his choices were not always going to be in favor of his survival, Kira began secretly assisting him when she knew he'd need it, not wanting to lose her new favorite pastime. She distracted guards by luring them away with thrown rocks or calls. Sometimes she even made it a challenge to sneak up to snip their belts, as it was always a joy watching them become tangled in their own trousers and falling armor. In rare cases, Kira secretly lent her hand in battle if it became too much for her *friend*.

Once he nearly got himself killed for lurking in the same dock her troop was assigned to raid. Looking back on it now, she realized he had probably been meeting Briar, as his ship *The Albatross* had been docked nearby. She allowed herself to bump into a crate. It splashed into the water, alerting everyone to her troop's presence. Reyn hadn't been pleased, but Alden was able to flee while their targets jumped to engage.

It was then Kira decided to introduce herself and invite him to join the Shadowen Thieves Guild. That way he'd be given proper training and could possibly get the information he was seeking. As long as she could convince him to join, she could protect both him and her guild's interests. More importantly, she could get to know the honorable thief further.

Having made her decision, Kira scouted out each of his known retreats the following morning. It had embarrassed her that she knew so much about his routine without even knowing his name. Eventually, she had found him in an old warehouse overlooking the shipyard after she spotted his cloak spilling over the rafters.

She understood the location's appeal, as it had a revealing vantage point, making it the perfect perch to survey the coming and going of vessels. Unfortunately for *him*, it had no secondary escape options.

Kira stealthily climbed the scaffolding and stole a quick look into the loft. He sat against a post and was focused on making notes in a journal with a dark red conté crayon. He took occasional glances at the ships as he moved his arm around the page.

Sinking down and crawling around, Kira crossed the beams until she reached the other side. Once satisfied with her positioning, she flipped herself up onto the platform, presenting herself. His crayon snapped on the page as he jumped up in surprise. Both shock and fear danced in his eyes. He backed against the wall and Kira grinned victoriously as he realized his poor choice of a roost.

An idiot once again.

"Hi! Remember me? I'm Kira!" she greeted in her high-spirited tone. Her attempt to appear friendly didn't work, and his face shook in horror. She frowned, hurt that he didn't remember her. Alden had tried to maneuver past, but Kira swiftly blocked his exit, coaxing him back. "That's a long way down... Let's chat!" she offered cheerfully.

He peered over the edge. "...How'd ya get up here?"

"Oh! Same way you did. But *stealthily*," she said with a smug expression. "I've been watching you since you hel—"

"Watching me?" he choked, understandably shaken by the idea. He raised his hand with the journal to ensure she kept her distance while the other drew a black dagger. She then nodded proudly as she eyed the book, curious what notes lay hidden. *He's so clueless. What if it was the journal I was after?* It was within arm's reach.

She blinked back at him, ignoring his useless blade. He was never quick enough that she should worry. "Mmhmm. A few months now, I think. You picked me up in the alley... Clothed me. Gave me tea..." She smiled shyly while rocking on her heels.

Kira watched the fear and rage burn hotter behind his hooded eyes. She was sure all he'd heard was "a few months." Like a wild animal, he tried again to bolt past. However, she read his movements like a familiar book and pounced. Effortlessly, she took hold of his belt and threw him to the dirty wood planks. A plume of dust leapt into the air and the rafters creaked in protest. His journal had flown from his hands and over the edge. It landed with a long-awaited thud, demonstrating just how high up they were.

Before he could figure out which way was up and why he was now on his back, Kira placed her knee to his crotch and his knife to his throat. She grinned, taking pleasure that she'd stolen it and conquered him—not that it had been a challenge.

That was the first time she had a chance to look freely upon Alden's face. There was something humbling about him. His face was fuller then, soft and clean shaven. His warm chestnut-colored hair was longer, hiding his narrowing and terrified brown eyes. Beyond it Kira could see a determined gaze, like someone never ready to give up. Although he was a lousy thief, his will to survive was as charming as his looks.

She blushed.

Alden's worried eyes tried to glare.

"Ya ever wonder how those guards became tied up all those times? Or how you miraculously managed to dodge the patrols as you snuck—oh-so-quietly—around? It was all more than pure luck. And last night at the docks...you were in more trouble than you knew, had you been seen by anyone else. I'm glad my warning spooked you." She snickered. "You really should be thanking me for not being dead. Many times over!"

The look that Alden had worn was priceless, like a child being told his pet chicken was no longer in its coop but in his hands—and mouth. He peered down at his traitorous blade she had firmly pressed against his throat.

Kira smiled innocently. "Look—don't mind the knife—I'm in the Shadowen Thieves Guild. We could use someone as dedicated to finding information as you! We can teach you more efficient ways of doing..." She bobbed her head side to side, looking for the right word. "Well, everything! And there is pay, of course!"

"Oh yeah?" He relaxed, probably in hopes that she would let him up. But Kira didn't buy his bluff and instead held firm. He growled. "What do you know about me?"

Kira beamed, pleased with herself for the copious amount of knowledge she had gathered. She knew his favorite foods, blend of tea, love for silence, that he was generous, and had an obsession with polishing his dagger. She could track his hideouts, knew what time he woke and went to bed. She opened her mouth, ready to spew most of it out, but shut it with a long frown. "I don't know your name!"

That made Alden smile. "I'd be more inclined to tell you if you weren't..." He glanced back down at his knife, then shifted his hips slightly. "Ya know..."

Kira grinned apologetically, gently removed her knee, slid off, and hopped to her feet. She remembered eyeing him seductively, hoping it wouldn't be the last time she'd be in that position with him. Alden eyed her, but she hid her look of desire with a sweet, curled smile, waiting eagerly for him to introduce himself.

He didn't.

Instead, Alden the Untrusting once again tried to leap past her. This time, however, he succeeded. He dove off the platform and flew through the air, cloak trailing behind. Kira gasped and called out, but to her surprise he caught a rope. His weight forced him to slip slightly, but he tightened his grip and continued the swing. Alden landed on a beam across the way and looked back at her briefly before descending down a post to escape into the busy street.

"Clever! I'll have to give him more credit." Kira had chuckled as she eyed the well-placed escape rope she failed to consider. She crawled down to fetch his forgotten journal and took off after him.

Knowing his habits, Kira had easily trailed him back to The Five Leaves. The shop, coincidentally, had five rooms. She'd learned Alden rented one at the end of the hall on the second story. Kira guessed he found it to be a peaceful and well-hidden enough place to reside, but in the previous few months, the small shop had grown in popularity. She figured it had something to do with their excellent brew of Brim Tea, since Mr. Grey had finally mastered the delicate recipe. From then on it became a perfect haven for displaced Brimleyns to enjoy a flavor from their destroyed kingdom. Although Kira did enjoy the homey brew, growing up with it herself, it wasn't the tea that kept bringing her back to The Five Leaves.

Kira waved warmly to Mr. Grey who narrowed his eyes as she jogged up the creaking stairs, as if she too lived there. She navigated to Alden's door and, with little effort, picked his lock.

As she invited herself in his black one-eyed cat leapt down to greet her. He rubbed up on her leg, as if they had met a hundred times. They had. "Hi Rek!" She bent to pet his head then scratch his white chin.

"How'd ya—" Alden sprang up from his writing desk and marched forward. With a fierce grip, he tugged her up and away from his cat. It scampered out the door. Alden gripped her arms and walked her back. She allowed the act without any resistance, blinking at his snarling teeth.

"Leave me alone!" he yelled while tossing her out and slamming the door in her face.

She could still remember the rattle of cups shaking at the bar below and the crash of one.

Taking in a breath, Kira politely knocked.

"What?" he snapped from beyond.

Kira bit her lip, worried she'd made a mistake approaching him as boldly as she had. She had considered leaving—forgetting about the man and letting him go about his business—but then remembered the night before. If the Shadowens and him crossed paths again, she wouldn't be able to help save him like he had her.

Rek looked up and gave a throaty meow of encouragement.

Kira drew in a breath. "Thank you for helping me out of the alley a while back. You've got a good heart and I can understand if you don't want to join the guild. But, if you reconsider, we gather at the Cantwell Inn... Meet me there tomorrow after sundown. You really would benefit from it. I'm...sorry." She then slid his knife and notebook underneath the large gap in the old door. "I didn't read your journal." It wasn't a lie—they were drawings.

The next morning, Kira had met with her guild leader, Pierz. Hopeful that Alden would join, she asked permission to bring in her first underling. He accepted, but when Reyn found out, he was less than pleased.

"Think someone's better, huh?" Reyn hissed, pinning her against the wall. Her cry amplified down the narrow alley as the commander tightened his grip around her neck. He leaned into her, noses touching. "You think you don't need me?" He slid his free hand to her waist.

Kira could still feel the pits of where his claws dug in her side and stench of his stale breath coating her face—memories she wished she could forget. Reyn began to slip his hand into her trousers, making her tense up. "You'll always need me..." he whispered in her ear.

Kira was sure Reyn would have had his way with her again then. She wondered what drug he had planned to test on her that time. One of pain? Pleasure? One that made her question reality? A sampling of each? His concoctions were endless. However, Kira stood as a victim for the last time, as—in an instant—Alden was there. He grabbed Reyn's shoulder and spun the man away from her. Without hesitating, Alden then punched him square in the face. Reyn stumbled backward, hitting his head against the stone wall of the Cantwell Inn. For a moment, he was dazed, unsure of what had happened.

Alden nodded to her, then positioned himself between her and the shadow commander, unaware or uncaring about the danger he was facing. His brown woolen cloak fluttered in a calm breeze creating the only sound around them. He stood tall and more confident than she had ever seen him before. His determined gaze was as cold and unforgiving as the black dagger gripped firmly in his hand. Alden had ended Reyn's ongoing reign of her that day, and it was a scene she'd never forget.

Reyn wiped his cut lip. He looked from Alden, to the blood on his hand, and then back up, glaring at Kira. Her mouth opened, yet she said nothing. As she closed it, a smile took its place. Reyn scowled, then shifted his attention back toward Alden, who remained a barrier between them.

"This him?" Reyn cawed in annoyance, tossing his greasy hair back.

It was Alden who had nodded.

Kira blushed.

Reyn glowered.

Alden raised his chin and narrowed his eyes, peering out from his hood. Though seemingly younger, he was both taller and larger than Reyn, who in contrast was as thin and lanky as a snake. Alden's size, however, did little to intimidate the commander; he too puffed up his chest and stepped forward, drawing what Kira knew was a poison-laced blade.

"Reynold."

The shadow commander peered past Alden. Pierz. When

Reyn looked back, his eyes appeared closed, just black slits across a stone-cold face. Reyn then stepped forward and made an effort to aggressively brush shoulders with Alden, but he held his ground, forcing Reyn to roll around him.

"You didn't need to do that; I can handle him," Kira tried to say confidently, but her voice wavered.

"Sure, but I was repaying the favor. We shouldn't need to fight enemies alone."

"Our shadow commander isn't an enemy…"

"You sure? 'Cause I think I just made one." Alden chuckled, smirking cockily at Reyn.

Pierz pushed Reyn along. Before the guild leader rounded the Cantwell Inn, he glanced up to meet Alden's unsure gaze. Then Pierz gave a welcoming nod.

Kira clapped her hand on his shoulder. "You'll make allies too."

He looked at her with a warm, friendly smile, as they had known each other for months—though only she truly had.

"Now, will you tell me your name?" she pleaded.

He shook his head with a charming laugh. "Call me Alden."

BURDEN

CHAPTER TWELVE

ayli leaned forward, peering under the rogue's hood. Sweat beaded his fevered face and his eyes were pressed together in anguish. His chest rose and fell with heavy and labored breaths. Mayli brought her free hand to his forehead, hesitated, then gently touched him. He was hot. She frowned and wiped his sweat with her sleeve. As she did, his face softened as if she had also sent away a bad dream.

With regret, she withdrew from the weave of their fingers. She had been content holding his hand, no longer feeling afraid or so alone, but her legs were tingling from kneeling with his head in her lap. As she lifted it, he let out a soft, lonely groan. *Did he not want me to leave either?* As gently as she could, Mayli rested his head back down, using his hood as a pillow. She scooted away, heart fluttering.

Upon touching the cool stone floor, something wet licked her and she immediately recoiled. Mayli brought her hand up, shaking. Her fingers were now coated in thick, red blood. She slowly turned her head. Reyn.

The man was horrible, and not only because he was dead or

because he had tracked them down, hurt her, and nearly killed her rogue. Reyn was horribly ugly. Greasy string-like strands of hair reached down to the floor and rested in his blood. His skin was dimpled and blotchy as if acid had burned him. The left side of his face was marred with rows of white scars. Judging by the spread, Mayli guessed it was from a human rather than a beast.

Hesitantly, she reached forward then pinched his cowl. With a quick flick of her wrist, Mayli flung it over his head. She squeaked and scurried away as if the dead man might seek retaliation for his death. She turned back to look. Mayli groaned, realizing she had to remove Reyn from her sight to truly be freed. Spotting a door leading outside, she moved to push it open.

Ivy vines crept over the door like a curtain. As she brushed them aside, dirt trickled down into her hair. She paused momentarily, cringing at the filth, then with an accepting sigh, Mayli continued forth. Finally, as if passing through a portal, she found herself in a quaint courtyard where a sprinkling of rain shimmered in the setting sun's warm glow.

Resting between overgrown weeds were bales of hay that had partially decomposed where they met the damp ground. A collection of small cages lined with bones and feathers were stacked against the stone wall. Around the corner, Mayli spotted the dirty pond-like fountain she had seen from the servant's quarters.

Farther down the yard was an oak gate leading to the main bailey. Deciding it was too far to drag Reyn, she turned back to consider her options. Mayli dug her boot into the hard foundation. *No way I'm spending the time and effort to dig a grave...*

Mayli stepped back into the kitchen, defeated. The thief rested with his hand on his wound. Reyn still waited expectantly for her to find his resting place. She hovered over him for a few minutes—though it seemed like hours—until she finally built up the courage to sit beside the dead man. Delicately, she removed the iron chest plate and began sorting through his belongings. She found a couple gold and silver coins, a set of flint and steel, a pouch of herbs, and several empty vials as well as one ornate bottle filled with a thick, brown liquid. Between his chest and clothes, Mayli found a small leather-bound journal. She opened it.

Reyn's handwriting was crude, but the things written inside were even more disturbing. He had many recipes for poisons and drugs that could do as little as give someone a headache or endure a sneezing fit to stopping their heart soon after consumption. Mayli lifted the bottle she had retrieved from the man's belt. "Doubt this is anything good."

Flipping further through the book, a folded paper slipped out. She picked it from her lap and opened it. A sketch of a nude woman with a long braid looked back at her. Her eyes were wide, scared. Curious, Mayli read from where the paper came.

It was all too fulfilling to watch Kira strip before her beloved as my men held him at knifepoint. I have to hand it to him, the idiot can draw, even watching me enjoy myself with her. The feud afterward in the Cads was worth it all, because now Kira will forever be mine, and he knows it.

Mayli's gut turned, realizing the fate she'd escaped. She looked back at the drawing, frowning. *Even thieves can't always protect themselves...*

Setting the items aside, she took a breath and grabbed Reyn's ankles. She grunted as she pulled the corpse into the courtyard. Mayli dropped his legs and wiped her brow of sweat. Using all of her remaining strength and courage, Mayli lifted the dead weight onto a pile of hay. Reyn lay face up, eyes rolled back as if staring at the arrowhead lodged deep inside. His arm slipped off and pointed at her accusingly. Mayli took a frightened step back.

"I'm not a murderer!" she yelled, then grabbed a stack of crates and toppled it over the man, hiding him from view.

Mayli turned her back to view the peaceful courtyard. The sun was breaking through an opening in the trees as it descended through an orange haze. She listened to the happy calls of birds fluttering past and the chirp of crickets preparing for nightfall. It was as if nothing bad had ever happened, not even the war. If it weren't for the overgrown weeds, the muck that floated in the water fountain, and dead body behind her, she'd believe it.

Mayli raised her gaze over the curtain wall. Beyond it was blue sky and endless golden forest.

I could leave. It would be easy; just a few steps outside and I'd be free.

A crow flew down and landed on a pile of crates hiding Reyn's body. It ruffled its wings as the wood shifted, then cawed at her like a warning.

I can't leave the rogue...

Distant, Mayli walked back to the servants' quarters. She pulled a blanket off a nearby bed and laid it out on the floor. She then filled it with as many pillows and quilts as she could, creating a mountain of fabrics she felt rivaled the height of Mount Hiore. When it looked like nothing else could fit, Mayli folded it into a sac and strung it across her back. Her muscles strained, but the burden wasn't anything she couldn't handle.

Entering the kitchen, Mayli paused. The thief was on his side, face down, vomit splattered on the ground by his chin. For a moment she feared he had died, but then saw the gentle rise and fall of his chest.

She heaved the linens back up before a sneaky pillow could find its way out and navigated to an inviting nook surrounded by cabinets. She constructed the bundle into a bed-like mass, taking care to push out wrinkles and fluff pillows.

Turning the thief away from his mess, she pulled him up. "Come on..."

The man squinted through tired, almost fearful, eyes. He blinked distantly at her. "Ki...?"

Unable to understand, she shook her head. "What key?"

He focused harder, then a faint growl rumbled from under his hood.

Unintimidated, she stuck her arms under his and lifted, commanding the man to rise with her. Together they stumbled as he weakly fought back. Finally reaching the nest, she dropped him.

He moaned pleasantly as the soft pillows welcomed him in.

She nudged his leg with her foot. "See? Not so bad. You don't need to make such a fuss!" Mayli then grabbed a rag, wet it, and knelt beside him.

She wiped dried blood off his face. He flinched but relaxed, allowing the tender touch. As she cleaned, she couldn't help but take interest in his appearance: the softness of his resting eyes, the dimples hooked in his cheeks, his charming mask of full stubble; even his matted, dirty hair lured her in.

"What's your name?" Mayli waited but he didn't even respond with a twitch of his lips. She threw up her hands. "Guess I'll just keep calling you 'my rogue' then."

He smiled.

She cocked her head. "Oh! So, you *can* hear!"

His smirk continued briefly, then slumped back down. He exhaled like it had been a great feat.

A small trickle of blood started to seep from his wound. She wiped it and then took his knife to trim a long strip of fabric from a sheet.

"Can you sit up? I'm going to wrap your side."

He nodded. Then, after three labored breaths, he pushed off the ground, arms shaking. Mayli helped until he leaned against her as if in an embrace. While balancing his weight on her, Mayli slipped the cloth behind and proceeded to wrap him until the cloth ran out. She tucked it in and tried to lean him back, but the man hung over her. She patted his arm awkwardly.

"I'm done."

He squeezed her.

Her cheeks flushed hot. *Is this a hug?*

Slowly, the thief laid down, bringing her back with him.

Mayli didn't resist resting beside the man but her heart raced. Soon, childish dreams began to dance inside her head, imagining that he was a knight sworn to protect her from every monster and cruelty sent after her by a powerful overlord bent on splitting them apart. He had taken vengeance on her mother's murderer, defeated her enemies, and retrieved the lost treasure of Gezmek—all in her name. She laughed to herself at the absurdity. She knew nothing about the man, not even his name. All she knew was his alliance with the fallen kingdom and that he was indeed saving her…just perhaps not for the reasons she toyed with. She giggled to herself.

Father would hate to see me lying beside a man such as this. And with that last thought, Mayli burrowed closer.

<hr />

Alden woke to the soothing melody of rain rapping against the window panes. Head spinning, he inhaled deeply, but his chest was heavy, depriving him of a full breath. Opening his tired eyes, he found he had become a pillow. He smiled and shifted to put his arm around Kira, who, in response, nuzzled deeper.

Although it hurt as much as it pleased him, Alden didn't mind only snuggling with the thief. He'd take any glimmers of joy nowadays. *Life in the guild isn't so bad when it is paired with moments like this.*

He brushed Kira's hair from her face. It was longer than he remembered and had a slight curl to it. He curiously gazed upon his partner until his cloudy vision woke with him. To his disbelief, the woman in his arms was not the Shadowen thief, but Princess Mayli Drake. He immediately retracted his hand as if he had touched something forbidden.

Why is she here?

Alden shifted a pillow and realized he wasn't in his bed—or any sort of bed, just a pile of blankets. He looked around. There was also no splintery woodwork, angled ceiling, writing desk, or even his easel and paintings. In its place was a worktable, cabinets, a cooking furnace, and piles of crates. *This is not my loft.* This room was drab, cold, made of stone, and painted with bloodstains…

Alden's heart beat fast with the pouring rain outside as memories and truth replaced his altered reality.

The princess is really sleeping on me…?

Thunder laughed. He chuckled along with it, seeing the room fade to rolling sand dunes and a perfect blue sky overhead. Alden brought his hand down, lightly resting on Mayli's beautiful tattooed shoulder. He stroked it gently.

No. This is just a dream.

PRISONER

CHAPTER THIRTEEN

"This one here?" asked a strong, feminine voice.

"Obviously. There's no one else to choose from," a man replied.

"She looks pretty rough," stated another woman.

"You would too in a jail cell," said the man.

"Key?" requested the first.

As her cell door creaked open, Kira rubbed her eyes awake. Before her stood Thomas, holding the iron door as two women dressed in elegant armor and flowing yellow capes entered. Their attire had extra layers of black and gold accentuating the v-lined cut.

Kira quickly stood to greet them, brushing off hay from her dirty tunic. She tugged it down and looked up with a smile.

"Come with us," the taller woman said in a commanding tone.

Kira leaned forward to peer down the hall, expecting to see a bush of blonde hair, but Briar wasn't there. "Is Prince Briar back?"

"Yes. He has instructed them to take you inside the castle to see him."

"Will he not meet me here?"

The women chuckled as they scanned the dungeon.

The stones were dark umber, absorbing all light and weeping with dew. A rat she named Gnaws feasted on a discarded bone from her last meal, creating a disturbing crunching sound which was amplified in her small cell. Kira caught a pungent whiff from the waste bucket, which was full from several days of use. She grimaced in embarrassment.

"Please…" Thomas gestured down the hall.

She obeyed and followed the women down the hall. Glancing behind her, she watched Thomas close the gate. His eyes met hers and he gave an odd smile before she turned the corner.

As promised, Kira was escorted inside the castle. Several gossiping nobles eyed her, pointing out the lack of flattering clothes. They sneered at her unkempt tangle of hair. Kira raised her chin, uncaring of their judgment. She was about to meet a prince.

The guards ushered her out of sight and continued toward the southern tower. It was the largest in the castle and overlooked Zollner's Bay. Kira made a point to peer out each passing window to catch a look of the beautiful ocean. She saw *The Albatross* docked beside an ugly black ship and a few other small boats. *Wonder what mischief Squirrel and Trod got into there…*

The curved stairway led up to an open foyer with thin stained-glass windows that rained light down from the A-framed roof. Large potted ferns and a long, woven rug with a swirling pattern led to a set of breathtaking doors where more guards stood unmoving at their guest's arrival.

"We present a princess," called the tall guard who led the escort.

Kira tilted her head in confusion. *I'm no princess. I have information about the kidnapped one, but they don't know that.* Kira shrugged it off, assuming she had misheard.

The guards stepped forward and patted her down. They

retrieved a small hidden blade she kept in her boot and also took her belt, which held her daily tools, including her lockpicks. She frowned but understood the precaution. Besides, she was in no position to protest now.

Together, the guards gripped the long golden handles and pushed the ancient doors open, allowing them entry. Kira had little time to take in the room's beauty as she was hurried toward an intruding curved wall with an arched doorway. The guard unlocked it and together they climbed the turret's tight stairwell until, after a final door, Kira found herself surrounded by a sea of women.

No...

Caught off guard by the sudden intrusion, the women froze in place. They sat upon layers of lush cushions and a low bed shaded by a canopy of sheer cloth. A couple paused mid-stroke, one brushing the other's hair. In the corner, several were huddled together and lifted their noses up from books. After a stressful moment, a few other women peeked out from hiding. Many wore nothing but scantily clad nightgowns, while others wore nothing at all. Some greeted her with smiles while others shook their heads mournfully.

The door slammed shut behind her, leaving a puff of cool air to swirl past. Kira spun and shook the handle. When it refused to move, she studied the lock, already visualizing how to break free. She pounded on the thick wood, cursing herself for being so trusting.

Kings aren't supposed to be like this...

Murmurs began to flutter, and she tensed. She peered behind her to stare at the harem.

A tall, long-faced woman with full lips broke free from the flock. Her hair was a mix of yellow and orange that changed depending on how her perfect curls bounced in the light. She presented her hand. "I am Eryn, and these are your new sisters."

Kira stepped back, unable to understand. "Sisters?"

"We are all considered princesses here," said a voice.

"In waiting to become queen..." informed another.

Kira's skin crawled as she remembered Pierz's words. King Olivar was in search of an heir and these women were his mates...*she* was his mate. Her nostrils flared. "No. This isn't happening." Kira turned around and rattled the door handle.

"Sorry, Sis, there's nothing that can be done," said a round woman with long eyelashes and a gown that accented her curves. She put her hand sympathetically on Kira's shoulder.

"NO!"

The women shuffled back. The rest just frowned. Then Eryn spoke up. "Only when a bee kisses a flower does its pollen reach others."

"Just stop!" Kira growled as she threw a hand back, annoyed by their acceptance of their fate. She had found a way past Reyn; it had taken many years, but she had done it. She wasn't going to wait that long here. She looked at the many faces. "Look, if we..."

"It could work out for you! Maybe you'll be queen!" chirped a wide-eyed girl, no more than eight or ten.

Kira slumped, heartbroken seeing such a young girl subjected to this life. *At least she is clothed properly.*

"I'm not even noble!" Kira pointed to all the women's tattooed crests upon their arms.

"Nor were we. Soon you will be too," replied a girl in her late teen years. She was beautiful, with a slender face and pointed chin, but her expression held a permanent frown.

"It's really for the better! Imagine the life you could live!" another girl said, setting down a book.

"I don't believe it. Commoners can't be noble without winning at the Festival of Gezmek! There are strict rules and ceremonies!"

"Olivar has an artist. He had him practice ink work on pigs and on himself until he mastered the coat of arms," said Eryn.

"So, there are noble swine running around? I mean, more than normal?" Kira joked.

The women giggled with her. The moment of play was interrupted by the rattling of full plate armor climbing the stairs.

"He's coming!" someone cried, and they scattered like mice.

Kira backed up beside the wall. Her fingers searched her side for her missing knife. She damned herself once more as she searched the vanity beside her. Finally, she found a brush. *A brush? Fine, it will have to do*, she thought as she gripped the bristled end.

As the door opened, a large man decorated in a fine golden robe stepped in after a guard. Kira reacted swiftly and twisted to jab the handle into the king's eye, but before she could launch her attack she was sent to the floor. Her face pulsed, wet and hot. She imagined there was an imprinted detail on her cheek that matched the guard's iron knuckles.

Olivar looked down at her. "You must be my new princess," he stated flatly.

Kira pushed off the floor and spat at his feet. She wiped the back of her hand across her face, removing a trail of spit and blood.

The king responded with a hungry grin as he sized her up. He reached forward and raised her chin to meet his gaze. "You'd make a strong queen. Let's hope you don't disappoint."

"Yeah, you just come and try that with me, you pig-headed cunt!" She snapped at his fingers, forcing him back. The king looked appropriate to the insult as his skin was a dull pink and he was heavyset. Fat cheeks framed his button nose and plump lips. His blonde hair was thin and balding, and he combed what he could across to support his crown.

"Ha, ha. Don't worry. We'll have a month, maybe less, until we engage in *that*. By then hopefully we'll have cleaned up your manners." He turned as a woman in a white silk gown entered, her expression indifferent. "Whose duty is it tonight?"

The thin woman looked down at a journal and traced her finger down a list. "Princess Eryn."

Kira shook her head as the woman who had seemed to be the leader willfully stepped forward. Eryn winked and gave a comforting and unfazed smile as she walked past Kira. She left as if she were just taking an evening stroll with the man of her dreams.

DENSEN

CHAPTER FOURTEEN

*M*ayli sat cross-legged on the shore with a satisfied smile. In her lap rested a dead goose she had just shot with her last usable arrow. Needing its feathers to fletch new arrows, she had watched patiently, letting easier targets like rabbits and squirrels pass by until a flock landed in the bay.

Kicking her legs into the sand, Mayli plucked several strong brown feathers from the goose's wing. After spending several days in the wilderness, killing two thieves, a few rodents, cooking them and forcing herself to eat them, getting dirty didn't seem so horrible anymore. Just survival.

Mayli looked down and followed the flow until the Draclynn River curled around a bend, disappearing into a thick and seemingly endless forest. The wind caressed its yellow and red leaves and the woods came alive, as if on fire. A trio of birds darted past, chirping happily. The land was serene, just as Colin had described.

When Mayli came of age, earning her royal tattoo, she wrote to each potential suitor. Many wrote back, bragging of themselves, their fortune and pride. However, the reply from Brimleyn's prince was unlike any she'd ever received.

Mayli,

I've heard many tales of the beauty that resides within the desert; It's soft rolling dunes, the vibrancy of colorful silks and art, the abundance of talented people and their passion to create. So, when I opened your letter, I felt the warmth of the Ammosian sun rise from it. Golden and curling words flowed off the page like the desert revealing lost treasure. Had I just discovered what all of Vatan sought? What I've always sought?

Princess, I'm humbled to have received your interest and hope that together we can unify our passions and make the world a gorgeous place, as my ancestors had before me.

Prince Colin Densen

P.S. These feathers are for your arrows. I've dyed them blue so that my essence could be with you during your upcoming hunt. Shoot true.

Their exchange of heartfelt messages went on for months. She had thought Colin had listened. Cared. He'd spoken little of himself and instead held interest in not only her culture, but her. Mayli had been excited for the Festival of Gezmek so they could finally meet.

Then her mother found his letters. One by one, she burned them. "Mayli, the Densens of Brimley are frauds. I will not have you marrying into that and dishonoring our family. I have a meeting there next week. Arkello Densen, Vatan's true heir, has provided me with the proof needed to end their foolishness."

Mayli snapped the last arrow she was fletching as a nightmarish storm of tromping hooves thundered in the distance.

Clinging to her bow and quiver, Mayli ran back to the castle, blood pumping. She flew down the noble hall and found an arrow slit just as someone rode in the bailey. A horse whinnied and she saw a black cloak whip by.

Mayli hurried to a balcony which overlooked the grand foyer. An overwhelming sense to protect herself and the thief swelled in her. As she hid, she damned her heart for pounding so loud, fearing the intruder might hear.

Keeping her eyes fixed on the doorway, she saw a tip of a curved saber reveal itself. Mayli jumped to release an arrow, knocking the sword free from the hand of its holder. A loud clang of steel on stone echoed through the halls as a warning.

"Sweet kings!" exclaimed a startled voice.

She saw a black gloved hand reach to retrieve the weapon and she nocked a new arrow. "Leave it! If you try, don't think your hand won't end up like your sword."

There was a chuckle. "Whoa, whoa... You wouldn't do that to an old friend!"

Old friend? Fear struck her. "How dare you call yourself a friend, Colin!" She pulled back on the string, causing the crude bow to creak under the pressure.

"Ey! Mayli, it's Briar!" Cautiously, the prince stepped into the room, leaving his sword on the floor. As expected, a mess of ash-blonde hair and a smiling face appeared.

Keeping the bowstring taut, she shifted her gaze back to the doorway. "Is your cousin with you?"

"I came alone."

"Are you bringing me to him?"

"No... I received a message to come here and bring you home to Ammos."

Weight lifted from her shoulders and she relaxed the pull. She descended the curved staircase to meet with the prince.

He bowed deeply, with his hand over his shoulder, then straightened. Briar had matured since she'd last seen him. Just a few years older than she, he had developed lean muscles with strong, wide shoulders. His head was square, especially his jaw, which was a bit wider than the rest. Soft angled cheekbones drew her eyes down to his lips. They were curled in a friendly smile. His hooded blue eyes washed over her form.

"Pleasure to see you again, Princess. It's been a *long* while. You look…good." He quickly hid a smirk.

Mayli blushed and shied away. She remembered the odd assortment of clothes she wore, the rat's nest of hair, blood from the goose, and face painted with dirt instead of makeup. *How embarrassing!*

Briar cleared his throat and took a step back, looking around. "Where is he?"

"This way." Mayli turned to lead him to the kitchen she had begun to call "home."

Briar paused upon seeing the thief. The man was lost under a mound of blankets and his hood, revealing only a sliver for him to breathe. Sweat glistened on his pained face. Briar looked at Mayli for clarification.

"He was stabbed in his side," she informed with a frown matching Briar's. "And poisoned…"

"Poison?"

"Reyn, a Shadowen, followed us here and they fought."

"Ah, Reynold… Where's that sleaze now?"

Mayli cast her eyes down at the path of blood leading outside, unable to answer.

"He's dead?"

She nodded.

Briar bent and patted his unconscious friend. "I'm glad he finally killed that son of a bitch. He's wanted to since the day they met."

"I… I killed him."

Briar fluttered his eyes. "You? Oh. Well, good job. Fucker deserved it."

Mayli wiped her face.

"Did he have any bottles on him? He likely had an antidote."

Mayli's mouth opened, remembering the vial. She went to the pack and dug through to retrieve it. "I found this."

Briar examined it. "This the only one?"

"There was an empty bottle which looked similar."

Nodding, he placed it on the thief's lips.

Mayli sucked in a nervous breath as a dribble poured in. "Are you sure?"

"From what he's told me, yeah." Briar pocketed the bottle and smiled at her with a twinkle in his eye. "Brewers know the effect of their poisons. They wouldn't want to fall victim themselves."

Mayli folded her arms. "You better be right. I have some words for your friend!"

"I'm sure you do," he said, pulling the covers away from the thief. With care, he peeled back the blood-soaked bandage. The wound oozed more blood as the scab tore off.

Mayli handed Briar a waterskin and rag to help. He dampened it and wiped the man's side clean. Pressing a few fingers to it, he assessed the damage. Then he released a breath of relief.

"Don't know what I'd do if I'd lost you too, bud..." Briar said under his breath, then gently slipped his hands under. With a strained grunt, he lifted him up.

Mayli collected their gear and followed Briar as he carried the man from the kitchen. Once back in the grand hall, he navigated flawlessly through the abandoned castle and made his way to a room on an upper floor.

Hearing a ruffle of feathers, Mayli looked up to see a bird nested in a bookshelf. It chirped angrily at them as if they had just intruded in on her room. As Briar entered, the bird fluttered out a broken window with several agitated peeps.

Mayli walked in. The bedroom was like many at Brimley Castle. Built with knotty pine planks lining the walls and a floor made of long, polished timbers. Centered on the eastern wall was a four-poster bed speckled with chew marks from termites. Around it blew white, tattered drapes.

Thick crown moulding trim led Mayli's eye toward a set of double doors carved with ivy details around its frame. They hung open, and beyond she could see a limestone-tiled room where Briar was laying down his friend.

Briar shifted his lips into a crooked and worried slant. Mayli watched as his tongue slipped out to the side absently. *Does he even know how to care for the injured?*

He looked at her with a firm nod, as if answering her unspoken question, then opened a low cabinet door, stacked with oak logs. Briar pulled a few out and began to prepare a fire in a furnace. He pulled a lever. A loud burble-like moan echoed within the castle walls. A moment later, water spewed from a spout, filling a copper sink above the furnace. Once the water had heated, he turned a dial to let it spill into a large stone tub.

Mayli touched her fingers to the hot water. "This is amazing! Fresh water is sparse in the desert, so the use of a private bath is unheard of, even for royalty!"

"I can relate," Briar said softly. "I don't have one where I live, since home now is only an attic above my office."

"Really?"

"Yep." He untied Alden's cloak.

The thief turned his head, moaned, and gripped Briar's boot. He then tried to crawl away, but the effort was too much and his body fell slack once again.

"I don't think he'll let you wash him. He refused much of my aid."

"Oh, he'll let me. I doubt he trusts you."

Mayli conceded with a nod.

He nodded too. "Don't take it personally. He's not one to open up so easily." Briar reached for the thief's shirt but paused. He shifted on his heel to address her. "There are some pears in my saddlebags, if you are hungry."

Mayli's eyes widened at the thought. "That sounds great!" She began to leave, then spun back around. "I just caught a goose too. I'll cook it for us!"

The prince looked at her like she had just spoken another language. As if the idea of her cooking was unheard of. She grinned. It had been until this week. She was still learning but enjoyed the challenge, and Briar's look was testing.

When Mayli returned with their meals, her rogue was now shirtless on the bed and covered in a sheet. Briar had bathed him, washed his hair, and cleaned all his wounds. Both arms were wrapped to his neck in gauze and Briar worked to stitch the small cut in his side.

Briar smiled, welcoming her over. "He'll need just a bit more rest but should recover soon. His fever is already reducing."

Mayli handed Briar a plate of overcooked goose, seasoned but burnt wild rice, and the pear. Together they sat at a table.

"How do you know him?" she asked.

Briar choked briefly, beat on his chest, and worked to swallow the bite he had just taken.

"Sorry!" Mayli gasped, fearing her cooking might be fatal.

"No, it's fine!" He pointed toward the man while clearing his throat. "We've been friends a long while." He filled his mouth with rice and smiled as if he truly enjoyed the dish.

Mayli leaned forward, arching a brow. "If you are such good friends, then why is he working for the Shadowen Thieves Guild while you are a captain of the guard? Shouldn't you be *arresting* him?"

Briar bobbed his head from side to side then pointed his fork at her. "I don't because of our relationship."

Mayli looked at him with a solemn expression. "You don't keep the best company, do you?"

Briar shrugged and spoke as he chewed, "Eh. In comparison

to the criminals I deal with every day, Alden is about as noble as we are!"

"Alden…" she repeated faintly, enjoying the sound roll off her tongue. She looked at the handsome man sleeping on the bed with a bright smile.

"What did he tell you?" asked Briar.

"Nothing! He never even introduced himself!" she yelled, pointing at Alden.

"No? So, what happened?"

Mayli leaned in, using her hands to help illustrate as she told her tale: "First, he and the Shadowens ambushed my carriage, then *he* took me from them! We stayed in some nasty basement in a mill, then we were hunted by his guild. Realizing I had to trust him, we fled through the woods and found a cabin for the night. Then he took me here and we fought Reyn. Alden risked his life defending me from him, so…" Mayli exhaled. "I stayed." She shoveled a large bite of food into her mouth.

"Despite all my advice and fair warnings, Alden insisted on staying in the thieves guild. But I'm glad he was there for you."

"So, Alden is a renegade? It's why he's helping me, not his king."

"Uh, he's helping both."

She cocked her head.

Briar chomped into the pear, juice running down his chin. "He said he could find answers about who truly murdered your mother by spying on the guild."

"And did he?"

"Not that I'm aware."

"That's because it was Colin. All evidence points to him. He even admitted to it."

"What he admitted to was visiting her room before her final moments."

"Only after he was accused of being seen."

Briar ran his hand through his hair and leaned back. "Mayli.

My family was hurt by the accusation of not being of royal blood. And Colin was heartbroken when your mother denied his proposal, but he wouldn't murder over it. None of us would."

"It doesn't matter what you want to believe about your family, Briar."

He nodded. "I know. It's why we have risked everything to find proof for you."

"Is losing your title and kingdom, living in an attic, and working as guard captain really worth that?"

Briar leaned in his chair, making it creak. "Of course. He is not just my cousin, but my King."

Hairs on the back of her neck stood up. "And if he asked you to bring me to him..."

He shook his head. "You don't need to worry about that, Mayli Drake. We are not your enemies."

She stared, brow wrinkling.

"By the crest on my arm, I promise." Briar placed his hand on his shoulder and bowed.

THE NOBLE

CHAPTER FIFTEEN

"Sammie," announced the doctor.

Kira glared, watching the tiny woman pop up from her seat and hook her arm around King Olivar. When they left, Kira turned back to brushing Hailey's hair and leaned in. "You don't ever go with him, do you?"

Hailey shook her head. "Nope!"

Kira exhaled, finding relief that there was *some* humanity in the king.

"At least for now. Hailey is insurance," informed Eryn, sitting beside them.

"Insurance? For what?"

Eryn spun her finger around. "This."

Kira's mouth opened in disgust. *So much for humanity.*

The door opened again and the doctor entered. "Kira Harlow."

Kira paled and locked eyes with Eryn. The woman just stared, offering no hope as she turned away. Clanging footsteps approached as two knights flanked Kira. She leapt up and tried to jab the brush's handle into an open grove of their armor. Her face flared in pain as one knight struck her across the jaw. She fell limply into the arms of the other.

Kira woke, cold and naked, strapped to a strange table. The doctor hovered over her waist. She flinched at an invasive touch. The woman then pressed on Kira's abdomen and inspected her groin. Kira tried to pull away, but the leather straps held her firm. The doctor wiped her and noted the faint red stain. She wrote on a parchment and nodded. "He'll be relieved to see you next week. Time for your mark."

Kira flailed her naked body on the table. Two knights stepped forward and tightened her straps. She screamed, then turned her rage on the doctor. "What do you mean?"

The doctor gathered her things and proceeded to the door without an answer. When Kira repeated herself and struggled further with the knights, the doctor turned around to reply. "The pollen is soon to drop. Best of luck, princess."

The door opened and the doctor passed by a man with a limp, escorted by a fleet of guards who entered the room. He was thin, fragile, with round tired eyes and a scraggly beard. Kira thought he looked like someone she'd find begging for food outside The Five Leaves who Alden would take pity on, or that the man could be friends with her rat Gnaws—perhaps related. His age was difficult to tell as he was starved to near bones. There were wisps of gray competing with his brown hair, which he held in a long, frayed ponytail. Across his legs, arms, chest, and even face were tattoos of the Dreggan coat of arms—some full, some just detailed segments of the draclynn, the fine line work of the zigzag weave in the intricate background, or even just color tests. Where a crest would be marked on the shoulder was a large black patch of ink, banning him any placement among noble society. In his long and boney hands, he firmly held a small, wooden case.

Kira's eyes ran back and forth, searching for an answer from the emotionless knights until the man walked to a table and opened the box. From it, he pulled a tray of sharp needlepoint tools carved from bone and bottles of colored vials. Kira froze as memories of Reyn and his poisons stabbed her. Feeling faint, she tugged to get away but her body fell weak against the straps. The man pulled out a few bottles. *Poison.* Kira's chest thundered and she used all of her might to scoot…an inch.

"You should be proud to be among royalty," laughed a guard.

A moment of focus hit Kira and she looked to the smirking woman and spat. "I know thieves with more honor and nobility than him!"

"Like you soon will be. Now please, you know the punishment for false crests, so don't squirm and ruin the design if you want to be kept alive."

"What?" Kira gulped. She looked up to the tattooed man preparing a needle, then drew her attention to the barbaric set of artisan tools. Reality dawned on her. *Not poison.* She tried to jerk free once more but the vise grip held firm. A long sigh escaped her until she peered up at the artist, accepting fate. "Any way you could etch the tree and seed? Brimley?" Kira pleaded, hoping to at least be loyal to her homeland.

The man blinked at her. His brown eyes, wide, suddenly full of life. He started to speak but the nearest guard stepped closer with a raised hand. The artist recoiled, mumbling under his breath, but a smile lingered. Kira felt her pride slip away as he selected the yellow ink. She closed her eyes and endured the needle's stinging jabs.

She was a Dreggan noble now.

Eryn looked over Kira's tattoo. "That's his best work yet! How do you feel?"

"Like a damn pig, tainted by a venomous snakebite. How do you think I feel?" Kira snapped, rubbing her freshly branded arm. She peered into the vanity mirror. A draclynn curved in an S-like loop spanned her shoulder, its tentacles curling and fin-like wings flaring out. The beast's wolf-like head seemed to growl at her, as if it knew she were Brimleyn. It itched and she wanted to claw it off. "I wish it was my home crest," she whined mournfully.

"Where are you from?" questioned Hailey as the little girl wandered up and looked to her through the mirror.

"Brimley," Kira said, smiling with pride.

"Coats of arms are highly complicated designs with expensive inks!" said a thin, chipper girl, who Kira learned was named Sammie since her recent departure with the king. She leaned in to get a better look at Kira's tattoo. "It's impressive enough that he is able to do this one. Besides, be glad you didn't get it of Brimley! You'd be marked as a traitor then!"

"I feel like a traitor now…" Kira pulled at her skin, trying to get a better look at the marking. Already tired of seeing it, she tugged her sleeve down to cover it. The sheer fabric did little to help.

"It will be fine, Kira," said Amber. The young, rounded woman rested a hand on her shoulder, but Kira pulled away.

"He screws you every day!" Kira roared with angst.

"It's not *every* day!"

"No! I'm done being poked and prodded!" Kira concluded.

Sammie cocked her head. "You haven't even been with…"

"No, not with *him*, but apparently I'll be *pollinating* next week! Is there not a day that goes by you don't want to flee? It has got to stop! We *are* getting out of here. We *are* going to fight back!"

Eryn scowled. "You don't think we've tried?"

"No! If you had you wouldn't be here. You all just sit around! I dunno, maybe you really think he has a seed in him."

"Hey!" several women snapped back.

"Not all of us *are* here," Eryn said with a snap.

Kira looked at the women who cast their eyes away. She frowned in understanding. "Look, if I'm now a noble, I'm going to make use of it. And so will you!" She looked at each face, commanding their attention. She presented the door. "I can pick this lock and any others needed. I remember the way out from when they brought me up here. Once we take down the first few guards, it should be a clear shot."

"And how do you think we are going to do that? We don't have any weapons, and your brush didn't work so well as one," Eryn reminded her.

"Sheer force! There's what, ten of you? I'll teach you to fight." Kira demonstrated a few swift punches in the air followed by a spinning kick.

"Teach us? I don't think I could learn *that*," said Amber, with wide eyes.

"I've taught an absolute idiot before!" Kira smiled, recalling Alden's first lessons. "Though he had once had some formal training, his ability to adapt to street fighting was laughable. I think you'll manage. Come see!"

Kira snapped off a chair leg. Gasps rang out. Kira looked at them in amazement and huffed. Then, she began scraping it along the rough stone wall, shaving off splinters and creating a chiseled point. Once ready, she tossed it to Eryn.

The woman examined it and touched the tip. She looked up at Kira with her eyes. "It's not sharp."

"Neither are swords. But even ramming that into a soft spot could inflict serious damage."

The women exchanged unconvinced looks.

Kira shrugged. "Fine," she said, snatching it from Eryn. She turned on her heel acting as if walking away. Then, in one swift motion spun to thrust the weapon inches away from Eryn's neck, then gently touched her with it.

Eryn stumbled back and pawed Kira's weapon away. "Get that away from me!"

"Dead girl talking." Kira smirked.

Eryn raised her brow and looked at the Kira anew, analyzing the lesson. Her mouth made a small "o" in understanding. "Break a leg, girls."

After a day's work, the women curled up like kittens and went to bed sore and exhausted. Kira found an unused nest away from the others and burrowed into the corner. She pulled a fur blanket over her near-naked body. Though her nightgown was beautiful and her new sisters were friendly, Kira wished for her old clothes, her ratty companions, and her unmarked skin. She cried quietly to herself and gripped her shoulder for the first time as a noble.

"Alden, I hope at least you are safe…"

CHAPTER SIXTEEN

*B*riar sat with his feet up on a desk and slouched into his chair, trying to relax as he read Reyn's journal. It was difficult, as Alden's descriptions hadn't been exaggerated about the man's cruelty, and if anything, he'd downplayed it.

Flipping past the next graphic page, he yawned.

"Good morning!" Mayli said as she hopped inside.

Briar snuffed out his yawn and watched her spin. The black button-up Dreggan dress he'd given her flared out like a snake's hissing tongue as it caught the wind, exposing the under layer of sheer yellow fabric. She smiled at him, waiting for a compliment. He had many.

"Hey!" Briar nodded in approval. "Do you like it? I wanted to get you something nice, but I also had to grab the clothes quickly before I left Dregs."

"Yes! You should have seen how my feathered jacket was torn asunder! I looked like a mangy sand strider!"

"Those birds are still pretty majestic, even when they aren't groomed."

The princess spun once more, and after a final twirl, grabbed onto the bedpost. Her head bobbed around as if she was still spinning. As she steadied herself, her gaze shifted to where Alden still lay unconscious. Not even the loud conversation had stirred him. Mayli took a seat at the end of the bed and began sorting out her tangled mess of hair while she became lost staring at the man.

"You read the part about the rats?" Briar turned a page of Reyn's journal, making a loud fluttering sound to draw her attention back to him.

"Hmm? Uh, *yeah*... Nasty critters!" she said as she tugged at a particularly bad snarl.

"What surprises me is that he kept still that whole time just to get that flower. It must have been quite a precious poison to withstand all of those tiny feet running over him. Not to mention the smell he had to put up with. What do you think he did after realizing he was covered in poo? I'm actually a bit disappointed he didn't write *that* down."

"Thanks for the visuals," Mayli said playfully and turned back to Alden, working at the next knot.

Briar laughed. Before the war, it had been up to he and his father, Prince Jamus, to be present during meetings around Vatan. After slipping out of a boring conference in Ammos, Briar explored their beautiful castle. Distracted by the unique architecture, where its domed halls were outside and sun-lit, he nearly crossed paths with Mayli's flying arrow. He'd not been expecting an archery range, for he was only in a quiet corridor. The princess hid, ashamed she had been caught practicing in secret. Curious to see the fabled skills of a true Ammosian archer, Briar vaunted about how he could outdo her in a hunt. Mayli accepted. He lost.

Embarrassed, Briar claimed that Mayli had all the animals trained to bow down before her and that it wasn't really a fair hunt anyway, though he knew better. She had laughed, amused. The princess had been one of the few royal, or even noble, women he had been able to pass jokes with; she would always laugh instead of turning a nose up. It was no wonder his cousin had admired her.

Excited to exercise his playful banter once again, Briar continued, "And can you imagine the fleas he had afterward? I mean, if he didn't have them already…"

"Okay. Got it," Mayli scratched her legs as if imagining that every uncomfortable itch was now a bite.

Briar chuckled. *Well, maybe she's grown to be a little more sophisticated in the last few years*, he realized, as she was clearly finished discussing the tale of Reyn and the rats. "Mayli. Why are you visiting the mainland? I thought your father kept you locked in a tomb or something."

"Ha! Just about. But it was by my Father's wishes that I leave."

"Oh yeah?"

Mayli's posture faltered as she rubbed her elbows. "Yes. Honoring my mother's last wishes." She looked up at him with lonely, hazel eyes. "He's handing me off to Gavin. We are to make arrangements…"

"Ah, old Prince Gavin of Hiore," he said. "He's almost twice your age. Think you could be happy with him?"

She shook her head and waved a hand. "That is irrelevant."

"Sure it is."

Mayli shrugged. "Hiore is rich and well-respected. I don't need to be happy if it helps my people."

"An unhappy ruler will make for an unhappy kingdom."

Mayli smirked at him. "Briar, you are so naïve."

He held out his arms proudly. "But I'm happy!"

"But is your kingdom?"

Briar flattened his lips and slowly brought his hands to his lap. "I'm not king."

"Perhaps if you ruled instead of Colin then Brimley would flourish."

"No." He gestured around the room. "This is Colin's and I will respect that."

"He doesn't deserve respect for what has been done," snapped Mayli.

Briar glared, holding back words he knew his cousin would kill him to say. He stood. "I'm gonna tend to the horses."

Mayli watched as Briar tugged his thick, leather jerkin off a chair, nearly knocking it over. He laced his arms through the sleeves, then using his thumbs, flared the collar up to cover his frown. He didn't look back as he left the room.

Hanging her head Mayli smoothed out a wrinkle in her dress. *Why did you have to kill my mother Colin?*

Queen Margaret had visited Brimley to present recently discovered evidence. Recently, Arkello Densen escaped the desert with The King's Blade, a rare and unique jeweled knife passed down to each generation of kings. Arkello also had with him scrolls and documents of Gezmek's downfall, proving that the sons of King Edune had died proving that Liam and Jamus Densen were imposters. The court agreed, reminding everyone that when the boys had been found, that they hadn't yet been crested. With the truth out, Queen Margaret then denied Colin's proposal to marry Mayli as he was no longer seen as royalty in her eyes.

The Densen's were enraged. Colin and Briar were rumored to have sat around, drunk, commenting on injustice, bias towards their lineage, and Margaret's small-mind. The boy's fathers, Liam and Jamus were argumentative, pulling what few documents they had to prove their lineage. Then, the night before Margaret was due to leave for Ammos, she was murdered.

Looking up, Mayli imagined the tower room where her mother died. She was glad the structure had fallen in the war following, saving her the temptation to sulk within the dreadful room.

Sucking in an unsteady breath, Mayli wiped her face. She crawled up the bed and cuddled beside Alden, just as she had each night to seek comfort. His warmth radiated like a summer's day, burning away every bad memory. As she nuzzled in, Alden moaned, wrapping a strong arm around her.

"Oh, you are finally alive!" Mayli sat up, suddenly shy.

Alden's hand slid down her back as if petting a cat. The man blinked, finding focus on her. He spent a moment staring with tired, dark eyes, then finally said, "No."

"No?" Mayli giggled.

Alden carried his hand back up, then cradled her face in his palm, pressing his thumb on her lips and parting them. "Life can't be this beautiful," he said, staring deeply into her eyes.

Mayli flushed. *This mess? Beautiful? I'd never question the complement before, but now...?* She looked down at her soiled hands. Though she had taken a bath, dirt—and blood—was still caked under her long nails, or what was left of them. Several were torn off. Her new form-fitting dress irritated the thin cuts from the woods, making her skin itch. Mayli hugged her body self-consciously. A tear rolled down her face and held at her jaw. Mayli brought her shoulder up to wipe her chin, but it was tender from where Reyn had hit her early on. *It's likely now blue, like Brimley. I'm beat like this castle. But somehow...he still sees a beauty?*

Mayli looked back at the man to dispute his claim, to tell him he's delusional, but he'd already fallen back into a peaceful sleep.

In the rooms morning haze, deep shadows contrasted against the highlights which fell over his body, emphasizing every angle. She let her eyes trail down the hard lines of his chest, down his torso and stopping at his exposed stomach. *He is beautiful.* She brought her hand up and lightly traced her fingers over his skin that lay tightly across muscles. As she did, his abs tightened.

Briar cleared his throat.

Mayli shot up, hair swaying wildly and face burning hot in surprise.

The prince took another step in and lifted Reyn's journal from the desk. "I, uh, forgot this," he said, wiggling it.

She brushed a curl behind her ear, nodding. More hair fell in front of her face. The ambient silence suggested Briar hadn't left. Slowly, she peered up at him.

Briar looked between she and Alden—who still slept—then shook his head. "He won't approve of that."

Mayli glanced at the way the sheets laid across her rogue's lap, smiling. "You sure?"

He tilted his head down, narrowing his eyes seriously. "With you, Princess? Absolutely."

<hr />

Sweat was flung from Alden's heated body as he jolted awake from a strange and alluring nightmare. Seeing a warm yellow glow, he squinted. The happy cooing of doves filled the room, along with the sweet scent of lavender soap. He smiled. *Nothing could have been that awful*, he convinced himself. Alden grabbed a pillow, stuffed it behind his head, and sat up.

"Good morning," said a familiar cheerful voice.

Briar stepped closer, coming into his view, and rested against the bedpost. He smiled lightly and looked down on him, popping a few berries casually into his mouth. *It must be late in the day if he was already up.*

"Briar, I have the worst hangover!" he moaned as a nauseating twist in his stomach lurched.

Briar stepped forward. "Ah, no. Al—"

Alden groaned, rubbing his head while trying to relieve his splitting headache. "Ugh... Centuries old liquor really brews the strangest dreams! Just awful... There were all these spiders and monsters after me. I even fought a kanavaur like the King of Vatan!" He laughed, raising his arm as if to stab. It felt heavy, so he let it drop. Alden frowned. "It was because of a war. Everything was lost: family, friends, the castle...but there were these *beautiful* women."

"Um—"

A gentle and cool breeze blew at the drapes, revealing the foreign stone and hole in the ceiling. Alden rubbed his eyes as he leaned forward to better stare at the destruction. His mind was still playing tricks on him. "It was a dream, wasn't it? Yeah. I'm still in it." He shut his eyes to stop the room from changing, hoping to dream once more of the Ammosian Princess and a mischievous thief.

"Alden, there was a war. This isn't a dream."

Alden's eyes shot open.

Briar leaned in, offering his waterskin. Alden snatched it and drank deep, as if he had been deprived for days. After depleting the bottle, he caught sight of another figure who stood at the foot of his bed.

"*May...*" Alden mouthed in disbelief, body tensing.

She smiled sweetly back at him.

As he slowly regained his memory, he recalled her sleeping beside him, screaming in horror as he restrained her in the carriage, trudging through mud and water, a burning figurine, watching the princess dance at the Festival of Gezmek, blood, Kira, a falling tower, and then Reyn stabbing his side. Alden put his hand to the wound. Seeing his arms lined with gauze, he looked up at Briar for clarification.

"You fought Reyn. Mayli saved you and I cleaned and patched you up, bud. Don't worry, you're safe," comforted Briar.

Alden shut his eyes, letting out a weak sigh. He sunk back into the covers and threw the pillow over his head.

"Why couldn't it all just have been a dream?"

After a recuperating nap, his fever was finally gone. Alden peered out from under the pillow. Mayli still sat at the foot of his bed like Rek would. She watched the drapes flutter in the wind with a natural smile and wide, wondering eyes. *She looks peaceful, happy, even.*

Mayli shifted her gaze to him, as if she knew he was looking. "Hi," she said softly.

Alden lifted his head, setting the pillow aside. His head still throbbed, but he was tired of lying around. He slipped out from under the covers and stood on wavering feet.

"Easy!" called Briar as he rushed to his side, lifting a quilt and catching his swaying body.

Realizing he was nude and about to fall, Alden snatched a quilt and wrapped it tightly around himself. "Thanks, now can you get her out of here and on a ship home?" he snapped, pointing a rude finger at the princess.

"Nice to see you too. Mayli, could you give us some privacy?" Briar asked with an apologetic smile.

Alden watched as the princess mumbled something, snatched her bow, and left. He frowned, easing himself back on the lonesome bed.

Mayli released her last arrow into a large vase, shattering it. Her arrow ricocheted off the wall and skidded down the hall. After collecting it, she looked up to find a staircase leading to the sky above.

The tower...

She followed up the stairs, which were coated in grass and flowers as if it were an old frayed rug. Once at the top, she gasped, seeing a familiar brown cloak. *Alden.* He was sitting on the edge, with his legs dangling. He seemed lost in thought as he took in the panoptic view of the town, populated now only by saplings, overgrown bushes, and the lonesome calls of migrating birds. In his hands he held a painting.

Mayli stepped back, but Alden's head turned, spying her. She brought her hands in front of her and waited. A moment passed before he took in an irritated breath and stood. As he did, he chipped the frame against a stone. His mouth flattened in disappointment as a piece of detailed gold-leafed moulding fell over the edge, adding to the decay. With a groan, Alden walked to a faded mark on the wall and hung it.

Mayli joined his side to view the art with him. Crowned in a gold branch-like crown was a handsome man with hair tied back in a ponytail, strong cheekbones, and a stern smile stood. His hand rested lovingly around his queen. Her chestnut hair grew long and continued off the scene like a waterfall. Between them were two small boys. The royal Densen family: Liam, Lily, Dominick and Colin.

"Shame the murderer hadn't stayed innocent," Mayli said.

There was no reply. Alden just stared at the portrait. He touched its corner and aligned the frame perfectly with the stain on the wall. For a moment he stood with eyes closed, then he turned on his heel. When she refused to move, the thief brushed past, forcing her to step aside.

"Hey!" Mayli chased after him. She tried to grab his arm, but he pulled away immediately, spinning to glare at her.

"Why don't you talk to me?" she snapped.

"I have nothing to discuss with you, Princess."

She shook her head, bewildered. "Well I do! Why didn't you tell me your plan or that you were friends with Briar!"

Alden scoffed. "You would have panicked. You hate the Densens, May. This kingdom. Me."

"I don't hate you."

He raised his brow, challenging her.

She held the hem of her dress. "Not anymore. I didn't understand before."

"Exactly, why would you trust my word when my blade was wet with Ammosian blood?" He pointed to his dagger at her hip and opened his palm. "That's mine."

"But you threw it to me."

He cocked his head. "I was drugged, seeing double. I missed."

"Missed? You could have killed me!"

"I'd never do that," he said, beckoning with his fingers twice.

Huffing, she tossed it to him.

The thief snatched it out of the air. He tightened the leather binding on the handle then scraped off a bit of dirt. Satisfied, he threaded his belt through the frog.

"Thank you," Mayli said.

"What?" He paused the tie of his belt and looked up at her, as if she'd spoken a foreign language.

"Thank you. For saving me. From the thieves, from Reyn. And those times you lent your hand when I fell. The knife. You risked your life to take care of me, despite my distrust..." Mayli shuffled her feet. "Thanks for holding me."

Alden shifted his eyes. "Holding you?"

"While we slept."

"Did not."

"You're calling *me* a liar?"

He shifted his gaze away and chewed his cheek. He looked around, then froze as if finding the memory. "...*Idiot,*" he muttered, placing his fingertips to his forehead.

She smirked. "So, you remember?"

He brought his hand down. "Ya know, guard dogs seem nice when they are asleep too."

Mayli chuckled, folding her arms. "Yes, but they are also loyal. Besides, you said I was beautiful."

Alden grimaced.

"You denying that too?"

He shook his head, keeping it low and eyes averted. "What else did I say...?"

Mayli grinned, then walked aimlessly, skipping her feet up. "Let's see, what else can I recall from your delirium? Oh, you said that you like playing with squirrels, that you fear spiders, and think keenreavers are actually people from the lost city. You promised you'd never hurt me and that one day you'll take me to an orchestra!" She spun to face him. "Will you?"

Alden rubbed his eyes. "No."

"You said cellos were your favorite. That their sad tune reminded you of us."

"That wasn't meant for you."

Mayli's chin lowered as a strange jealousy draped over her.

He dropped his hand to his hips and fluttered his eyes at the ceiling. "That all I say?"

"Um." She shrugged. "You were really concerned about your cat. Do you really have one?"

He gave a single nod. "Rek."

"Hmm, interesting. I pegged you as a dog person."

Alden huffed a small laugh. "Ya know, you're not so bad, Princess."

"*I'm* not so bad?" she asked, watching him pass by with a drunken swagger.

"Yup." Alden gripped the railing overlooking the inner balcony to the tower.

"Uh-huh. Like I was ever mean to you," she said, chasing after.

As she neared, he pulled away and followed the railing down the curling oak staircase. After a few steps, he had to grip the banister to keep from wavering. He called up without looking back, "You were, and your mockery sure wasn't welcome. Neither was commanding Brimley's demise."

Mayli halted her descent. *He blames me?* She sighed and continued down the grass-covered stairs with elegance. She hovered over him with her chin held high. His head turned, acknowledging her presence above him. "Alden, I appreciate you saving me but your prince's jealous rage caused your home to fall, not I."

The lobby at the tower's base was large, round, and had thick oak arches that circled around the ceiling and met at a point. If it weren't for the domed structure, this too would have likely fallen during the collapse. Between each beam hung dusty cobwebs that dangled down like moss hanging from a tree. There were fine chiseled details in the exquisite wood mouldings lining the architecture, but the craftsmanship was hidden behind years of dirt piled high. She imagined it had once been a beautiful space but was now only a haunting mess.

Alden looked down, voice quiet. "Won't you be open to the idea that someone else was behind what happened?"

"Are you making a confession?"

He sneered.

Mayli smiled, then took a step down to be level with him. "Then let the past go," she said, turning her back on him. She then hopped down onto a soiled rug, dust billowing up. She took a few steps away to escape the cloud. When he didn't follow, she turned around and held out her hand. "Ready?"

Alden looked at it smugly.

Mayli rolled her eyes, lunged at his hand, and tugged him away from the stairs. He leaned in, allowing her to pull him along.

Alden withdrew his hand from hers just as Briar lifted his head from Reyn's journal. "Good, you're back." He tossed Alden the antidote. "Drink that. I gave you some earlier and it seemed to help."

Alden brought the bottle up to his face. "You fed me this?"

"Hey, I remember you telling me Reyn's antidotes look fancy!"

Alden lowered the bottle. "He also keeps his most deadly ones in nice containers…"

"Eh, but you got better!" Briar waved a hand.

"Let's keep your gambling to Noble's Dice. I could have died!" Alden said before taking a swig. His tongue flashed out and he shook his head in anguish.

"About as good as dune ale?" Briar laughed.

"I'm not drinking that again," Alden said before sucking back on his water skin. He wiped his mouth, then leaned in to begin a private conversation with Briar.

Mayli flopped onto the bed. She took in an irritated breath but released it with a relaxed sigh. She rolled over and sat up on her elbows to look at the two. Neither paid her casual position on the bed any mind as they whispered among each other. *Most men would.*

Bored of being left out of their hushed conversation, she sat up. "What are you two blabbing on about over there?"

Alden pursed his lips, whereas Briar lifted his head and smiled at her. "Oh, not much. Silly, nonsensical things."

She shifted her eyes to look at Alden, whose foul scowl and hunched-over posture suggested otherwise. "Mmhmm," she agreed sarcastically. "Alden."

He looked to her, brown eyes reflecting in the sun. They pitched in worry, as if nervous to answer her upcoming question.

"Did you learn anything while in the guild? About the murder?"

He dropped his head, then shook it.

"That isn't surprising," she mumbled. Mayli folded her arms and looked to the prince. "Your cousin did it Briar, you just need to accept that."

Briar smiled. "I completely agree, actually."

Mayli fluttered her eyes. "You do?"

"Yep. Arkello has motive."

Mayli laughed. "Arkello? You don't really think you are his cousin, do you?"

Briar nodded. "Yes, I do."

"Even if you are, which I doubt since the real heirs of King Edune were proven dead, it doesn't make sense. Arkello was in Ammos at the time of the murder. It couldn't have been him."

"I'm not so sure that's true," Alden said while picking at his dagger.

Mayli glanced at Alden then back to Briar. "Was he there? Did you see him?"

"No," replied Briar.

Alden sheathed his knife. "A master assassin can lurk in the brightest shadows."

"Assassin? I've heard about Arkello's skills, but what motive would he have?"

Briar leaned in. "Same as Colin. Your mother denied your hand to both of my cousins. Likely me too had I not been with Evelyn, then again I have royal Colte blood from my mother's side."

"But Arkello has always been so nice to me."

"Wasn't Colin also?"

Mayli's face soured. "Letters lie. No, unlike Colin, Arkello is a good man and has never pressed his advances on me. Besides, he's too focused on finding Gezmek again to even look or talk to me. But he did wish me luck with Gavin before I left last week."

"Luck with Gavin?" Alden asked.

Mayli picked at her broken nail. "Yes… we are to make arrangements."

Alden leaned back in his chair. "Shit," he sighed.

She looked up. "What?"

Alden shook his head and sat back up to cross his arms on the table. "Nothing. But it makes sense as to why the Shadowens were hired to ambush you."

"You think the murder and the kidnapping are connected?" asked Briar.

"Sure. Her first arrangement was sabotaged, now this. If it is

Arkello then it is clear that he doesn't want Mayli married to anyone but himself. No matter the cost."

"Or Colin doesn't," Mayli scoffed.

"Likely both," joked Alden.

Briar raised his brow.

Alden shrugged. "I don't know. It could even be Gavin."

Mayli scrunched her nose up. "Why would Gavin kidnap me while I was on my way to meet him? That is a little farfetched, Alden."

"Maybe, but if shown that Ammos is unable to protect their most prized treasure, they won't be as revered. That could be leverage to demand more power and Hiore loves having control. Prince Gavin would even look like a hero if he'd arranged it to be the one to save you."

"Thats absurd. You two might as well be suspects."

Alden and Briar exchanged exhausted expressions, then Alden met her eyes. "You can trust us to get you home Mayli Drake. No reward. No mention."

She huffed. "The honorable thief."

"And prince!" Briar chimed in.

ONWARD

CHAPTER SEVENTEEN

"I should have taken a third horse."

Mayli spied Briar alongside his huge, black warhorse, patting its muscular and arched neck. Its thick mane flowed to the ground in perfect waves. Mayli brushed her fingers through her own hair, trying to tame the frizz. *His horse is better groomed than I.*

An excited whinny drew Mayli's attention to the young, beautiful rose-gray mare in the next stall. The smaller horse nodded her head up and down as Alden entered the stable.

Alden's once tired face quickly grew bright with a sweet smile. He walked to the pen and put his hand on the horse's dappled forehead, instantly calming her. Mayli smiled, watching him stroke her face and whisper sweet nothings into her ear.

Briar continued, "Though, a man galloping along with two saddled yet riderless horses would have risen suspicion. So, Mayli, we'll have to double up."

"I'll walk. She can take Emory," Alden said, leading the mare out to her.

The horse cocked her ears at Mayli and nudged her side with

her snout. Mayli retrieved a pear she had found and offered it to the horse, who accepted it gratefully.

"Ah, no, Alden. I'm glad you are feeling better, but you still need to give your body more rest," Briar said, patting Alden's wound, making him flinch. The prince laughed and handed off a saddle.

Alden took it, straining, then rested it on the mare. Once all her tack was secure, he stepped forward, gripped the saddle, and pulled himself up, wincing slightly.

Mayli grabbed the saddle and hooked her foot in the stirrup.

Alden scowled. "What are you doing? Ride with Briar."

Mayli pulled herself up, forcing Alden to scoot forward. She leaned in, whispering. "I can't. He's still a Densen."

"You hate them that much?"

"After our talk last night, I'm just not sure who to trust."

She looked over to the prince. He wore his black and yellow tabard, signifying him as Dregs's guard captain. Light shaggy hair stood up at all points while his bangs hung in his eyes. He finished hooking the bit in his horse's mouth and then kissed its muzzle with an audible "muah!" The animal snorted and playfully nibbled at Briar's hair, making it stick up even more than usual. The man laughed, patting the large head away. Then, with an effortless hop, swung himself onto his horse. Briar looked up, smiling wide, and pointed. "Onward!"

"Yeah, he's a real villain," Alden said, ushering his horse forward.

The sudden rocking forced Mayli to grab Alden at the waist to keep balance. He let out a small, throaty grunt.

"Oh, sorry!" Mayli moved her hand away from his wound, choosing to place it instead on his leg.

He swiped her hand off.

Defeated, Mayli rested her head on his back. He stiffened, taking in a long, controlled breath, but after a moment, his shoulders finally relaxed.

Briar met her eyes, narrowing them slightly. "Best keep that hidden, Mayli."

She raised a brow.

"That silk. It's a dead giveaway to who you are."

Mayli watched as Briar rode with one hand on the reins while the other was a fist on his hip. His horse took long graceful strides, which carried them both with a proud and royal finesse. She looked at her own attire, which was already dirty or torn. She eyed Alden's clothes, which were just as rugged. He slouched in the saddle, letting the horse follow rather than lead. *I more closely resemble him than royalty.*

Sighing, she unwound her scarf and tucked it under her tunic, giving the impression that she had large breasts. She jerked her head towards Briar. "How's this?"

He looked for only a moment as his face took on a pink glow. "Fine," he said before sending his horse into a trot.

Emory took the same pace, disallowing Mayli to rest against Alden's back again.

She watched the horse's legs tense and stretch. They bulged out like ocean waves in a storm—hard, fierce, and with undeniable strength and beauty. *It's no wonder the pair won so many jousts.* The beast raised his snout and with it flew his wavy, black mane. He revealed a wide, focused eye that seemed to stare back at her as if he knew she was admiring him.

"What's your horse's name?"

"William!"

"William?" Mayli laughed. "Not Midnight or Shadow? It's such a happy name for a strong, dark warhorse!" Mayli teased.

"Well, he was called Excelsior, but when my uncle died in the tower's collapse, my father passed on the name in his honor...just before, you know, he also was murdered."

Mayli's cheeks flushed. "Oh."

"Yeah."

She remained silent the rest of the day.

"We'll rest here," Briar announced through battering rain.

Bringing her head up from Alden's back, Mayli looked past her soggy hood. Lightning flashed, revealing the silhouette of an old log house as thunder rolled in the distance.

Briar hopped off William, splashing into a puddle. Slopping through it, he led his horse to the door and opened it. Together they entered.

Mayli looked around, searching for the second building where they would sleep. The only other foundation she could find were fallen trees—no other houses.

Alden slowly dismounted, groaning slightly. He steadied himself, stretched, then reached up. Mayli took it and he helped her down. Upon touching the ground, her legs buckled.

Mayli's face pressed into Alden's chest as he caught her.

"You okay?"

Nodding, she began to hug him, but he peeled her off.

"Good. Tomorrow's ride will be worse."

"Oh." She stepped back and glanced at the house. "Are we seriously staying in there? With the horses?"

"Would you prefer to sleep out here?"

The rain picked up.

She shook her head.

"Well then, come on," he said, leading her and Emory inside.

As they entered, a strange thunder roared in the distance. They both turned their heads as riders approached.

"Shit. We have guests!" Alden called to Briar.

Briar drew his saber with a humming ring. "Hide behind the horses. I'll greet them."

They obeyed as the deep rumble halted beside the house. Mayli hunkered down and Alden crouched beside her. He took deep, nervous breaths, squinting in pain as he peered past the horse's legs.

As the door swung open Briar revealed himself. "Hello!"

"Woah! Didn't expect anyone to be here!" said a startled man. He called backward, "Hey, it's been taken, ya know!"

Briar stepped backward as a large man bullied his way into the doorway. The first man followed behind, along with two women and a child wrapped in a father's arms. Three more lightly armored men also walked in. Suddenly the small house was beyond capacity and reeked of sweat, mud, and horse.

Briar moaned and lifted his arms out in a welcoming manner. "Make yourselves at home, then..."

"This isn't your home," disputed the large man as he shook his head, spraying everyone with water. He lit a candle and looked around the house. The warm light crept into the shadows beside them. Alden slowly shied away. "Why are there horses in here?"

"It's raining," answered Briar.

"No shit, but why are there horses in the house?" repeated the man looking back at the prince.

"Why are all of you in here?" Briar crossed his arms.

"Shelter."

"Well..." He shifted through the mass of people to be between Emory and William. "Same reason."

The man pointed to the door. "Take them outside with the rest, there's no room for such scrub."

"*Scrub?*"

Briar took a deep breath through the nose and straightened his jerkin. He stepped forward, greeting the bold man who dared insult his horses. "Let's have proper introductions, shall we?" Smiling, he placed his hand over his right shoulder but did not bow. "Hello! I am Prince Briar Densen, Captain of the Guard in Dregs, and you are?"

"Prince?" The man moved the candle uncomfortably close to Briar's face, but he didn't flinch. "Not according to most. Your father is a fraud."

"That is still up for debate, but my mother was Princess Trisha Colte of Dregs. I am still royal."

The man scoffed and tugged his belt up. "Well, *prince*, what brings you out here? Hoping to find the lost princess?"

Mayli and Alden exchanged a worrying glance.

"Could be. What do you know of it?" Briar asked seriously.

The stranger leaned forward, palm open. "What will ya pay?"

Briar slowly blinked, unamused.

"Worth a shot, but I guess you're as piss-poor as us now."

They laughed

Briar remained focused. "Speak what you know."

The father spoke up, hugging his kid in. "Highwaymen tore apart the princess's escort and escaped into the Colville mines."

"Yes and thieves were found dead along the road leading to Brimley Castle," said the mother.

"And now thanks to your fucking cousin, Hiorean knights have been stomping all across Vatan harassing us Brimleyns. Why do you think we are here?" He gestured around.

"Watch your words!"

"Oh?" he snorted. "Or what? Murder us? The child? Wouldn't be a difficult task for a Densen, now would it? After Colin killed Queen Margaret and then Princess Gina, what's a few commoners?"

"My family is innocent." Briar snapped. "And my aunt is still alive, you fool."

"Is she? I haven't seen her in a few years."

Briar shook his head. "That isn't surprising. Royalty doesn't mingle outside the Festival of Gezmek usually."

"Makes sense why you are out and about then." The man laughed. "Ya know, I bet I could get a lot for your head. Vatan would eat it right up that a Densen had something to do with the princess's disappearance. Nobody would even question it."

Mayli gasped as the armored men crowded around, faces smug. A bead of sweat dripped down her face as the tension rose along with her heart rate. *I have to do something.* She began to rise but Alden hooked his arm around her waist and held her to him.

Briar gripped his sword. "Get out."

The Brimleyn looked down to Briar's curved weapon. His cocky smile wavered, then he chuckled. "Come on, there's another cabin in the woods I know of," he said walking outside into the now pouring rain. Before his companions followed, they each spat at Briar's feet and exited with the same arrogant expression as their leader had.

There was a wet slop of boots shifting through mud, a squeak of clammy leather, and a cry of protest from the child. After the thunder of hooves dissipated, Mayli heard Alden exhale and then gasp for another breath. Still in his embrace, she turned to look at his worried face inches above hers. He briefly met her gaze before letting her go. He cleared his throat then stood.

They parted through the horses. "Brimleyns are so charming," Mayli said.

"Oh yeah, delightful," agreed Briar with a grin as he began undressing William.

Alden rolled his eyes and left outside with a bowl.

"How do you let them disrespect you like that?" asked Mayli.

Briar ran a hand through his hair, sighing. "Mayli, because of the war I lost everything, especially respect. I'm used to it."

"But you are still a prince of Dregs!"

"Thanks to my uncle Olivar, all I am to people is a measly guard captain."

"That's absurd!"

He nodded. "Yeah, I know. And I'm also an heir of King Edune of Vatan, but still, nobody cares."

"That's because you're not. Your father James wasn't crested when found. Who is to say that he and Liam weren't street orphans?"

Briar straightened up, giving her a hard look. "My father

and uncle had treasures and tomes fleeing the Desert of Gezmek. Their stories with the sandstorm have been accredited."

"So? I still don't believe it. They could have found or stolen them."

Alden huffed as he returned with the bowl now brimming with water. He set it on the dresser. "And of course what Arkello brought back wasn't stolen or forged."

Mayli narrowed her eyes at Alden's sudden attitude. "Arkello had The King's Blade. You can't forge a treasure like that."

Briar set the last of William's tack down and stepped beside Alden as the man removed his gloves to wash his hands. A hushed whisper growled between them. Briar glanced at Mayli momentarily, smiled guiltily, and then rolled his eyes back at Alden.

More whispers.

Mayli leaned in, curious, but as she did, Alden pulled away in frustration. The table rocked at his departure and water spilled onto the wooden floor. He collected their waterskins, then opened the door to leave. The wind screamed and sent a cool draft into the room, whipping his cloak back dramatically. Alden stepped out and slammed the door shut behind him, leaving the room cold and gloomy.

An annoying drip rapped on the floor, amplifying the dead and awkward silence. After a moment, Mayli joined Briar's side. She looked into the bowl where his eyes reflected from the candle's glow. She searched his stormy eyes, looking for an answer to Alden's wrath, but there was only a lonely ripple of thought. Briar caught her gaze in the reflection and struggled to smile back at her. Failing to succeed in an honest expression, he dipped his hands in to break the water's image, bent forward, and washed his face. Mayli turned and leaned against the wall, staring at the door, imagining Alden outside, alone in the storm and being hammered by an unforgiving rain. *He doesn't need to face it alone.* Mayli stepped forward, reaching for the door, but Briar caught her by the arm.

"He... You should leave him be." Briar's head shook sympathetically as he released her.

Mayli hesitated, considering the guard captain's words, then continued her journey across the room. Taking hold of the handle, she braced herself for the wind.

Three thin waterskins lay on the wooden deck waiting to be filled. Above them rested Alden. His arms were folded and he leaned against the house, pinning his cloak back with a raised foot. He turned his head from under his hood, revealing the silhouette of his chin. It rose and then his frown deepened.

She picked up an empty sack and lifted it out to collect rain that poured off the roof like a waterfall. It didn't take long to fill, and she turned to hand it to Alden. He kept his absent gaze over the lonesome road. With an irritated breath Mayli threw the waterskin on top of Alden's folded arms. Jerking in surprise, he unwound, letting the sack fall. Alden lowered his foot to stand away from the wall and scowled. Mayli turned her head away from him and rested her hands on her hips defiantly.

There was a hollow thud and Mayli looked to see that he had sunk back into the wall. Annoyed, she strolled forward and gripped his hood with both hands and gave it a tug. "No, you don't get to hide!"

With haste, Alden grabbed her wrists and peeled her off. He opened his mouth to yell but snapped it shut as he looked past her, eyes shifting as if they sought the right thing to say. He pulled her struggling hands down to her side before he let them go.

"Talk to me."

"About what? About how many Brimleyn lives were destroyed? That anything we say to defend ourselves is discredited or ignored? Or how Briar is living in a shack ruling over guards instead of subjects?"

"That's his choice."

"Loyalty isn't a choice, it's an oath."

"Oaths can be broken."

"Not with him. The Densens aren't ones to break promises."

"Like how Colin promised to always love me?"

Alden was about to speak again when a rogue wave of rain carried by an angered wind drenched them both as if they were on a ship. He blinked slowly, water tearing down his face. "Wanna go back inside?" he offered softly.

Mayli rattled her frozen head up and down.

Back in the house, Briar lay on the floor. He was now relieved of his armor, boots, and jerkin, leaving him dressed in a slack tunic and barefoot. Emory stood while William lay on the floor, curled up with his large head resting comfortably across the prince's lap as if he were more dog than horse. Briar rolled his head across the oak floor and smiled faintly at them as Alden threw off his cloak and armor.

Mayli shivered, rubbing her wet arms up and down.

"Here..." Alden said stepping in front of her.

Mayli watched in awe as he put his hands to the clasp of her cloak. Rough fingers grazed her throat and she paused for breath. She stared at his downcast eyes. *Look at me...* she begged internally. He didn't. Mayli swallowed as he removed her cloak leaving a cool breeze in its place. He left to drape it over a cross-beam to drip-dry beside his. Chilled, she wandered over to the candle and cupped her fingers around it. The small flame did little to warm her but then a soft quilt wrapped around as Alden gave her a gentle squeeze around her shoulders. Mayli put her hand up to touch his but he had already stepped away. *Alden?*

When she turned, the thief was in the corner with his head bowed.

Mayli walked over and knelt before him, but Alden continued to keep his gaze shielded. *Look at me...* She gasped as her rogue unexpectedly did as if he'd heard. "Um. I just wanted to say that for your sake, I hope you are right."

"About?"

"Everything," she yawned, resting beside him.

He put his hand on her shoulder, hugging her in. "Thank you, Mayli Drake…"

DREGS

CHAPTER EIGHTEEN

"*W*oah," Briar said, bringing William to a halt.

Mayli shifted her tired head across Alden's back to peer out with a yawn. At the sight of purple knights, she hunkered down. "They can't be thieves if they are stationed with your guards, right, Bri?"

"That's right."

"Well…" She pointed to urge them forward.

Alden brought her hand down. "No, I don't trust anyone right now. We'll find another way in."

"The Isle of Dregs is one big fortress. There's no other way that won't be guarded," Briar informed.

Emory let out an exhausted snort that Mayli would have guessed had come from Alden. He leaned his head back, looking skyward, then released his own sigh of exasperation. "What then?"

"We just go in."

Alden turned in the saddle and growled. "They are checking crests!"

Mayli looked to watch a group of travelers that were held up in line. The next one awaiting entry had a cart dressed with a canopy that sheltered their load. Before they reached the bridge, a Hiorean knight rode forth to greet them. There was a brief conversation, then the knight pointed at the man's sleeve. He hesitated but lifted it. At the sight of the tree design, they pulled him aside for questioning. Meanwhile, Black-Coats tore open the Brimleyn's canopy and rummaged through his belongings, tossing them carelessly. When nothing seemed to be found amiss, they let him go, but glares followed.

The next man in line stepped forward and proudly displayed his crest of Dregs. He was welcomed in without further inspection. As he passed the Brimleyn, who was now taking care to secure his jumbled goods within his cart, the Dreggan noble shoved him. The force caused the man to tumble against the stone bridge and lose a bag over the edge. It splashed into the river below.

Laughs erupted at the man's expense and Alden began walking Emory backward. She flung her head around uncomfortably at the strain he put on the reins.

Briar reached forward and snatched the mare's bridle. "Do you forget who I am?" He tugged at his guard captain's uniform. "I own these checkpoints! Let's go."

"Sweet kings…" Alden grumbled. He rested his hand on the hilt of his dagger, letting Emory follow.

"Prince Briar, where have you been?" asked a tall woman. A purple cape flapped in the wind against her strong, thin armor.

The metal glistened in the sun, causing Mayli to squint and tilt her head away. The Hiorean Army took pride in the mirror-like sheen of their wares for that exact purpose: to glow, be seen as righteous, and command respect.

Briar, however, didn't squint or cast his view down. Instead, he lifted his chin and smiled. "Madam Veridia, hello! Just making the rounds."

"You've been gone for almost a week, Your Highness."

He shrugged. "Big kingdom."

Veridia flashed her eyes to Mayli and Alden. "Who are they?"

"Old friends."

"I'm…" Mayli began.

"You can call me Nick, and her Emma," Alden interrupted as he squeezed her leg.

Mayli closed her mouth.

Veridia eyed them. "What brings you to Dregs?"

Alden's grip tightened further around her leg, and it began to hurt. Fearing he may lash out, she continued their act, "We're looking for a new home." Mayli put her hand over Alden's and wove her fingers into a gentle embrace as she molded her body against him. The knight's gaze followed the interaction and Mayli began rubbing her thumb along Alden's hand. She then nuzzled her head up to rest her chin on his shoulder and smiled innocently.

Alden gulped.

"Why were you gone in the first place, Briar?" the knight asked, breaking her gaze from Mayli after she had given Alden a tender peck on the cheek.

"Thought I'd scout in search of the lost princess. I assume that's why you are at my gate?"

"Alone? Why no party to aid you?"

"Have we not battled in enough tournaments for you to know me? Maybe not—you never lasted that long." Briar smirked. "I don't need fancy armor or an army of tin soldiers to get work done."

The knight rolled her eyes and relaxed back in her saddle. "Perhaps you are right."

Briar, too, let the tension go, leaning back in his. He looked at the four other Hiorean knights. "I heard you lost a knight."

"His sacrifice will not be forgotten to whoever took Gavin's fiancée."

"It wasn't official yet!"

Veridia looked at Mayli and began to open her mouth.

"Try the Shadowen Thieves Guild," Alden interjected.

The knight blinked and shifted her focus. "What do you know of the guild?"

"Enough to know they are the only ones who could have done such a thing." Alden lowered his gaze as the sun's reflection glinted in his eye.

She narrowed her eyes. "How so?"

Alden squeezed Mayli's hand and looked back at her. "Anger them and you'll learn what they are capable of..." He held her eyes.

Mayli couldn't help but blush.

"Would you know who runs the guild?" the knight continued with her questioning.

"He goes by Pierz," Briar offered, saving Alden from the barrage of questions.

Veridia looked back at the prince. "Pierz? He have a full name?"

Briar yawned and rolled his neck. "He's a thief. The name sounds more like a play on words about stabbing... I have more information including names and drawings of some guild members if you'd like to discuss it later, but right now, Emma, Nick, and I are tired and hungry, and I am desperate to crawl into The Binx and nurse some drinks."

"Of course, Prince Briar," said Veridia as she stepped aside, allowing them entry to the Isle of Dregs.

Once safely across the bridge and free from watchful eyes, Mayli wrapped her arms around Alden's chest and gave him a joyous squeeze.

"You can cut the act now..." he groaned.

"What act?" Mayli replied with playful innocence and further hugged him.

Alden stiffened. "I'm not your lover," he stated through clenched teeth as he lifted his chin to make way for her intrusion.

She ignored him as she continued to cling on. Alden looked over at Briar for relief.

Briar shrugged. "I don't know, you two cuddled pretty close last night."

"She was cold."

"I'm not sure Colin would agree." Briar raised a testing brow at Alden.

Alden shook free from her hold and quickly dismounted.

Mayli pouted. "Oh, who cares about what he thinks?"

Briar looked to Alden and then back at Mayli. "We do."

"Well, he and I will never be a thing, so let him be sad and envious forever." She swung her leg around and hopped down at Alden's side, touching a hand to his chest to hold balance.

Alden pulled away. "That's an awful thing to say."

"Yikes! The thief thinks I'm the awful one," she pretended to whisper to Briar as if sharing a secret.

Briar laughed. "No wonder he has no friends!"

"Hey, I have friends!"

"Oh yeah?" drawled Mayli.

Alden began counting on his fingers, then paused, looking around as he pondered more.

"Five?" Mayli gave a slight laugh. "Wow, was I at least one of those fingers?"

"Briar, Dean, Mary, Squirrel, and Kira." He read off his fingers and added one more on his other hand to point at her. "And now six, if the awful Lady *Emma* insists."

"I do!" she said with a proud nod. She then broke into laughter. "Wait, you really are friends with squirrels? I thought that was just your delirium."

Alden laughed softly with her. "The kid's name is Squirrel." His smile then wavered as he recoiled his fingers by two. Alden squinted, as if pained and formed his fingers into fists. "Four."

"She'll understand, Alden," Briar said. "From what you've told me, Kira has always been there for you as you have for her."

He shook his head. "I don't think so."

"Kira... Was she that woman that was with you in the carriage?"

He nodded.

"And...she's your lover?" Mayli asked softly.

Goosebumps raced across Alden's body like lightning at the memory of Kira's lips against him.

The day was one he'd never forget. They had just retired back to her flat after an exhausting mission in the Cad Islands—days he wished he could forget. Happy to be alive, they both collapsed on her bed. Although tired, the thief had a sly, rambunctious spark dancing in her eye as she glanced at his dagger.

Alden protected The King's Blade well, hiding its true identity and value by wrapping the jeweled handle in leather. The dark sheen of the curved blade reflected glimmers of blue and lavender like auroras in the night sky. To anyone else, at first glance they would assume it was crude as black blades usually were. But it was from Gezmek.

Because of the secrets it held and precious value, there were few Alden trusted it with. Kira wasn't among them. However, his desire to keep it from the thief only made her want it more. Even with his guard up, she still had the dexterity to flick her hand toward his belt and relieve it from his scabbard.

Alden threw her a damning scowl. She spun the weapon around, then presented the hilt, daring him to take it. He had leaned forward to do so, but she drew it farther behind with a widening smirk.

Annoyed yet patient, Alden inched closer, passing his head by hers in an attempt to steal his blade back. Their hands touched as she allowed him to grip the hilt. Then, he felt a peck on his cheek. It was soft, tender, and left him wondering. The act had frozen him, and during the freeze, Kira pressed her warm advantages.

The thief slowly slid her face up to his mouth and stole a kiss. Without ever having had a lover's touch, Alden hadn't taken much convincing to press his lips back into Kira, and passionately—he'd wanted to for months. And as it turned out, so had she.

Alden smiled as he replayed the memory of him unlacing her blouse so that he could take hold and kiss Kira's plump breasts. She rewarded him with a soft moan—a rare sound from her. A rush of desire had encouraged him to stab the dagger into the wall before pinning her to the bed. They stared at one another with longing, then kissed once more. Kira wiggled as she tried to kick her leggings off. He helped. Once they slipped past her ankles, Alden loosened his belt, letting his drop too. He then connected himself with her, locking them into a wonderful embrace...

He sighed.

It had ended as soon as it started. While his mind had rung in alarm, he pulled away from the thief, concealing himself, and plucked his knife from the wall. She wouldn't have either blade again.

Alden squeezed his eyes shut, glad they never went further. *Her affection was all a sham to find answers.* He couldn't blame her. As a shadow seeker, it was her job to gain knowledge at any cost. Alden worried what secrets she learned and told the guild aside from his meetings with Briar.

Alden looked at Mayli, who had a twinkle of worry in her eye as she watched him develop his answer.

"No," he finally replied. The realization stung.

"You don't trust in love."

He turned from her and began walking down the cobble street, unsure if it was a question or a statement. Regardless, he didn't wish to answer, even though his action had.

"Neither do I," she said quietly.

Alden paused to look back, unconvinced. She was a flirt. She had suitors knocking at King Bakhari's door constantly asking for her hand. Alden had also heard rumors that she was always accompanied by at least a few men as if she had them strung behind her on leashes. Others gossiped that she slept with her guards. And the way she already acted toward him further demonstrated her fluidity with men. Alden saw Briar even raising his brow as he ushered his horse forward. Alden narrowed his eyes, wondering if Prince Briar and Princess Mayli had ever mingled.

Mayli looked between them and she folded her arms. "It's true! I may tease, flirt, and play now, but..." She shook her head. "My heart hasn't mended since Colin."

"You loved him?"

"I..." She nodded. "I loved his words, but that wasn't really him."

"It was. He's always looked at you with high regard. Always adored you."

"Does he now? Last I heard he only wanted what power I could give him."

"Last I talked with him, that was a lie."

"You talk to him?" Briar asked.

"Occasionally. You?"

"Yeah. Occasionally."

"That's surprising. Colin wasn't on your list of friends," Mayli said to Alden, wiggling her fingers.

Alden groaned. "That's because we aren't on good terms."

"Why?"

Alden took Emory's lead and continued towards the guard tower. "He's a coward who ran from his duties."

Mayli sat tapping her fingers on the leather chair. She looked around, then shot up from the desk and began pacing once more. She'd been stressed ever since the realization that she'd be sailing in the southern waters. Her brother Jair had told her enough stories about pirates and sea monsters near the Cad Islands to put her on edge for life.

As she circled the small office for the third time around, Alden reached out to gently halt her continuous loop. Mayli was sure she was making him dizzy—she already was—but she brushed past and continued her lap. When she walked by Alden again, he spoke confidently to her, "It will be fine. Briar will ensure we are on a safe ship."

"What reasonable captain goes by Captain *Bosun* Scraggs? That sounds like a pirate to me. I mean really? Which is he—a captain or a boat swain?"

"Captain. He owns his ship."

"Yeah, a pirate ship."

Alden shrugged. "If he's friends with Briar he can't be so horrible. He and his crew are probably renegades like me but have an appetite for booze and are…smelly."

"So, pirates… And you don't think you smell?" Mayli plugged her nose as she passed by him.

"No more than you," he teased, waving his hand.

Mayli paused to take a delicate sniff of herself. A sweet stench of sweat and horse pierced her nose. She looked back at Alden's mischievous face and frowned shamefully. He chuckled and presented the leather chair beside the fireplace for her. She stepped forward and flopped into it, resting her tired feet on the stone. She sniffed again self-consciously.

Alden took a seat on the hearth and peered inside, smiling. She looked too. Melted wax was pooled at the bottom. *Perhaps his letter?*

She looked back up to him with worry. "If we get ambushed,

how do you know they won't slit our throats? I've heard such awful stories..." Mayli whined.

He broke his gaze from the ashes and smiled sincerely. "Briar and I will be with you, you'll have your bow, and a whole ship to defend you. We'll have ya home in three days."

"Three days? I don't know if I can last that long out at sea..." She held onto her stomach, imagining the seasickness already taking over.

"You'll be fine. Compared to what I pulled you through, it will be like a leisurely adventure," he said. "Think of it as a vacation!"

"After I met the Hiorean prince, that was what this trip was supposed to be."

"We'll, see!" Alden cheered as he tapped her knee. "This adventure is not much different!"

"I prefer vacations in which I don't get kidnapped, attacked, made to serve myself, wear wool, make friends with my enemies, and then put on a ship to vomit..." Mayli leaned forward in the chair and caught her head in her hands. She heard him chuckling again. She liked that. Mayli perked up. "Do you think they will have the tea like Mary made?"

Alden put his hand on a pouch strapped to his belt. "Perhaps." He smiled sweetly.

She gazed up at him, enjoying this side of Alden. Since the bridge he'd been in a good mood, smiling and talking with kind words. He was playful even. *It is like I'm experiencing the real him. The man before the war.*

He watched her as she pondered what his daily life had once been. The man acted proper and was respectful. For the most part, he was chivalrous. Especially now as he tried to comfort her. He knew how to fight, read, and write. And he was charming, if not snarky. His parents were millers now, but they proudly displayed a shield that had seen war. Her war. She considered the options. "Were you a soldier?"

"A what?"

"What did you do before The Brim War? A guard or knight maybe? Did you joust with Briar?"

"Uh…sure," Alden said as he drew his dagger and began picking at the blade.

She raised a brow. "*Sure?*"

He shrugged, looking around. "What makes you think I was anything worthwhile?"

"You are a good person."

Alden sneered. "Look, knights, soldiers, guards, queens, and princes are not free from wrongdoing—you should understand that best of anyone—and thieves, murderers, and liars can rationalize their actions to be good. Everyone is just in their own mind. Title is irrelevant when it comes to virtue," he said, then continued rubbing his nail against the black steel.

Mayli grinned, clamped her hands on the chair and pushed up to stand with a hop. "See, you said it yourself."

He looked up from his blade. "Huh?"

She lowered her chin and peered up at him with wide, smiling eyes. "You said: thieves can be good!"

He flattened his lips, defeated. "Fine. But still, who I was before the war doesn't matter anymore, May. That life no longer exists. Never will. I'm no longer worthy of…anything."

"But you are!" She put her hand on his right shoulder. "At least to me you are! If you aren't a knight already, you should be for all you've sacrificed!"

Alden's face was a wave of emotions. It turned from confusion to scrunched-up as if he were lost in a serious thought. Then he looked at her hand on his shoulder. His face loosened again as if he had given up. He closed his eyes—now pained. She wanted to hear the flurry inside his head—wanted to ease his burden. Mayli traced down his arm to find his hand and opened his palm. She placed hers inside and squeezed.

Alden opened his eyes and drifted down her body until he spotted their woven hands. He blinked up at her face then lowered his gaze slightly to her lips. Mayli split them apart as she took in a light breath and leaned in. As she neared, Alden shook his head out of a daze and quickly pulled his hand free. He narrowed his eyes as if saying "no" then turned away to hide behind the wall of his hood.

Mayli sat back down and lowered her head, letting her hair hide her own heartbroken expression. She replayed the way he had looked at her, touched her, and spoke to her searching for any mixed signals. She found none.

After a while sitting in silence, Alden perked up like a watch-dog. "Come!" he said quietly, taking her hand and peeling her off the leather chair. It was only then that she noticed the approaching footsteps and loud voices. Together they flew up the stairs to Briar's living quarters.

"I was beginning to fear *The Lucky Fish* would never swim again," said Thomas, stomping his boots free from mud as he walked to the door.

"Captain Bosun Scraggs finally paid off his debt." Briar led his lieutenant into his empty office. Mayli and Alden were gone. He looked up the stairs, assuming they were hiding. Unconcerned, Briar removed his jerkin and hung it on the coat rack.

"Did he?"

"You can't keep men like that anchored to the land forever."

Thomas nodded. "Say, I need to fill you in on a few matters while you were out. Have time?" He walked to the desk and flipped over the hourglass.

"Not now, Thomas." Briar rubbed his brow. "I'm beat from my journey and am looking forward to relaxing at the Binx & Drinx, hopefully get lucky with a lady, and then having a decent night's rest before I take on the city's troubles. I trust Dregs can last one more day without me."

"Right, sir. I'll see you in the morning!"

"And please let me sleep in...at least a little this time?" Briar pleaded with a yawn.

"Oh, ah, no promises!" Thomas nodded with a cheesy smile.

"Thanks..."

Thomas walked to the door.

Before he opened it, Briar spoke, "Hey, how's Aunt Gina?"

He paused, looked down, then smiled. "Fine. Still mourning her husband."

Briar smiled with relief. *She is alive.* He nodded. "Say hello for me."

"Will do, Sir." Thomas shut the door behind him.

Briar slumped into the leather chair and looked at the pool of wax in the fireplace. *Hmm, Alden is probably disappointed I didn't burn those earlier... At least he found 'em. Nosey thief.* He closed his eyes and took a moment to rest.

A knock sounded at the door.

By the kings, already the city won't allow me to relax... Oh... Briar looked to the hourglass, now spent.

"Come in," Briar yawned.

A thin, squirrely fellow with a gnarly unkempt beard entered. He smiled at Briar with the few crooked teeth he had left. The man had shy but wild eyes that darted around unsteadily as if following a fly around the room. Briar looked to see if there was one, but after hearing—and seeing—nothing, he realized it was a unique feature about the odd man. He couldn't help but stare judgmentally as his visitor fidgeted and swayed from side to side.

Briar waited for an explanation. None came. He dipped his head while raising his gaze. "You okay? Are you drunk?"

"OH! Yes! Ah, never been on land before—everything keeps moving!" he replied, staring at the ground in disbelief.

"I see," replied Briar, unsure which question he had replied "yes" to. He rolled his eyes. "Why are you here?"

"Ay! Captain Bosun Scraggs is ready to set sail." He straightened up but the formality lasted for only a few seconds as he began to sway once more.

"Ah! Very good. Thanks! See ya down there." Briar popped up from his chair with newfound energy. The pirate stumbled back and found his balance among the coat rack, sending Briar's jerkin to the floor, which he proceeded to step on.

Briar frowned at the muddy print across the back. He blinked slowly back at the man. "You do know your way back to the docks, *right?*"

"Hmm..." The man's eyes shot to the ceiling in search of answers. He reached a boney finger upward as he mumbled and drew a line in the air, pivoted his wrist, and drew several more lines, all the while his tongue twisting and turning out of his mouth.

Briar watched in awe. *How had this man even found his way here?* "Uh-huh. Good. Great... We'll escort you back then, I guess. Wait here."

Briar jogged up the stairs.

In his open room, he saw Mayli kicking her feet as they dangled from the tall bed. She sat beside Alden, who wore an impatient frown.

Alden stood and pointed at the chimney stock. "Why do you have that thing hung?"

The attic had no firebox, but still, Briar wanted to dress the chimney to appear as such, adding any sort of homey touches to his dull room. He had built a stone hearth and decorated it with an array of wide candles to set the illusion. He even installed a wooden mantel where his father's sword, Gallivant, rested proudly on a decorative gold stand. Above that was a simple still-life painting.

Briar stepped around to view it. The subject was a bowl of fruit with a few jugs and plates whose ellipses were uneven. The horizon line was skewed as if the items were set on a broken table. Colors were muddied and haphazardly thrown down with aggressive brushstrokes as if applied in a rage. As sloppy as the piece was, Briar loved it and framed it with as much respect as if it were a treasure from Gezmek.

He crossed his arms and smiled in appreciation, then lifted one hand to it. "What? You did a good job."

"Wait, you painted that, Alden?" Mayli covered her mouth as she began to laugh. "And I've been sitting here insulting it this whole time…"

Alden continued his plea, "See? Take it down."

"No! Not unless you paint something to replace it!"

Mayli lit up at the idea. "Paint me!"

The princess posed with her chin elevated and shoulders back. She sat still, focusing on a distant point. Briar watched as Alden studied her longingly. He saw the man's eyes trace the contour of her body, his smile slowly growing.

Briar cleared his throat. "Not sure it would be appropriate to have a portrait of the Ammosian princess hung in my house, Mayli." Briar then turned to gaze at the painting and held his chin as he squinted, imagining something new. "But, now, William would be great!"

"If I paint your damn horse, will you throw that rubbish away?"

"No!" Briar exclaimed and twisted to protect the amateur painting as if it were an innocent child.

"That should never have touched the grace of a frame! There is a reason I didn't sign it." Alden stepped forward, pulling out his knife.

"Fine, fine!" Briar held out his hands, stopping Alden from destroying it. He then relieved the painting from its hook and rested it against the wall. He took a step back, continuing to appreciate it.

Alden rolled his eyes and grabbed it. He twisted it around to hide the art from being on display. "I don't wanna see this again. Throw it away."

"Can I have it?"

"No," he and Alden answered in tandem.

The princess winced.

Alden frowned, then walked over and grabbed his pack. He swung it over his back and looked down on her. "I promise I'll sketch ya something on the ship. Let's go."

"Good, don't mind the squirrel," cautioned Briar as he trailed behind.

"Squirrel?" Alden paused in his tracks.

"Oh, not *Squirrel*! Just a squirrely old man from *The Lucky Fish*. Apparently, this is his first time on land... He's very drunk. I think."

Alden nodded in relief.

Briar led Alden, Mayli, and the fish-out-of-water to the harbor. Rows of handsome and well-manicured ships with yellow and black trim lined the docks. He grinned at his white and blue ship, *The Albatross*, which was the largest of them all. *It's been far too long since I've taken her out.*

Beside it was a small rig coated in thick black pitch, which stood out like a weed among flowers. *The Lucky Fish* had a long, narrow hull fitted with oars. Its foremast was angled forward where the main stood slightly back with canvas sails tucked neatly around.

As they approached, Captain Bosun Scraggs leapt down to greet them. He wore a leather tricorn hat decorated by a rainbow of feathers, a long tan coat, tall boots, and, of course, a scraggly beard. The messenger hurried past his captain and climbed aboard. Briar exchanged a humored look with Alden, then looked to Mayli. The princess stood behind Alden, clinging to his arm as she eyed the pirate and his ship.

Briar approached Scraggs, so close only he could hear. "Anything happens to these two, you'll see *The Albatross* on your ass." He nodded to his giant ship above them.

Scraggs's eyes trailed upward, then floated back down. "As much as I'd love to see yer ship in action once more, Prince Briar, I'd prefer it to not be against me own again!" Scraggs looked over Briar's shoulder and greeted his passengers with wide and exaggerated arms. "I'm Captain Bosun Scraggs! Welcome aboard *The Lucky Fish!*"

Briar nodded in agreement and waved him away. The captain boarded, leaving them to their farewells. Briar turned to Alden, who was looking at him with concern.

"You're not coming with?" Alden asked.

Briar shook his head. "Not with Hiorean knights in town. And If this ship leaves and so do I...well. It's already suspicious enough that I was gone a week." He stepped forward and gripped Alden's shoulder to ease the man's worry then pulled him into a hearty hug. "You'll be fine," Briar whispered.

Alden squeezed back, then broke free.

Briar placed his hands on each of them. "Nick, Emma, take care of one another."

SWEET KING

CHAPTER NINETEEN

*B*riar woke to a knock. He waited, then rolled over and faded back to sleep, assured it was the construction of a nearby house gaining a third story. The rapping sounded again. *It's horses clopping down the cobble road. Maybe a woodpecker. At least if it were a bird it would be doing me a favor by clearing out the termites.*

Briar stuffed a pillow over his head to drown out the ear-splitting intrusion as it continued.

"Briar!"

No...

He took a deep breath and flung the soft fur blankets off his naked body and twisted to put his feet to the cold and dusty floor, sending chills through him. Briar pushed off from his bed and leaned forward until he caught himself on the windowsill a few feet away. After a mournful growl, he slid the glass up and peered out.

Thomas waved.

Briar felt the crust of morning sleep poke his eyes as he glared at the man in the predawn light.

You obey every other order—why not this? Why not the simplest of them all?

Briar released the glass and let the window slam shut. "The rooster can wait."

He took his time as he heated a kettle, relieved himself, dressed, poured the hot water, and fixed his tea, taking pleasure in the few minutes it took to brew. He looked around, but his powdered cream was missing. Frustrated, he added extra sugar before he descended to the office below. Finally, with a moan, he opened the door.

"I told you I wanted to sleep in…" Briar drew in a deep breath, making an effort to show displeasure of the hour.

"The sun is fully in the sky," boasted an unexpected feminine voice, ruining his yawn.

Briar closed his mouth irritably as he saw Veridia enter behind his lieutenant. He peered outside, seeing the bright orange ball but a hair's breadth above the horizon. He blinked back at the knight, unamused, and clicked the door shut. Briar trudged across the room, curled up in his leather chair, and pulled a knit quilt from his Aunt Lily over him.

Veridia looked around, seemingly judging his messy assortment of papers across his desk, mud that was caked on the wood floor, scattered tack from his horses, the wild flare of his hair, and sleepy crust in his eyes. Briar blinked over at Thomas who stood at full attention as if he had been up for hours—which he probably had.

"What's so important?" Briar asked.

"I need to discuss your recent absence," said Veridia.

Briar tilted the mug and sipped. "Again?"

She lifted the raven's note from his desk. "Is your cousin behind this?"

Briar snarled at the accusation. "No, he has no ill will against the Drakes…" He leaned in and looked at her definitively. "Never has."

"What then? Why travel the northwestern road?"

He shrugged. "There are plenty of Brimleyns who do hold the princess accountable. It seemed like a fair place to scout and was within reach."

"Where are your friends? Perhaps *they* had something to do with it?"

"Nick and Emma? They left with The Lucky Fish last night."

"Weren't they looking to make Dregs home?"

"Were. However, a better opportunity presented itself to them."

"Perhaps they were fleeing something."

"Likely you, Madam." Briar winked.

She glowered.

Thomas shifted to address the knight. "Madam Veridia, we were spread thin searching for the princess. Prince Briar told me of his travels and when he'd be back, and here he is. Do you have anything to discuss other than making unjust allegations?" said Thomas.

Briar raised his mug, thanking his lieutenant for the added support, then leaned back in his chair.

"I do. You said you had illustrations of the thieves in the guild?"

Briar pointed at his desk beside her. "Help yourself."

Veridia's gaze followed his direction. Her mouth dropped. "Are you kidding me, Briar?" She swept a half-eaten cookie aside and picked up a stack of papers. She shifted through helplessly.

Briar watched her struggle for a moment. "They are near the bottom…in a folder. Green. Stacked between William's pedigree and an old shopping list."

The knight blinked dully at him. She lowered her chin and sent her brows high as if doubtful. Briar nodded to assure her. She shook her head and took a few more minutes to search, despite his clear instructions. Finally, she found the file and withdrew the sketches. "This is red," she said, holding up the folder.

Briar saw no difference in the color and shrugged.

Veridia scoffed. "I swear, Briar. It amazes me that you can even be captain of the guard in all this mess."

"Watch your tongue, milady! He is still royal!" Thomas warned.

Briar gave an approving nod to Thomas yet again. As he cast a championed grin at Veridia, Briar danced his fingers in a wave goodbye. "You have what you came for…"

She crossed her arm over her shoulder, offered a small—almost unseen—bow, and left the room.

At her departure, Briar laughed softly with Thomas. He then yawned and brought the mug to his face, breathing in the soft earthy aroma. "Did I miss anything else exciting?"

"Right, so, uh, that thief you warned me about. She was a Shadowen, and I found her snooping in here soon after you left."

Briar spilled his tea before he took a sip, burning himself. "Shit!" He dabbed his tunic dry with the quilt. "Everything okay?"

"Well, she wasn't here to fight nor cause trouble—she turned herself in, actually." Briar cocked his head. Thomas shrugged. "She said she was just looking to talk with you, sir. I told her she wasn't under arrest if she just wanted to chat, but she insisted to be locked up in the castle dungeon. Seeing no harm, I granted her that. I tried to get her to inform me of her concern, but she was really passionate about keeping it between the two of you."

"Take me to her." Briar stood, now fully awake.

Thomas shuffled his feet. He looked up to the ceiling, the floor, and then back at Briar. "I, uh, can't."

Briar stood straight and eyed his lieutenant curiously. "What do you mean you can't? You locked her up, right?"

"She escaped, sir."

"Escaped?" Briar stepped forward rashly. "When?"

"Several days ago."

"How did the guards miss that?"

"They already admitted to slacking off at the Binx that night, sir. Seems they thought they could get away with it while you were away. Would you like to question them?"

Briar sat back down and fidgeted with his mug. "Why escape after requesting to be put away?"

"Maybe she didn't want to wait any longer and saw an opportunity," Thomas offered with a shrug.

Briar shook his head, unconvinced. "No, she could have just asked. Thieves are sneaky. Add a few more rounds of patrol. I don't trust this woman. If you see her, apprehend the thief right away. I will talk with her then."

"Yes, sir."

"Anything else?" Briar asked, smothering a yawn.

"Just the usual."

"Don't crowd me!" hissed Kira.

The gaggle of women backed up only slightly as Kira worked the lock. Her tongue poked out of her mouth as she maneuvered a set of long hairpins. She heard a click, and the door loosened its hold. Everyone froze and she looked around with a sly grin.

"Oh, I can't do this!" someone squealed.

Kira stood and rose her sharpened chair leg into the air. "You can and we are! Remember what I've taught you; together we are a greater force than any guard or king! Use your anger but be controlled. We can't go into a frenzy if we wanna make it outta here together."

"Hear that, ladies? We are leaving this wretched place!" said Eryn.

"I know we practiced walking silently, but that just isn't gonna happen with the lot of us. You are about as quiet as Amber's rumbling stomach." The women giggled. "So! We move with speed! Ready?"

The flock bobbed their worried heads and gripped their

makeshift weapons. Kira swung the door open, and together they flew down the stairs. They met with a guard who was beginning to investigate the commotion.

Kira leapt like a cat, taking the staircase's height to her advantage. She landed with the chair's leg buried deep in her opponent's neck, coating her and the women behind with a blast of blood. Kira and the dead guard skidded down the stairs a few feet. She recaptured her footing, leapt over the body, and continued her descent.

As Kira reached the door she realized the patter of feet no longer trailed behind. She did, however, hear an unnerving slew of tearing and jabbing coming from up the stairs. Chills ran down Kira's spine.

She turned back and walked around the curved stairs. Kira gasped at the horror. Eryn and the others tore at the dead guard like wild beasts. They pounded back her face and ripped off parts of armor to better beat at her. Unable to understand, Kira stood stunned as the unnecessary violence continued. Even Amber, who was usually shy and well natured, was in on the attack. Sammie was in bliss as the girl exposed more soft flesh to tear apart. Hailey, at least, wasn't in on the slaughter and instead cried on the far most step.

"Stop…"

They continued.

She watched as they ripped hair from the woman's scalp. "Stop!"

Eryn looked up with her sharpened brush tip in hand and grinned with bloodlust. Kira shook her head in disbelief, stepped back and almost slipped on the step, then took off down the stairs, leaving the chaos behind her.

The door at the bottom remained open from the guard. Kira crept quietly into the king's chamber.

The room was appropriately large, taking up the full tower's length. On the opposite side was a matching turret from where she had been tattooed. Bookshelves lined the far wall and even under the windows. In the middle was a huge canopy bed. Sheer drapes silhouetted a round, sleeping figure.

Leaving the fate of King Olivar to his princesses, Kira snuck to the double doors. With her chair leg in hand, she unlatched the lock, grabbed the handle, and pulled. As expected, two large guards stood on the other side. Catching them by surprise, Kira kicked forward, sending one to the ground. She swiped at the other, forcing him to dodge, but not before the leg's tip snapped as it hit across his nose. The guard took a fumbling step back, cupping his hands over his now bleeding face.

Taking her opening, Kira leapt over the man whom she kicked and dodged a panicked swing of a sword from the one who bled. They began to follow, but Kira grabbed a large potted plant lining the hall and sent it crashing behind her, slowing their pursuit.

A chilling battle cry rang out from the king's room as the harem of women exploded from the doorway. Overwhelmed, the guards were swallowed up by a barrage of claw-like hands, which dug and tore at their faces. Screams cried out and Kira looked back as the frenzy once again took their revenge on their keepers.

One guard parried the first mindless attack and cut open one woman, then the next, throwing their soon-to-be corpses aside.

The guard walked towards his next target: Amber. The plump woman squinted, preparing for the hit that never came. Eryn had blocked the attack with a poleaxe she had stolen from the guard in the stairwell. She pulled away when Amber came to. The guard pressed forward, and they clashed their weapons together once more. Amber dove and tackled the guard to the ground. The others swarmed. Eryn stepped forward, then dug the blade deep into the guard's neck.

Kira pulled her eyes away and fled down the stairs, leaving them to their duty.

After escaping the horror, Kira found her way to a secluded nook and collapsed into it, shaking. She cried as she hugged her body in, recovering from their ruthlessness. She thought back to the mass of blood stained on the women's fingers and hair. The wild eyes of Eryn haunted her the most. *This is like the Cad Islands...*

After a deep breath, she opened a set of balcony doors to the brisk night. The wind carried a wave of chilled air kissed by the ocean's breeze. She wrapped her arms around herself, holding in any warmth the sheer fabric could provide, then glanced over the edge.

Across the garden was the castle's curtain wall where a patrol of Black-Coat guards marched around the bend. She ducked and patiently waited for them to pass. After they did, she gripped the rail and—by using the break between stones as footings— climbed down the castle. Once at the bottom, she found a thick flowering bush and hid within it.

Thorns poked into her and she couldn't wait to be the one doing the prodding for once. She gripped her chair leg. *Briar will soon face justice, followed by Thomas.*

The patrol marched by once more. Once they were out of sight, she darted for the wall and leapt. Kira scaled the rocks like a cat up a tree and over the barrier to the city beyond.

Freedom.

<hr>

Briar flipped his blankets off irritably as a loud knock yet again stirred him awake. He turned in his bed, groaning as another knock sounded—seemingly closer. "If it's that rooster again, I swear I'll..."

"No cocks here. Just a pissed off hen," an unfamiliar voice interrupted.

Briar shot up and gripped Valor from his bedside out of reflex and spun.

"How *dare* you lock me up and feed me to that...*pig?*" She spat the words.

"What? Who?" He blinked his eyes awake, then Briar gaped. A woman stood before him, gorgeous and scowling. All details of her body were shown through a seductive yet bloodstained nightgown, revealing a firm and toned figure, along with a healthy set of breasts that had earned his attention the first time he saw her. "*You!* You are that thief!"

Briar pulled a blanket off his bed and attempted to cover his naked and vulnerable body. While he worked to become decent, the thief lunged with what looked to be a sharpened—and bloodied—chair leg. Briar dropped the blanket and swiftly parried. His sword cut into the wood and ripped it from her grip.

She spun and stole Gallivant from its stand on the mantel. "Yeah, I'm *that* thief!" she twirled the weapon in her hand masterfully.

Briar's nostrils flared. *My father's saber...how dare she!*

She lunged and Briar jumped backward, not wanting to strike the weapons together.

She growled. "How can you let that happen to them? You disgust me!"

"What are you talking about?" He circled the thief into the center of his room, deciding being nude was better than being dead. She maneuvered to attempt another jab but hesitated.

Briar capitalized on her mistake and gently clanged Valor against Gallivant. He brought his hand from underneath, gripping her wrist. In one fluid movement, he swooped the sword up, yanking it from her hand. He pushed the woman to the floor and lifted Valor to her neck. "Hold! I gave orders to keep on the lookout for you after I noticed you gawking at the city gates. Thomas said you were in my office and turned yourself in only to flee the dungeon."

She looked up, appalled. "Flee? I told your lieutenant I needed to talk to you! I asked to be locked up! Why would I escape?"

Briar shook his head. "That's what I was wondering! I hope this isn't the conversation you wished to have?" he said, resting Gallivant back on the mantel.

"No… It was about Alden," she said, hugging her legs in.

Briar cocked his head. Her hair was braided in royal fashion and on her arm was the noble crest of Dregs. But beyond the beauty were cuts, scars, and acid burns. *Could this be the woman Alden spoke so highly of for her cunningness? Though he never mentioned how beautiful she was or that she was a noble...*

"Are you…*Kira?*" he asked in a hushed tone.

"Of course I am!" she snapped back with annoyance as if he had just asked if she were a woman, if her hair was brown, or if she was upset. "I was hoping to help…"

Briar dropped his sword arm. "Why risk the guild's wrath?"

"Same reason he did!"

"Doubt it," Briar chuckled, pulling off a blanket from his bed and wrapping it around his waist.

"Sure, it is. We did it for Brimley, our home…"

Briar fluttered his eyes at her open-faced lie and pointed at her noble crest of Dregs. Kira looked down. Defeated and ashamed, she covered her tattoo. She peered up, frowning. "I'm no noble, Briar. King Olivar had an artist brand us. He needed his new queen to be noble if he thought his scheme would work."

Briar arched his eyebrows and shifted his stance. "What?" He kneeled down and took her arm for a better look. She flinched at his touch, and he respectfully let go.

The design looked fresh. Regardless if she had grown up as a commoner in Brimley, the mark now made the thief a true noble of Dregs. He turned to sit beside her at the foot of the bed with a disgruntled sigh and closed his tired eyes in thought.

After a moment, Briar glanced back up at her. She blushed and turned away, letting her gaze fall on the false fireplace. *Had she been admiring me?* Finding himself turning red from sitting beside such a beautiful and barely dressed noblewoman, he looked at the hearth too. Together they admired Alden's painting, which hung proudly above the mantel once more.

After a brief silence, Kira spoke up. "I, ah...burned some letters in that drawer."

"Letters? Wait... YOU?" Briar scurried to his feet and lifted Valor back toward her throat. "You read those?"

She didn't even flinch. "Yep, and don't worry, no one else ever will. Sorry, but ya really shouldn't keep information like that around! Or get some better locks like I'd told him," she said flatly while ignoring his blade.

"And how do I know you didn't hand them off to Pierz and burn something else to deceive me?" He inched Valor closer.

"I wouldn't do that to you guys!" Kira began to stand, but Briar pressed the tip to her neck, threatening her back down. She rolled her eyes. "You're lucky I was the first to find them."

Briar clenched his teeth and took a subdued breath from his nose, fighting to keep himself even-tempered.

"Look, I'm on your side! I came here to tell you that he is saving Mayli. Though he doesn't know it, I helped make it happen."

"You knew it was Mayli, but they didn't?"

"Perks of being a Shadow Seeker. I'm hired to be nosey."

"Why not tell him?"

"I wasn't convinced he'd trust me... and I also wasn't sure how he felt about her... so I left it up to him."

Briar took his chances and lowered his weapon. "How did you help?"

Kira looked down, face softening. She picked at the detailed gold hem on her nightgown. "I convinced Reyn that Alden and I were best suited to overtake the carriage. At first, he refused, arguing that Alden was a poor fighter and would be useless. He was right, but I argued that would be his strength in this case. I reminded Reyn that Alden wasn't known to be overly aggressive, whereas anyone else—like a perverted assassin—might get carried away with their blade, since we were hired to take the woman alive, and for the most part, unscathed."

"So Reyn just agreed?"

She rubbed her neck. "Eventually… There were conditions I had to meet."

Briar stood and walked to his nightstand. He lifted a book from it. "I've read enough of his journal to know what that means." He tossed it to Kira.

Kira hugged it close. "How did you get this?"

"Reyn is dead."

"Wh—" Breath escaped her as her jaw dropped. "De… Reyn is…"

"Dead," he finished, then offered his hand.

"Truly?"

"Princess Mayli shot an arrow through his head."

Kira's face brightened like a spring day melting away winters freeze. She put a hand to her mouth as her body quavered then wiped a tear of joy. Finally, she took his hand and he lifted her. "I knew I'd like her!"

Briar retrieved his long black cloak off the end of the bed and wrapped it around her conservatively while holding her shoulders. "Me too."

Kira blinked twice while her eyebrows rose.

Embarrassed, Briar awkwardly let go. He moved away and picked his trousers off the floor. "If you didn't escape, what happened? What's this about a pig and the king?" he said, stepping into them.

As Kira explained how Olivar denied his obvious problem of being infertile, Briar clenched his fists and took in strained breaths. She went on about the women's pent-up oppression and how she was able to rally them to fight back and break free. "I came here right after to seek revenge, but I guess you, and also likely Thomas, had no idea…"

"None…" Briar gasped through his hands holding his face. Then, he popped up. "Wait, this *just* happened? Like, *now*? Where are the other women?"

"Probably still causing havoc in the castle." Kira shrugged.

"*Shit!*"

Briar hurried to the wardrobe, pulling out the rest of his ensemble. Kira collected his belt off the banister and hugged it around him after he'd thrown his tabard overhead. He sat on the bed and laced his boots while Kira adjusted his pauldrons over his shoulders. As she tighten a strap, he shifted his eyes to her. "Will you stay here?"

"Will I be safe?"

Briar stood, facing her. "As Captain of the Guard, and as your Prince, you have my word." He placed his arm across his chest and bowed.

Kira slid off the bed and untied his cloak from her neck, once again exposing her body. He breathed in her peppery aroma as she draped the garment over his shoulders. As he rose, she pulled his hood over his head, then stayed close as she tied it. "Then I'll be here."

Briar grinned, inhaling a deep breath, making his chest large and proud. With a wink, he twirled to run downstairs. He hurried to the tower next door, beating breast plates together in alarm to rally his troops. His guards dressed quickly, and together they rode to the castle. As they marched to the upper floors, Briar paused, seeing a Yellow-Coat guard leap from the balcony above. He rolled and dodged a thrown clay pot, shattering dirt on the marble floor. Briar ran to the man's side and looked up.

A tall lady, wearing a blood-soaked gown similar to Kira's, clapped with excitement. "AH! My sweet king!"

Three other women all crossed their chests to hold their tattooed shoulders. They bent at the waist, bowing formally.

Briar threw the fallen guard he recognized as Carl a questioning glance. The Yellow-Coat shrugged and shook his head as he stood. Briar glanced behind him, reading the same confused expressions on the Black-Coats. He looked back at the bowing women. "Nay, I'm Prince Briar Densen of Brimley, Captain of the Guard of Dregs! Who are you?"

"Me? I'm Eryn Wright of Brimley, daughter of Henry. I'm a blacksmith who worked for the castle, or was until the war when that pig took me... Who you see here were Olivar's potential queens." She gazed down at Briar with a more serious look and presented the group of women with wide arms. Eryn lifted her head and spoke without emotion, "Your uncle is dead."

"We will not live as slaves!" a woman called.

"We killed him in order to free ourselves from years of rape!" explained another.

Chatter arose from among the guards. Briar let out a whistle, commanding several to dispatch from the group to meet the murderers upstairs.

"Good riddance!" shouted a woman.

"King Briar!" chanted a few.

King Briar?

Briar shook his head and raised his voice to cut through their harpy-like howling. "My Aunt, Gina, would be the new ruler of Dregs, not I!"

"Oh, sweetie, she died of fever years back! He had it covered up. Olivar didn't want to eventually submit his throne to a Densen. That's why he had us—to conceive an heir. But no dice." Eryn abandoned her weapon upon seeing the guards approach. The others followed suit.

Briar shook his head slowly.

I can't be king...

He turned to his lieutenant for reassurance, but the man

stood stiff, face red, and unwilling to look him in the eye. "You knew? Could this be true? You just said she was alive!"

Thomas winced.

"Don't be mad at him! Olivar was very persuasive to make sure secrets were kept." Eryn pulled a small girl forward.

"Hailey!" gasped Thomas. A bead of sweat found its way down the lieutenant's brow and caught in the creases of his eyes. It mixed with a tear, then fell down along the rest of his face.

"Daddy!"

Briar looked up in horror at the young girl covered in blood. *Is that his lost daughter?*

Thomas turned suddenly. "I'm sorry, Your Majesty! I wanted to tell you, but he threatened to…to…"

Your Majesty…?

Thomas cried. "I sent the thief up, hoping she would… Oh, forgive me!" Thomas stepped away, bowing deep, face nearly to the floor.

From behind, Briar heard a shuffle of movement. He spun back to see Thomas and his guards lined in a perfectly straight row. He watched in disbelief as they all crossed their left arms, gripped their shoulders, and bowed gracefully low following Thomas's salute.

Briar stared in awe. Never had they looked so refined. Never had he been shown such respect. As reality began to dawn on him, his stomach twisted in knots. Feeling the pressure and wanting to have a strong first impression as king, Briar gripped his own shoulder and stood tall.

"Sweet kings…!"

CHAPTER TWENTY

Since leaving Dregs, Alden had stayed busy by offering his hand on deck, managing the sails and helping to relieve nets of freshly caught fish. When there wasn't a job to be done he'd lock himself in his private cabin or overlook the horizon from high up in the crow's nest, sending Mayli a clear message of solitude.

She spotted his cloak thrashing in the wind. He was bent over the starboard rail, shouting over the crash of waves. A few crewmen hung by ropes dangling over the side as they applied fresh paint to the ship. Alden pointed, directing them.

The first mate obeyed his command, climbing over the edge. Alden caught a rope and yanked. As he held it firm, waiting for the man to adjust his seat and be lowered, he caught sight of her. She smiled and lifted a hand to wave. He quickly turned his focus back on the job, as if he hadn't seen.

Mayli let her hand drop along with her smile. She missed the sweet and comforting man she had seen in him in Brimley, along their travels, and at Briar's. The separation bothered her more than she wanted, leaving her with a longing desire to be around someone she knew. She wanted to be with *him*. But without Alden feeling the same, Mayli was left to herself.

Defeated, she walked away.

Jim the chef passed by and waved with a shy grin. He was a large and quiet man who spoke little other than of matters relating to food, and even then, his speech was limited. Most of the time he communicated with a grunt or twist of fingers to help illustrate what he wanted to say. "Hot stew," "Fish and grits," and "Full turn, we eat," were the more well-developed *phrases* he could muster. Mayli waved back but hurried along. Although Jim was good to her, he offered poor company and stared at her a bit too long for comfort.

Mayli sipped tea the chef had made. Jim always had a hot mug of the Brim tea sitting out for her just after dawn, timed perfectly for when she woke. Unlike her other adventures on the water, the Brim tea she drank aboard *The Lucky Fish* was delightful. As usual, the brew settled her queasiness, but for once, she was able to enjoy the sweet, earthy taste. The chef seemed to make it better than anyone. His even rivaled Mary's back at the mill. *If only he could cook or bake like her too.*

Mayli downed the last remaining drops of tea and set the mug on a crate. She floated along the deck, stepping lightly as if dancing as the ship rocked back and forth. As she passed behind Alden, she gave him a sidelong glance. He remained focused over the edge, but Mayli could see nothing of importance happening other than the slaps of wet brushes across boards. When he continued to ignore her, she sighed and made her way toward the stairs.

"The ray glides above."

"What?" Mayli looked around, unsure who had spoken.

Captain Bosun Scraggs peered down at her from his hammock, which was constructed of fishing nets and blankets strung between the mast and the quarterdeck's rail. He held one hand behind his head while another gripped a brown bottle laced with twine around its neck. He raised it, welcoming her over. Mayli smiled, then trotted up the steps and around the rail. She leaned on it, gazing down at the lounging man.

Scraggs tilted his head to her and a pillow fell away. "Rays. Shy fish who usually keep to the sandy bottom. Occasionally they breach for us to see their beauty," Scraggs clarified, eyes dancing along her figure.

Mayli sat and threaded her legs between the banisters. He continued to observe her with stormy blue eyes that reflected the sea below. His cheekbones were strong and glowed red from the sun, but she speculated he very well could be flushed from the bottle of rum he nursed—or maybe her. Mayli pushed her head through the gap in the rail and grinned flirtatiously. "Are you saying I'm beautiful?"

The man nodded with a charming smile. "Most certainly." Scars made him appear older than he was—he had no wrinkles nor any gray hairs hiding in his yellow sun-bleached hair. Mayli guessed he couldn't be older than Briar. Scraggs, she thought, was properly named as he grew a scraggly short beard, which held his chin onto his long face. She wouldn't call him handsome, but he wasn't unattractive either.

She looked down at Alden, who quickly adjusted his hood as he tied a knot. *Had he been watching? Oh, this is perfect.*

"*Captain* Bosun Scraggs," she said with emphasis.

"Hmm?"

"Your name doesn't make any sense."

"I don't know... I think Scraggs is very fitting!" he said, stroking his mess of a beard.

"Not that...the Bosun part. Are you a bosun or a captain?"

"Captain! See the hat?" he said, pointing. Several tropical feathers jetted out from his tricorn hat's side, signifying his many voyages to far-off lands.

"Then why both ranks?"

"I was a bosun for so long, that even when I built this ship and finally became captain, it felt wrong to say Scraggs without Bosun before it. The crew insisted on calling me 'captain' whenever I was on board. Rightfully so, mind you. So, I became Captain Bosun Scraggs."

Mayli considered this, then beamed. She stretched out and lifted her foot to kick off his hat. "Now you're Bosun Scraggs?"

Scraggs caught his hat before it fell down to the deck and twisted to face her. He held an amused grin. "Yes."

"And what needs to be removed to see just Scraggs?" she said, making sure it could be heard from below.

Mayli watched as he drew her in with thirst and a devious smile sprawled across his drunken face. She giggled but it was interrupted by a loud clanging of buckets and zips from ropes. Shouts erupted as workers below scrambled to hold tight to a line that held a man upside down like a caught fish. He held a bucket of red paint, which dripped down to the deck.

Mayli watched as Alden fought to find the right rope to lower the struggling man down. Once the crewman found his way to the rail and was stable, Alden scowled up at her.

An impish smile danced on her face as she was rewarded with an even better reaction than she had hoped. Alden narrowed his eyes further, then turned to help clean the mess he had helped create.

"Bad omen."

"Hmm?" questioned Mayli, still smiling as she watched the scurry of men.

Scraggs pointed. "Just a day out at sea and already my deck looks bloodied."

Alden threw off his cloak and rolled up his sleeves, revealing fresh bandages. He knelt and began scrubbing, coating his hands in the dark red paint. He looked up at Mayli once more. Their eyes locked. As he held her stare, she retired her grin, ashamed.

She hoped his reaction was from jealousy but knew it was probably a matter of safety before anything else. These men weren't exactly the courtly type and Mayli was sure they were pirates. If they saw her royal crest, she'd be sold to the highest bidder on the Cad Islands. Her brother Jair had always told stories of the unruly place and how it was a thieves' paradise. The land had no ruler. The only laws were ones made for oneself.

Mayli stood, waving goodbye to Scraggs and continued back to the hull. When she entered the living quarters, she paused. It was a large open room lined with swaying hammocks, some filled with sleeping bodies. Crates lined the sides where they kept their belongings or goods to be used throughout their voyage. In the corner, two men played a game of dice, letting the ship's sway do the rolling.

"What game is this?"

"Ah! Hello, fair maiden. Most know it as Noble's Dice," said the larger man. If it wasn't for the smell alone she could have still guessed he was a fisherman. His wide beard sparkled in candle-light from the shimmering fish scales caught in it. "Wanna play?"

"I'm afraid I've never had the pleasure," she said, sitting on an overturned bucket.

A thin man smiled with bucked teeth. She'd named him Rat after seeing how he scurried up the shrouds to tie off the sails like a rodent. "It's simple, Emma. The game is exactly how king-doms are ruled! If ye be lucky you'll be born noble and riches flow. But, if ye roll low, yer a peasant and must give up every-thing to the kingdom. Usually, there be coin en betten' involved to really play like kings."

"I'm not sure that's how noble rule works." Mayli giggled.

"Sure it is! Roll this." He handed her a strange ball-like die.

She examined it for a moment, then tossed it casually onto the crate and read the number. "Twenty."

Both men looked down at it in disbelief. Then, they eyed each other, each drawing determined looks as they furiously shook their own dice in the cup of their hands. In sequence, they tossed their roll.

Rat's landed on a twelve. He shrugged.

The fisherman's continued to spin. Mayli could see the number twenty winking in and out, painting a wide smile across the man's face. He leapt up in excitement, but bumped the table, causing his die to roll across the crate. It hit Rat's mug, resulting in a deflating low result: one.

The fisherman snatched his die and scowled at it, mumbling vulgar profanities Mayli had never heard before. He rashly tossed it to her. His cursing continued as he crossed his arms and stomped away.

Mayli looked at the remaining player. "Did I win?"

"Can't do no better than a twenty! Ye be a queen!" He grinned, revealing his bucked teeth.

That will be truth someday. She snickered to herself then handed Rat the white die the fisherman had given her.

"Oh, no! That's yours now. Dolo rolled a one, so whoever rolled highest—as you did—would have earned you coin from each of us. But you rolled a twenty! That means you would have kept the pot, and the die too. Take good care of it. He had carved it from a thick scale of the draclynn who killed his brother."

"Oh!" Mayli exclaimed in horror, then narrowed her eyes. "Wait, draclynns are real? I thought it was just a river and Dreg's creative representation of the delta for their emblem."

"Nah, the river was named after the beast."

Her eyes widened. "And they really look like that serpent?"

"Mostly. Ye seen a squid?"

"I've eaten them," Mayli offered with a shrug.

Rat cocked his head with a smile. "The tentacle parts?"

She scrunched up her nose and shook her head.

"Missen out, I tell ya… But ye know 'em?"

"Yes."

He smiled, then drew his hands wide to explain. "Okay, now, imagine those on a large snake with huge fins, and a wolf's head."

Mayli clicked her tongue. "Sounds ridiculous."

Rat shook his head and leaned forward seriously. "Ye won't be saying that when you be looken' her in de eye! They are smart!"

Mayli nodded. "Well, thanks. I too have lost family to a monster. Solo can keep it."

"No, that's not how it works. He failed and must pay the price."

"That's awful..."

"Such is the world of kings, peasants, and sea beasts."

"Thank you, Ra...uh, what's your name?"

"The name's Sican!"

"It was a pleasure, Sican! I'll probably be back for more. Because, apparently, I'm good at ruling," Mayli said with a wink.

"Oh, no, the pleasure was mine, me queen!" Sican said with a comical bow.

Mayli giggled, bowed then walked away. Alden hadn't been wrong. The men aboard *The Lucky Fish* weren't so bad. They of course were smelly but treated her kindly and with respect. While most slept in hammocks or tiny nooks, Captain Bosun Scraggs had given Alden and her private rooms. The space was small but provided her a space to reflect on the trip, thieves, her mother, Gezmek, the Densens, and her rogue...

She opened her door. It was in shambles. Blankets spilled off her bed and onto the floor. Clothes she'd collected from her adventure were piled everywhere, and drawers hung open as if the sea had also made the dresser fall ill. *It's like I'm back in the hoarder's cabin.* She'd never had to pick up after herself before as Lidia magically kept things in order, and now was ashamed at how much work she had made it for her.

Irritated by the mess, she stepped back into the dark hall. The room across was Alden's. She opened the door. At first, she thought maybe she had mistaken the room for another's, as the thief kept his surprisingly tidy. His desk was free of clutter, the bed was made, and he kept his clothes off the floor by hanging them on a string tied between beams.

Even this scoundrel has good habits.

She sat on his bed. As she did, a puff of his scent caught in her nose. Though it was stale and musty, it now captivated her. She smiled and laid down, remembering the nights when she slept beside him and he'd held her. She figured he hadn't known what he was doing; he was lost in a crazed, drugged-up state of mind. But still, he allowed her to sleep by his side when they traveled to Dregs. It was because of those nights, understanding his intentions, and realizing he was the man who fought to keep Kira safe from Reyn, that Mayli knew there was warmth in him.

She shivered, feeling a cold draft as the door squeaked open.

Mayli turned her head on the pillow and smiled shamelessly as Alden took a step inside. He held a plate of food in one hand and a cup in the other. Red paint was stained on his shirt, hands, and along his bandaged arm.

He froze, seeing her upon his bed, then turned to leave.

"Wait!" She ran to block his chance to escape.

Alden obeyed but gazed up at the ceiling in annoyance.

"Won't you even look at me?"

He looked to the floor.

Mayli grabbed Alden's shoulder, rotating him to face her. He avoided eye contact for a moment, let out a breathy sigh, then met her challenging stare. "What do you want?"

"Company?"

After a brief silence, Alden awkwardly shifted past her. He set the plate on his desk, scraped the chair out, sat, and began eating. She watched patiently as he finished his meal and drained his water.

Alden stood with his dishes and approached her by the door. He jerked his head for her to step aside, but she held her position. Mayli leaned against the door, easing it shut.

Alden let his stance go slack and shifted his weight from one leg to the other. He set the dishes down, scratched his brow, then groaned with irritation. Staring at her, he untied his dampened cloak and tossed it over the chair. "Fine," he said offering her the chair then threw himself on the small bed. He crossed his ankles and folded his hands behind his head. Alden chewed the inside of his mouth in frustration as his face took on several expressions. His eyes narrowed at the wooden beams looming above, as if trying to understand an unheard conversation.

After several tense moments, Mayli crept forward. When Alden realized she was about to sit, he rudely shifted to deprive her of an empty spot. He glared. Mayli shoved his legs aside and took a seat at the foot of the bed. Together, they sneered.

Finally, Alden broke the contest and resumed his watch of the beams. "Why are you here?"

"Hmm, you kidnapped me, remember?"

"But why are you *here*." He raised his hand and swirled it angrily to display the room.

Mayli tilted her head low and looked at him with wide, hopeful eyes. "I've missed you."

"I don't miss you. Leave."

Mayli gasped as if she had just been stabbed. "You hate me."

"No. Look, it's..." He sighed. "It's just easier if we both forget each other and move on."

"What? No! I can't...I *won't* forget my rogue!" Tears began to form.

"You have to." Alden glanced at the unguarded door.

She looked too then collapsed on him, depriving him the chance to flee. Crying, she bore her face into him. "Why?"

"Because we can't be friends, especially not lovers."

"No..." Her body shook uncontrollably, releasing tears and wetting his shirt. As she continued to cry, strong arms wrapped around her, giving her a reassuring squeeze. At his touch, Mayli released a broken breath along with a whimper. Her breathing relaxed and she nuzzled in, wiping her face dry. Foreign emotions swelled within her. *How could I fall so hard, and now have this feel so good?* Alden began rubbing her back. *He lied*, she realized with a smile.

Mayli breathed in a soft laugh. Alden moved his head away and eyed her as if searching for the humor in the situation. She smiled. "It's because I'm a princess, isn't it?"

He stopped stroking her.

She leaned up, batting her wet lashes at him, beaming mischievously. Alden looked back at the door, but Mayli shifted to stay within his sight. "*You* think you can't enjoy whom you want because of titles?"

"I *know* it."

She shook her head. "But you said title is irrelevant when it comes to virtue." Alden's eyes closed as she touched his cheek. Thick stubble scratched against her delicate palm as she caressed his nervous and stiffening chin. It wasn't the only part about him becoming stiff.

Her rogue took in a deep, trembling breath through the nose. Then, he gripped her arms. Mayli's heart raced as she gasped, pleased he could see to agree. She eased herself forward and closed her eyes in anticipation...

As she neared, Alden—in a flash—twisted her around and pinned her to the bed. Her eyes shot open with excitement, enjoying the rough act, but to her disappointment, he pushed off.

"This isn't about virtue," he said, then snatched his dirty dishes from the desk. Alden tugged the door open and slammed it as he left.

Mayli lay on the bed—abandoned. She shivered and her teeth began to clatter. Wanting to remember his touch, she wrapped her arms around herself and rolled against the wall. Her head clunked against it. Disgusted and ashamed, she cursed herself for being such a silly girl, lost between shades of love with a thief stealing her heart.

Something jabbed at her side and she readjusted to retrieve the thorn. She drew out the die she had won in the game of

Noble's Dice. Mayli observed the detail carved in the draclynn scale. There were twenty faces, each numbered in gold paint.

Mayli wiped her eyes, stood, and moved to the desk. She tugged at Alden's cloak and wrapped herself in it with the hood up, uncaring that it was wet. After plopping in the chair, she twirled the die around in her fingers, then rolled it across the table. It spun in a dizzying spiral as it decided her fate. Finally, it stopped.

"One."

THE DRACLYNN

CHAPTER TWENTY-ONE

*M*ayli jolted awake as a haunting cry clicked and echoed around the ship's hull. She peeked from under Alden's cloak. The cabin was dark. She peered out the porthole. But there was nothing; not even the moon. Only darkness and a speckled sky of stars that twinkled at her from behind wispy, gray clouds. She crawled off the bed and stepped out into the hall.

Chills crawled down Mayli's spine as she entered the common area. The ship's belly looked to be alive as the silhouette of filled hammocks swayed as if the vessel was breathing. She scurried past the sleeping crewmen, desperate to escape the unnerving room as another wail sounded.

She ran up to the top deck and panted. Only the crash of waves, the periodic clank of metal, and the flapping of sails could be heard now. Mayli looked around. A few men worked the ropes. Everything was normal. The moon had already set. People were asleep. There was no real danger lurking.

"Hey."

Mayli yelped in surprise and spun with Reyn's dagger

extended, ready to fight. She sighed and dropped her arms in relief. "Alden!"

Alden drew an amused smile. "What ya doing up? It's late."

"I heard an awful noise. I was frightened. Maybe just a nightmare. I can't sleep well on ships."

"You heard that?"

Mayli's eyes grew wide and her jaw began to fall away from her mouth.

He nodded without concern. "Likely whales."

"Whales?"

"Yeah." Alden walked to the ship's stern and leaned against the rail overlooking the black sea.

Mayli lingered behind, unsure if she'd be welcomed. *He doesn't want me by him.* She turned to go back down the stairs.

Noticing, Alden turned and offered his hand to her. She looked at it, confused. He even curled his fingers in. Out of protest, Mayli ignored his hand as she stepped beside him.

A chilling breeze danced across the ocean. The sails flapped and metal clanged. She sucked in the cold air through her rattling teeth as she shivered. Then his touch warmed her as his arm drew her nearer. Mayli gazed at him in wonder but he didn't look back.

Together they watched the waves fold away from *The Lucky Fish*, cutting across the smooth, dark sea. After a long silence, Mayli nudged him and pointed. A huge puff of smoke-like mist erupted from the water as the back of a whale emerged from the depths. The haunting cry that had stirred Mayli from bed echoed across the water.

A white glow from its body lingered under the surface. "It's albino!" she gasped in amazement. "And there are more!" She pointed as a few smaller white shapes began following it.

Alden leaned forward and squinted to catch a better look of the creature then took a frightened step back. She blinked at him, confused. He stared back as if he were dying—eyes wide and mouth slowly opening. She glanced back to the whales who followed at a distance. When they began to dive from view, Alden grabbed her wrist.

"Hey!" she cried out, wincing at the pain, but her protest was short-lived as he began to run, pulling her along. She caught her footing just before she almost tripped going down the stairs.

Alden hugged the corner and threw himself against Scraggs's locked door, causing it to rattle and shake. He pounded on it as he tried the handle.

"Oie! What are ya doing down there?" called Sican, perched high in the crow's nest.

"DRACLYNN!" Alden cried back.

Mayli gripped the tiny token in her pocket made from such a creature. The nasty die that kept rolling ones. She took a step toward the rail, curious for another peek, but Alden pulled her back, a look of terror haunting his eyes.

"Alle...?"

Sican began ringing an ear-piercing bell, stirring everyone awake. At the sound of alarm, Scraggs finally opened his door, and Alden burst past him with Mayli in tow. Scraggs opened his mouth to protest, but beyond the panorama of windows, a huge plume of water erupted from the ocean's surface. Everyone stared, aghast.

A stampede of groggy yet determined pirates burst onto the deck like bees out of a hive. Scraggs shouted rapidly, instructing each of them with different tasks, too fast for Mayli to comprehend. Many unwound ropes, allowing the sails to stretch out and catch more wind. Others rolled out harpoons and secured them to posts. The rest took position to row.

Alden stepped away to join the preparations, but Mayli pulled back on him. "Don't leave me!"

He turned and embarrassed her with a tight hug. For a second Mayli thought that his lips had pressed against her forehead, but he drew away before she could confirm.

"Mayli, I have to protect you. Stay here." He put his hand to her cheek and lightly stroked it. He then slipped into the shadows.

The door closed on her, and Mayli spun to look out the window. There was no sign of spray. The white glow under the surface was gone. She heard a gasp of surprise, followed by more shouts of direction from outside. Mayli opened the door to look. Half the crew was on the starboard side, pointing down and searching the water, unsure where the beast had gone.

Suddenly, the portside was struck with such force that the ship dipped down, scooping water onto the deck. One man slipped into the sea. A few others barely escaped a similar fate. They hurried to throw him a rope as he swam desperately back to the ship. Just before he reached the lifeline, a white flash darted under the water's surface, and in an instant, he was gone.

Fearing it had been Alden, Mayli stepped out and scanned the faces of men. She saw Scraggs, Dolo, Sican, the squirrely man who had fetched them, a few unknown faces and even Jim the chef, but her rogue was missing. She screamed as the ship was hit once more, throwing her to the ground.

"Alden!" she cried.

"Get *inside*!"

She looked up, hearing his voice. He was perched above her, clinging to the shrouds, surveying the beast. In his hand he held his black dagger. Mayli couldn't see how such a small, close-ranged weapon could defeat a monster whose body seemed to be twice as long as the ship. Reyn and his rapier had been enough of a challenge.

Mayli pulled herself up and ran down to the ship's hull. A thin layer of water swirled on the floor, shifting crates around with ease. It splashed up to her feet, chilling her body. Taking a deep breath, she ran through the frozen puddle to her room.

Like before, her things were thrown everywhere—only now

in slightly different places. She tossed a heap of clothes aside then snatched her bow.

As she emerged back on deck, she collided with Alden, spilling her quiver.

He bent to pick the arrows up.

"I'm not helpless!" she cried.

"I know," he said, dumping them in her quiver and handing her one. "Shoot true."

The draclynn's long neck towered over the ship like a cobra rising out of the sand. It's wolf-like head snapped and hissed. White, pearlescent scales shimmered regardless of the lack of light. Below the surface was the glow of its body, which was held in position with massive wing-like fins. Suddenly, a whip of tentacles burst from hiding and came thrashing down.

The railing split and a chunk of the ship's siding exploded. A rope snapped and caught a man by the arm, tossing him to the beast. The monster dove its long neck into the water to retrieve its treat.

"Fire!" shouted the captain.

With a clank, followed by a twang, a harpoon launched straight at the monster's head as it bobbed at the surface. It pierced the beast's cheekbone just under its eye. The draclynn cried out in agony, commanding everyone to clamp their hands over their ears. The beast shook its head and the ship jerked, throwing the two manning the harpoon over the edge.

While everyone else was still countering the ringing in their ears or holding themselves up, Alden rushed down and used his knife to separate them from the draclynn and the ship slowly settled.

Now freed, the beast looked at him and began to lift its tentacles. Alden looked around to find a safe place to tumble. To his left was a group of men. *They'ed be killed too...* As a tentacle snapped forward, Alden opted for a debris-covered floor. As he rolled, he felt a slight pinch in his side from where Reyn had stabbed him as well as new pokes and bruises from the clutter on deck. However, the whoosh of air and the critical blow he'd been expecting never landed. Instead the beast cried out once more. He looked up. A small arrow was buried in its black eye. The draclynn thrashed wildly as it submerged, sending a giant wave across the surface.

Alden scampered to his feet as he held his side in pain. He saw Mayli drawing another arrow. He motioned for her to run back to the captain's quarters, and she hurried to obey. They dove inside just as a huge wave hit. The impact threw them against the wall, knocking the wind from his lungs. He heard furniture begin to shift, but with his breath gone, he couldn't bring himself to move. Mayli grabbed him and pulled him out of the way just before Scraggs' heavy treasure chest had the chance to pin his legs to the wall. Alden coughed as air returned to him.

"Thanks," Alden said as he turned back to Mayli. His forehead wrinkled up in worry. "You okay?" He touched her pale face.

Mayli leaned against the doorframe as the ship continued to sway. She wrapped her arms around her waist then without warning collapsed to the floor, releasing the contents of her stomach.

Alden pulled her hair away and rubbed her back. "I'll take that as a no?"

She shook her head.

Shouts from below drew his attention. Seeing that Scraggs had been pierced by flying debris, he ran to help.

"Where's your medic?"

They shook their heads.

Alden snarled, imagining that the man had been fed to the draclynn. He lowered his head back to the bloodied captain. The gash that split his brow was of no concern, but the splinter that threatened the artery in his leg gave Alden reason to worry. He was no healer but knew which areas to cut and slice to cripple a man.

"Get me rope!" Alden demanded. A few men ran to fetch it. He looked up at Jim. "Do we have cayenne on board?"

The chef looked to the other crew members, dumbfounded as if Alden had just spoken another language.

"Red, spicy powder!" Alden snapped.

"Oh…" Jim nodded and ran down to the kitchen.

The first mate offered him a rope, and Jim returned with a wooden box. Alden snatched the twine and wrapped it around the captain's leg. He felt around then wiped his brow. "It only struck muscle." He looked to Scraggs, smiled apologetically, then yanked the piece out.

The man screamed, then cried louder as Alden poured the cayenne pepper into the open wound. Some crewmen looked up, fearing the draclynn was back. Alden took a quick glance around too before wrapping Scraggs' leg in cloth.

Suddenly, the ship's bow began to lift. *No, it isn't lifting. The stern is being pulled down.* The boat moaned in distress, and he heard Mayli scream. Alden looked toward the captain's quarters as a bloom of tentacles sprang out from the water behind the ship. They lurched forward at all angles, snapping rails and severing ropes as they coiled around toward the main deck.

Mayli began poking at a tentacle with her bow, trying to keep it at bay. It coiled around her weapon and snapped it in two. Mayli drew Reyn's dagger. After a series of frightened swings, she severed it. Several pirates ran to join in on the fight, seeing they could wound the beast with blades.

The additional weight continued to pull *The Lucky Fish* farther down, and Alden slipped to the floor. He began to slide toward the draclynn. Suddenly, from behind, he saw a tentacle wriggling toward him.

Alden rolled to his feet. His hair danced as the tentacle darted past. He peered up at the long, white appendage. Blue veins pulsed under the skin as it tightened its grasp around something. He followed the line out to where it held its prey.

Mayli.

Fear seized him. *Why did I dodge? Why hadn't I let it take hold of me instead?*

With The King's Blade in hand, Alden yelled and stabbed. The sharp point tore into the soft flesh and blood oozed out. He stabbed again, making the beast flinch. The sudden jerk knocked the dagger out of his hand. It twirled into the air and then fell into a pile of ropes. He could see Mayli reeling in pain as it attempted to strangle the life out of her. Disarmed, Alden grabbed at the tentacle that continued to squeeze the princess. He desperately pulled and clawed at its grip, but it refused to let go.

Finally, he freed her arm that clung to Reyn's knife. Alden reached for the weapon, but she dropped it to grab hold of him. The dagger skidded down the floor and became stuck on a ledge created by a fallen bookshelf. He looked around for help, but none could aid as they were just as occupied fighting the beast.

With all his strength, Alden pulled hard. The princess lifted and Alden was able to hook his arm under hers. She cried out in pain from being pulled in both directions. The beast then reeled them out of the captain's quarters, but Alden hooked his foot on the doorframe—refusing to give her up.

A piercing crash sounded and glass suddenly rained down from within the cabin. Alden looked to see the snarling lips of the draclynn come chomping through the set of long windows. The arrow in its eye pointed straight at them.

Alden tugged Mayli to him, holding her tight around the shoulder. Her scared, hazel eyes glistened back at him like gold as he reached his free hand to her and wiped away her face of tears. Cupping her chin, Alden then lifted her lips up to his. They were soft, full...trembling in fear... He kissed the Princess of Ammos until the beast pulled her from him. She stared in wonder and then in horror as he released her.

"ALDEN?!"

Trying his best to ignore her cry, Alden dove. He skidded down the angled floor quickly, approaching the draclynn's snapping mouth. It thrashed wildly, eager to get a taste. Alden tumbled to catch the ledge where Reyn's dagger had landed. He reached for it, but the monster's weight tilted the ship farther down and the blade slid just out of reach.

A hot, stale, fishy breath blew over him. He looked back to see razor-sharp teeth smiling at him. As he kept the draclynn's gaze, he fished his hand behind until he found a loose plank. In one swift motion, he tossed the wood in its mouth. The beast chewed happily, giving Alden enough of a distraction to snatch the dagger.

Without thinking, Alden leapt onto its wide snout. He slipped on wet scales as it chomped, sending splinters into the air. He scurried up to grab at a horn budding from the back of its head and held on.

In front of him, he saw his horror-stricken face reflected in the draclynn's remaining black eye. *Coward.* Alden then yelled, thrusting the dagger into his reflection, sending a spray of dark blood across his body. He spat the sour taste out while he dug the blade deeper in. The beast thrashed and he was thrown from its head, landing on a pile of wood.

Realizing the short blade hadn't been enough to kill it, Alden grabbed a metal curtain rod. As the draclynn struggled to free itself from the room, Alden used the rod as a spear and jabbed it into the eye. He took a step and pressed hard, easing himself closer. The draclynn's teeth were now just inches away. With a fierce cry, he thrust.

The ear-piercing screech only lasted a moment before the beast fell still. Its body—now limp—began to spill from the ship.

Alden grabbed the windowsill, keeping himself from being dragged along with it.

As it slid away, he laughed in relief. *I killed it. I saved the ship, the crew, myself, and...* His heart froze.

"MAY!" he cried, turning around.

Glass from the window continued to break and shatter around him. The cabin moaned under the pressure and wood started to twist and snap. *The Lucky Fish* swung wildly as the beast slipped back into the ocean, sending Alden to the floor.

"MAYLI!" He tossed rolling debris away from him and used the shifting furniture to help himself back up. Battling the swaying ship, he called for her once more as he looked out the destroyed window. His heart sunk along with the white, lifeless body as it disappeared into the depths of the Zollner's Bay with his princess.

"Alle…"

Alden spun around to see Mayli clinging to the doorway. Her wide, wet eyes shone bright, beckoning him closer. He took long strides, kicking the wreckage and seawater that surged past. She stood weakly as Alden wrapped his arms around her. He took in a weeping breath while his hands traced through her hair and pulled her head into his embrace. He cried, hugging her tighter.

Suddenly, she pulled away. Her face was lit with concern and her brow wrinkled. Her lips parted and just as Alden suspected the princess would yell, Mayli bent over and spilled out whatever else remained in her stomach.

Alden chuckled as he rubbed her back. He pulled away her long hair and gave her a wry smile. "You really don't do well on ships, do you?"

The princess glared up at him, then laughed.

THE BREW

CHAPTER TWENTY-TWO

"We keep going," Alden said.

The first mate shook his head. "Ammos is still two days away and this fish won't live more than one without stopping to repair... She's swallowing water on both sides and the sails are torn."

"So, we'll get on the lifeboat."

"Ain't got one no more." He pointed to the ropes and dangling planks of where it had been.

Alden paled.

"There is a port nearby," Scraggs said.

"We'll go there, then."

Scraggs sucked booze from a bottle then leaned from his seat upon a barrel. "I'm not sure Prince Briar would be pleased with me if he learned I brought *a princess* to the Cad Islands," the man said quietly with a knowing smile.

Alden reached for his dagger, but he hadn't yet retrieved it since the fight. He cursed, hoping it was still there.

Scraggs shifted into a more upright position. "Calm down, t'was only a guess. The Ammosian princess is missing. Briar sent us to Ammos and…I heard you call Miss Emma *Mayli*. A few women hold that name, but none as well trained with a bow, nor as beaut—"

Alden clamped his hand around the captain's neck, silencing him.

The first mate stepped forward but stopped when Scraggs smiled and winked.

Alden leaned in, hovering just above the captain's ear. "There will be no mention of the princess. Is that clear?"

"Aye, lad. I'm smart enough not to be messing around with royalty anymore. Got me locked up in Dregs last time."

"Good." Alden released the captain, patting his chest. "Set sail to the Cads."

<hr />

Mayli sat under the mast. After the battle, Alden had told the crew about how well she did with waves and requested that they arrange a seating area where the ship was the steadiest. It was comprised of crates and barrels as well as part of the torn sail to provide shade. They even completed it with a hammock—which she adored. The swaying helped counter the ship's constant rocking, keeping her stomach at ease.

Alden walked over, sheathing his knife and leaned against the mast. He pinched his lips in then offered a smile. "So, we are going to the Cads."

"The Cad Islands?" gasped Mayli. "But the coast is right there!"

Alden shook his head. "That's the desert of Gezmek, Mayli. If we don't get swallowed by waves, we will by dunes. We have to take our chances with the islands."

"Have you not heard the tales?"

"I've been there, it's not so bad. People travel from all around to trade their goods there. It's where Dean sells most of ours,"

Alden said, trying to make it sound more inviting than she knew it actually was. "The captain's treasure didn't fall overboard, and the draclynn scales are worth money, so he might be able to fix this ship up or buy a new one to get you home."

Mayli peered down at the damaged hull. The wood made awful bone-breaking noises, as if pleading with them to sail to port, *any* port. Hole-torn sails flapped violently in the night's wind. The portside was smashed in, leaving a large cavernous gap, exposing the hull. Some gashes reached as far down as the water's edge, and when a large wave hit, the ship drank it in. Several men scurried with buckets to keep the boat dry. Each bucket thrown was countered by another splash of seawater, yet somehow *The Lucky Fish* still sailed on as men rowed.

With a defeated sigh, Mayli nodded. "Okay…"

Alden patted her leg and stood. "Ya want more tea?"

Mayli peered into her mug and drank the last sip. She handed it out to him. "Yes please. Tell Jim thanks."

"Jim?"

"Yes, he makes a lovely brew."

Alden's eyes widened in surprise. "Ha! I don't think that man knows the difference between tea leaves and a salad."

Mayli raised her brow.

"I'll make you some more." He smiled and descended down the stairs to the kitchen.

Mayli dropped her jaw. *He's been leaving it out for me?*

<hr />

Alden pulled out a small bag he kept clipped to his belt. He sniffed it, breathing in tender memories. With a smile, Alden gathered a pinch and measured it carefully in his hand. Satisfied the ratio of dark, curled leaves to floral and citrus accents was correct, he funneled it into a tightly-woven mesh cloth, then tied it.

The kettle whistled and Alden removed it from the flame. He poured the steaming hot water into Mayli's empty mug and dipped the strainer in. Several minutes went by before he retrieved the cloth soaked with leaves. In the same pouch that he kept his brewing set, Alden retrieved a small bottle of white powder and added several taps to the drink. *Thank you, Briar!* Alden stirred it with care before taking a sip.

He grinned.

It was hot and creamy and hit the perfect notes of a zest—an earthy herbaceous flavor with balsamic undertones. The taste transported him back to a time when he and his mother would sit overlooking the Draclynn River, sipping the comforting drink.

Oftentimes, she read to him about the far-off lands of Gezmek, telling tales of King Edune and his heroism when he ruled over all of Vatan. The differences in cultures fascinated Alden. Unlike Brimley, where they needed to wear heavy woolen cloaks for half the year, desert folk wore long cotton kaftans to counter the heat. Sometimes they were accented with braided ropes, tassels, or a wide band of fabric at the waist. Many decorated themselves with shimmering silk scarves and feathered accessories. He learned from his mother's reading that the use of feathers signified their pride in both archery and falconry.

Alden took another sip.

As a boy, he wanted nothing more than to visit Ammos and search for the lost treasure of Gezmek. He had drawn pictures from descriptions he read in books and chatted with anyone he could who had been there. His sketches had amused his father and together they would draw.

He sipped once more before pulling the tea away, realizing it wasn't his. Smiling, Alden jogged up the stairs to deliver it to his princess. When he found her, she had once again retched and was holding her head in her hands.

"Here," he said sympathetically as he crouched down and pulled her wavy hair away from her face.

When she tilted up to look, he saw she had cried in his absence. He thumbed away a tear. "I told you I'd protect you."

Mayli sniffled and took the mug. She drew a long sip then swished it in her mouth as if to rinse away the stale flavors only the stomach should know. Alden sat beside her in the hammock, causing the rope chair to sway and force Mayli to lift the tea away from her face to counter the rocking. After they steadied, she leaned against him and took another sip.

"You really made this?"

Alden looked around absently, then nodded. "Yep."

"Why didn't you ever make it before?"

"Would have, but I didn't have the key ingredient. I know ya don't like it without the cream, either." He pulled out a bottle of white powder and shook it. "Stole it from Briar," he said with a wink.

Mayli laughed quietly.

"It's usually better when it's made with fresh ingredients. Cream loses a bit of lushness when it's dried." Alden traded the bottle for the pouch of tea. "I found these in the castle."

Mayli peered inside as he opened the pouch. She pulled out a small purple flower and sniffed. She looked beautiful doing so— like a painting he'd someday paint.

"Lavender," he said.

"Thought so. What else is in there?" She touched a finger to the bag.

Alden widened the drawstring and lifted the bag to her nose. She gently shut her eyes and inhaled with a pleasant hum. "Vanilla?"

"Yep."

She sniffed again. "And orange?"

"Yep." His smile grew wider.

"Really? We drink citrusy brews in Ammos."

He brought the bag to his own nose and sniffed the blissful aroma before tying it back to his belt. "I combined the light Ammosian tea with the dark Brim tea to make this special blend."

"I love it."

Alden blushed. "I do too."

She rested the mug on her knees and watched the ripples crash against the brim. A moment passed. Then she threw a hard look at him as if he'd done something wrong. Alden shook his head. "What?"

"You kissed me!"

"Ah!" He blushed further and looked away. "I…eh. Don't cha be thinking into that now!" He waved a dismissive hand.

"Mmhmm." She stared at him with a raised brow until he broke under it.

"Hey, I wasn't gonna just let ya slip away without you trusting me, ya know?"

"A simple 'ey, don't cha worry, I'ma kill this thing, yeah?' could have worked just the same," Mayli mocked.

Alden opened his mouth, then closed it with a flat frown. "Do I sound like that?"

She giggled. "*Oh yeah.*"

He chuckled along with her, gazing into her smiling eyes.

She began to lean in. Realizing her intention, he sprang up. The hammock swayed and with her free hand Mayli grabbed her stomach, trying to steady herself while tea spilled over her fingers.

"Nope! Sorry, Princess Puke, that's the only one ya get!"

"Princess…HEY!" She grabbed at a small shard of debris and tossed it at him.

To her frustration, he dodged it with ease and trotted away with a rambunctious smirk. She laughed and it sounded like a song. He walked back to her, smiling warmly.

She blushed. "Thanks for not ignoring me anymore."

He sighed. "You are impossible to ignore." Alden pulled out a stained parchment and handed it to her between two fingers.

<hr/>

Mayli took the paper but kept her eyes on Alden. He fidgeted— gaze distant. His throat bulged as he swallowed nervously. Finally, she looked down at what he had given her and gasped. Ink drops and messy chicken-scratch-like lines darted across the page but each stroke seemed to have a purpose as it formed the image.

Her.

He'd drawn her leaning over the rail overlooking the water's edge. She was bundled in her cloak with the hood down and hands nursing a mug of tea. Her hair was dancing in the wind along with her scarf, even though she hadn't been wearing it like that since they'd left Brimley. Her eyes were wide, conveying a sense of loss combined with hope.

Mayli looked back up at Alden, and as she did, a tear rolled down her cheek. "Thank you," she said in a light whisper. His eyes shifted to meet hers but darted away as if embarrassed. She continued, "Every portrait that has been made of me has always been an idealized version; one that the world expected to see of a princess." She looked back down at the drawing where a fresh tear had dotted the bottom of the page, causing ink to spread. "But you see *me*."

Alden cleared his throat. "I learned to paint portraits like the ones you mentioned, ignoring the truths and painting people cleaner, stronger, and purer than they really were."

"So, you worked as an artist?"

He shrugged. "Da taught me. He was a fine teacher, and I, a lousy student. I wanted to do it my own way…" He looked at the parchment and she followed his view. She admired the attention to detail, not only in the linework but the emotion. The way he had captivated her lonely soul pulled at her heart.

How many see me this way?

Alden fidgeted with his scabbard, then drew his dagger. He held it out, placing his thumb on the blade. His tongue stuck out and he closed one eye, as if measuring distance. "Be precise. Observe, and then carefully interpret what the shapes tell you. When you work fast you disrespect the colors!" Alden said, as if mocking Dean's stern tone—it wasn't quite angry enough. He lowered his arm and looked her in the eye. "He was protective of his paints, so every application of color to the canvas had to be mixed perfectly. I never knew how valuable the materials were until I tried to purchase some of my own after the war. It was then I finally understood why he didn't like when I mindlessly mixed colors." Alden looked down and used his nail to chip at some dirt on the blade. "Da would slap my hands when it wasn't done to his standards. He treated the pigments better than his own family."

Mayli frowned.

Alden snickered. "I had joked once that he had an affair with a woman named Alizarin. Mum spent days searching for the fabled lady. Nearly tore Brimley apart until I explained that alizarin was a shade of red... I could have painted her portrait with just that, the way her face flushed."

Mayli burst with laughter and Alden did too. She watched as a humble grin found its way across his face and his eyes twinkled like a star in the night's sky.

Alden smiled and pointed at her tea. She handed it to him. He coiled his hands around the mug, took a sip, and closed his eyes as if the steam had kissed his face. After a twist on his heel, he sat. The sway in the hammock jolted her to fall beside him, and she made no effort to readjust herself. To her relief, nor did he. It felt right. He passed the tea back over. When she grabbed it, her hand touched his. He didn't flinch. Instead, his fingers spread wide and wove them between her own. Together they held the mix of Ammosian and Brim tea.

A FULL PLATE

CHAPTER TWENTY-THREE

*a*s daybreak pierced through the windows, Kira rolled over in Briar's soft bed made of furs and heavy quilts. She hadn't been able to sleep, fearing she had helped free monsters set on a rampage to take over Vatan. She smiled to herself at the playful idea. *If only I could release such beasts.*

The front door finally creaked open.

Excited, Kira flung the blankets and pillows off and quickly tiptoed toward the staircase. She leaned over the rail, listening intently.

"Upon your request, the scribes forfeited this. There is great detail describing each birth and death in the royal family, including Gina," said a voice she remembered as his lieutenant, Thomas.

"Sweet kings…" she heard Briar gasp.

"There are also these. Olivar had proper documents made for each new noble owning small properties we had acquired from Brimley. Looks like there are five dead and one missing. The remaining four are locked up. Do you want us to search for…" Papers fluttered. "Kira Harlow?"

Kira bit her lip.

"Ah, no. She wasn't involved in the king's murder, according to the others. Let her be free. She's gone through enough, I'm sure... Thomas, if you come across her, treat her nobly. I will be honoring their newfound titles."

"Yes, sir."

Kira touched her arm, feeling the fresh scar of ink. *Briar really is honorable...*

"What should I do with William?"

"Bathe him, dress him, and for king's sake, feed him. I'll look after him tomorrow."

"Will do, and I've stationed more guards around the city in preparation for the announcement," said Thomas.

Briar huffed. "How many can I actually trust, though? A hundred? Fifty? Could I be lucky enough to have five? How do I know if even they are trustworthy?" Kira heard the quick rustle of fabric. She imagined him pointing.

"Exten and Tarek are your royal knights, and many guards have always been loyal."

"Loyal? After what you kept from me, I don't know how far I can even trust you!" snapped Briar.

"My lord..."

"I know...I know." Briar sighed. "How's your daughter?"

"She's well."

"Good. There won't ever be anything like that again. I promise."

"Thank you. It is liberating to know Hailey will be safe now."

Kira covered her mouth to keep from gasping.

"And I'll have to trust that you will make the appropriate arrangements to keep Dregs that way. No more secrets from me?"

"Yes, my lord."

"And, Thomas, I hope now you will finally respect my desires to sleep in?"

Kira heard the men chuckle and the door close shut. She thought maybe Briar had left with his lieutenant, but the sound of clanging plates and nearing footsteps alerted her that the prince was still here. She smoothed out his tunic she had exchanged for her nightgown and brushed fingers through her hair, trying to look presentable.

Briar carried a large tray of food and a scroll case up the stairs. He paused briefly to look at her. His ever-curious eyes looked her up and down, blinking slow. "You stayed."

"My Prince asked me to."

Tired lips stretched into a smile. "Join me for breakfast?"

Kira eyed the seductive platter, nodding with wide eyes, and eagerly sat. Briar placed it before her and took a seat across. Ham, steak, potatoes, bacon, muffins, and fresh fruit dipped in chocolate all sat on ornate plates. There was even a doughnut. She reached for a perfectly crisp slice of bacon and bit into it with a satisfying crunch.

Kira looked up after finishing the meaty treat. "This is a lot of food, a lot of nice food... You get all this for me?" she asked with a grin as she dragged over a slice of ham.

Briar waved his hand. "Have it all."

Kira bit happily into the meat. She closed her eyes as the sweet, caramelized glaze rolled in her mouth. *Even when I've stolen from nobles, I never enjoyed such a rich and flavorful meal as this.* Curious to try more, she took another hurried bite. Even the simplest food, like the eggs, had an overwhelmingly creamy and complex flavor. "I didn't think guards received this kind of assortment of food! This is fantastic!"

"They don't," Briar said as he stabbed the steak without interest, then twirled the blade.

"Right. Royalty does," she said with a full mouth.

"Yep."

Kira swallowed and studied his long, bothered, and scrunched up face. "What happened last night?" she finally asked.

Briar didn't look up. The man only continued to stare at the crevasse he was creating. Kira lightly poked his hand with her fork to stir a reaction. He dropped the knife and shoved away from the table. He strode across the room and took position by the window, looking out.

His posture was loose and hung low like a cloak of sadness had been draped around him. His hands fidgeted.

"Did they kill your uncle?" she asked quietly, though she knew the answer.

"Yes."

Her stomach tightened, feeling she was partly to blame for his pain. Once again, he had lost a member of his ever-shrinking family. "Sorry."

"Screw that kin-shaming bastard!" he snapped.

Kira blinked. When she began to open her mouth, Briar looked back at her in distress. Kira rose from the table and joined him by the window, looking at him with worried eyes. "Are Alden and Mayli okay?" Kira asked, now scared.

"What? Uh, yeah, they should be fine."

"Then what?"

Briar shifted his eyes around as if unsure himself. His breathing became challenged.

She pulled him around to face him. "Briar, what is wrong?"

"Nothing!" He laughed.

Unamused, Kira challenged his statement with a raised brow.

"Really! Nothing is *wrong*," he assured her with an awkward smile, which he accompanied with eyes squinting happily.

Kira stared.

Finally, his grin relaxed and his face turned hard. Briar turned away to stare back out the window.

The sun had just risen and silhouetted high soaring gulls in search of discarded treasures. Beyond the angled clay tile roofs Kira saw the tips of sails and heard the ringing of bells announcing the departure of a ship leaving port. Across the street, a man used a thick stick to beat the dirt free from a rug off his balcony. A plume of gray dust drifted down below where a shopkeeper cursed at the man above.

A family strolled by. Their child stopped as the shopkeeper's wife offered a small candied fruit at a discount. The father shook his head while the mother scolded her son, who continued to beg. When the child thought no one was looking, he pocketed the small treat and skipped forward to catch up with his parents who had already turned their backs on the storefront. Kira watched as the keeper's wife shook her head in amusement and ate a piece herself.

Briar shifted to grab an item from his coat. Kira looked as he held a thin gold circlet. After rotating it in his hands nervously, he placed it on his head and fixed his posture to stand tall.

Kira's eyes widened. It was a waiting crown, used to mark the king-to-be. She blinked twice as King Briar looked up to observe *his* city.

THE CAD ISLANDS

CHAPTER TWENTY-FOUR

The whole harbor stared. Sailors stood holding heavy boxes while others paused their tying of knots, letting their sails droop or cargo fall. A gang of rough-looking children climbed to the peak of a roof to catch a better view. Across the bay, a small boat drifted absently into a ship, whose captain was too distracted by what was coming into port to notice. Even would-be thieves didn't seem to take this opportune moment to pick the pockets of onlookers—at least none who were seen.

A splintering cry echoed across the bay, drawing attention from anyone who had somehow missed the oddity in its approach, as *The Lucky Fish* scraped across the dock. Almost half its body was underwater so that the deck was near level with the land. White scales from the draclynn littered the ship and glimmered like silver coins in the rising sun.

Scraggs stepped out proudly and surveyed the sea of gaping eyes. He tilted his tricorn hat up to them, then strutted down to the nearest tavern with a pompous swagger to mask his limp. As the remaining crew scurried to secure the sinking vessel, Alden and Mayli slipped off. No one seemed to notice them as the attention around port was still locked in a trance.

Alden decided to not follow Scraggs into the Sea Monster's Grinn, as the captain would be the source of a lot of unwanted attention. He was already drawing a crowd of curious followers dying to hear the legend of how his *Fish* was so lucky. Alden assured himself that Scraggs would tell the proper pirate's tale of stretching the truths and claiming Alden's heroic moment with the draclynn as his own.

It had been only a year since Alden had last visited the Cads with the guild, yet everything seemed different. The map he once memorized was now skewed. Buildings had expanded, sealing the gaps between alleyways and rerouting roads. Some shops he had once visited were now nowhere to be found, whereas remnants of some blended with newer construction.

Here, anyone was free to do as they pleased. They could erect a shop or house as long as they could protect it and make good with the neighbors around. In the same sense, a business could easily be destroyed if it offended someone enough. Oftentimes there would be destruction just for the thrill of a bored criminal.

Alden grimaced at the memory when his troop had helped Pierz scout out a few properties, enforcing the guild's rule over a small precinct. The mission turned sour after Reyn sabotaged it in an attempt to leave Alden for dead. Luckily, Pierz had caught on, no doubt thanks to Kira, and fought off several thugs and saved his life. Before then Alden hadn't seen his guild leader fight. He had assumed he couldn't, leaving all the dirty work to his shadows, but the man was masterful—sparing no one.

He shook his head before being hit with another memory—the unforgettable smells. Blood, fish, rot, salt, spices, barbecued meats, and a fresh aroma of cooked onions—*or was it sweat?*—wafted from Canopy Street.

Alden pulled Mayli back, seeing her lean in to accept a kabob with a questionable assortment of meats and vegetables from an even more questionable man.

The vendor scowled at Alden for robbing him of a sale, and Alden hugged Mayli in, wrapping his cloaked arm around her. "Try not to stray…"

Together they parted through a sea of strange people and entered Canopy Street where playful music beat from all around. The princess gaped like Squirrel would have, taking in the oddities of the bohemian town in amazement. There were many who sported stylish and trending noble fashion while some mixed silk gowns with layers of bulky leather or even fur. Others even wore hardly anything, breasts out.

Alden looked Mayli over. Even though Briar had bought her the new tunic, she still wore bits from the cabin and Brimley. He tugged her across the street.

"Where are we going?" she asked with anticipation.

"To get you out of those rags."

"I think the inn was back there," she said mischievously.

Alden refused to address her and kept his chin up and eyes focused on the shops. There was a vibrancy of colors; merchants called out, bragging about the rarity of their wares, while others boasted about their good prices.

A handsome, dark-skinned man stood outside one gaudy storefront. He wore a flashy red suit embroidered with gold and blue and a flamboyant hat that curled up on the side. As Mayli walked by, he tipped it at her and bowed. As he did, a rose appeared from his sleeve and he presented it to her.

Mayli's mouth parted as she drew in a surprised gasp at his trick. As she began to reach to accept the flower, Alden stole it. He winked at the man, then handed it gracefully to Mayli as he whisked her away. She clung onto it, giggling.

"What else would you like?" he asked as they stopped in the middle of the street to survey their choices.

"Hmm?"

He faltered, watching her spin the flower under her nose. *Beautiful...* "You, ah, can't have anything like what the man in red wore." Alden looked around. "How about here?" He ushered her to a tent that had simple knee-length dresses. He pulled one off a hanger and eyed it. They both shook their heads, and he returned it to the rack. He flipped through the others, all at which she continued her shaking. Finally, she stopped him and pulled one out.

It wasn't quite a dress, but rather a simple, long, buttoned-up, sleeveless tunic. The fabric was made of soft cotton and dyed black. It had a hood.

"You like *that?*"

Mayli stared at it with fascination. "I love it!"

"I'm afraid I've made an influence on you. That's not silk, nor is it cheerful looking."

"You're cheerful," Mayli said as she put it up to herself, as if trying it on.

He rolled his eyes. "Fine, but that will need an undershirt."

"You don't think I'd look good with just this on?" she said while loosening a button on it.

"Stop it." He snatched the tunic from her and began sorting through a pile of simple sleeved blouses.

"What?" she whined, butting up against him. "You're the one who kissed me!" She leaned into his view, eyes batting. "Remember?"

"Nope. Don't remember. Ya must have hit your head when the beast attacked. You've imagined it." Alden gave Mayli a sidelong glance, then smiled back at the pile of clothes. In his search, he found several appropriate sized shirts, a light jacket and set of leggings.

Mayli groaned at the sight of conservative apparel. She picked a garment up and held it to herself in the mirror. She tugged her scarf out from her tunic, trying on the look.

"Keep that hidden!" he said, hushed, tucking it back in her shirt.

A suspicious man passed by in the reflection, watching them. Alden spun but the shadow disappeared as a parade of shaved llamas wearing colorful striped sweaters trotted by. A dwarf-like man who sported the same look danced beside them. He rang a small bell attached to his little finger and sang an odd song about never really losing anything, and that what you have only transforms into something else.

Alden tapped Mayli and pointed. "Want me to get ya one of those too? You'd almost look as cute as them."

She hit him lightly and laughed.

Across the way, Alden spotted a cobbler. He wiggled his toes, feeling the sole split. He turned back to Mayli, who had added a few other scandalous dresses to her pile. Alden paid for everything, along with some tabards and tunics for himself, and crossed over to the next shop to finally get his boots mended, thankful he finally had his allowance from Briar.

After they concluded their shopping, Alden and Mayli continued down Canopy Street. The next quadrant was filled with dangerous weapons: swords and shields, maces and axes. Several talented acrobats tossed knives across the crowd with three men stacked tall on each other's shoulders. Alden and Mayli watched as one flipped off while tossing a blade to the next man down, who in turn did the same, leaving the man on the bottom to juggle three sharp blades.

"You can do that, right, Alle?"

He turned to watch for a moment longer before nodding. "Oh yeah, Briar and I practiced that all the time."

She giggled, then frowned. "I wish I still had mine."

Alden shifted his head to Mayli but kept his focus on the acrobats. They climbed up to their partners while spinning their blades on their noses. "Your what?"

"Knife."

He looked down at her. "You mean Reyn's?"

"He's dead. It became mine."

Alden chuckled. "Sure. I found it very useful, though. I don't think I could have killed the draclynn having my own."

"You're the clumsiest of thieves," she teased.

"I'm not a thief, May."

"Yet you stole mine!"

"You dropped it."

"At least I didn't almost kill you with it!" she teased.

"Please..." Alden rolled his eyes. "I was aiming at Reyn."

"You said you missed."

"I lied."

Mayli dipped her head low, eyeing him. "You threw your blade to me?"

He nodded.

"You could have died. If not from Reyn, me!"

"I trusted in you."

She blushed and looked back up to watch the performers. "Still, I feel a bit naked without a blade after having had it on my side for so long."

Alden frowned. "I *have* been a bad influence on you..."

"Nah. I've always had a guilty pleasure for this kind of thing."

He blinked. "What kind of thing?"

"Being dark and mysterious," she said, while wiggling her fingers in a spooky manner towards his face.

Alden snorted. "You? Edgy? You've always enjoyed the clean and comfortable life, where everything is orderly and proper."

Mayli wrinkled her nose in protest and shook her head. "Being a princess, you are told to put on this fake shell, like the people you used to paint. But I've always wanted to shatter it. You know that—you drew *me*."

Alden shrugged. "I guess so." He looked up to watch the performers as they called out for their next dangerous trick.

Alden then laughed. "You were so mad when Lidia forced you to wear the frills and laces to go on that hunting trip."

"I...don't remember talking about that with you," she said hesitantly.

"Huh?" He watched a performer hold the hilt of a sword in his mouth while he balanced—and spun—another at its tip. Then he bounced several knives into the air and began to juggle. The crowd gasped, including Alden. He looked at Mayli with an impressed smile, but she hadn't been watching—the princess was staring at him. "Oh. Uh. Briar had told me after he had returned."

She nodded. "I'm surprised he talked at all after that trip. He mistook a stump to be a boar, and he didn't even hit that!"

Alden chuckled. "I teased him about it for weeks. Even instructed friends in the kitchen to serve him a log."

"No!" Mayli gasped.

"They were kind enough to coat it in gravy so it looked like ham. It was amusing to see him try and cut into it." He smirked.

The princess laughed. "Oh, he was never any good at hunting."

"That's a tough contest with you, May, but put Briar on a horse with a sword or a lance and there is no competition," he stated confidently.

"He lost at the last Festival of Gezmek, though. To Sir Stridan. That was embarrassing. Briar's saddle slipped and he fell off at the first exchange of lances. It earned Stridan nobility."

He snarled. "Evelyn Allwell had hired a young Shadowen to cut the strap so he'd win and they could wed."

"Sir Stridan wouldn't agree to that!"

"He didn't. The man was clueless. After the festival, I heard the hired thieves laughing about how they blackmailed Evelyn into giving them more money so they wouldn't tell Stridan. I sent him a letter. I doubt they are still together."

"How awful."

Out of the corner of his eye he saw a performer lurking behind the many onlookers. He called out the next act, drawing in more curious eyes. As more flocked in, he brushed up against a woman. Alden watched him cut a purse free from her belt as he apologized for the intrusion.

Realizing the performance was a ruse, Alden took Mayli's hand and crossed under the dance of flying daggers. Screams of death echoed in a nearby alley. She wrapped her other hand around his arm, squeezing his bicep. He peered down, expecting to see her frightened; however, her lips were curled in an adorable smile. Long black lashes blinked contently as she walked arm in arm with him.

THIELEN'S LODGE

CHAPTER TWENTY-FIVE

"One room. Two beds," Alden said, with two raised fingers as he entered Thielen's Lodge.

The innkeeper looked up from wiping his counter and eyed them questionably, paying particularly close attention to Mayli. Alden glared from under his hood, but he was sure the look was lost under the shadow. The man shook his head. "We only have one room with a single."

"How much?"

The man leaned back and polished a glass. "Seeing as you have such a lovely lady accompanying you…three silver."

"That's a bit high for a place like this…" Alden gestured around the lonely room, noting the peeling wallpaper and the odd assortment of broken furniture. The place was almost as decrepit as Brimley Castle. His glove snagged on a sharp splinter poking out from the bar. He plucked it off and tossed it at the bartender, concluding his statement of the old inn.

The man set his glass down with a cocky grin. "Simply supply and demand. Besides, it is you who walked all this way to be here! Feel free to go pay those silvers to thieves and sleep in an alley…

or grave." He rolled his eyes to gaze upon the princess, then winked. "You, of course, don't deserve such a fate and are welcome to stay with me. No charge."

Alden leaned forward, glaring until the flirtatious man stood back.

The man chuckled and put his hands up. "Okay, okay, I understand. But when a man calls for a separate bed with someone as beautiful as she, you can see how the wrong impression could be made." He wiped his counter seemingly out of habit, then peered back at Mayli. Alden gritted his teeth, seeing Mayli blush.

Alden slid over three silver but held his finger on one. The man took the two and reached for the third that was pinned. He wisely reconsidered. The innkeeper tilted his head and raised his brow with an entertained look. He huffed. Stepping back, he snatched a key off the wall behind him and tossed to Alden. "Your room is the middle. Number three. And you, milady..." He turned to address the princess with a wink. "My offer still stands."

"I'm good, thank you," she said kindly.

"I'm sure you are."

Alden stood, taking Mayli's hand possessively and leaving the last coin.

Alden ascended from the room's center to the top floor balcony which overlooked the parlor. They followed the rail to their left and he unlocked the third door with his key. As they entered the room, Mayli let out a loud, exasperated sigh, threw her bag on the ground, and flopped onto the bed. The old wood cried out as it sagged with her weight. Dust fluttered into the air, revealing just how few visitors the lodge received. *Supply and demand...*Alden mocked as he locked the door. He dropped his own bag of goods to the floor and watched out the window as he removed his armor. Worn drapes fluttered in from where a glass panel was missing.

He heard a shift of movement, then felt Mayli's hand gently slip around his. The princess's sweet touch caused him to shiver. Alden cursed himself for opening up and fought to embrace her. He focused intently out the window. It had a charming view of the harbor, framed perfectly through the palm-leafed trees. Though distant, he could see the black and red hull of *The Lucky Fish* getting work done, ships of all shapes and sizes, the mess of structures lining the harbor, and Canopy Street still buzzing with activity. There was even a large fire and some sort of celebration, though Alden reckoned it was something less innocent.

Mayli cupped her other hand around his and pulled him to sit on the bed. Alden obeyed like a puppet. The princess scooted closer, then rested against him. He allowed her to lay him back, knowing he shouldn't. *There's nowhere to run and hide.*

She twisted and nuzzled her head under his chin, planting it on his chest. Alden took in anxious breaths and closed his eyes as her curious fingers began to explore. Mayli touched his face, neck, and arms, summoning goosebumps in their wake. She followed the lines of his tunic, circling buttons, and tracing the bands of leather hugging his waist. She moved further down and Alden's stomach tensed. When he heard the sound of his buckle clicking free, he grabbed her wrist, depriving her the chance to further seduce him.

"Mayli... Stop," Alden growled with the same warning a guard dog had protecting a locked door.

She lifted and smiled at him, cocksure. "Don't you want this?" she said, putting pressure onto his lap with her free hand. Her fingers drew lines up and down his hard contour.

Yes... Alden replied in his head. He tried not to tremble as he answered, "No."

"You think highly of yourself to deny a princess, thief," she jeered, sneaking fingers under his waistline to caress him, free from fabric.

Alden inhaled sharply. He narrowed his eyes, but then they closed, too distracted by the way she was fondling him to protest.

"No kings will know," she whispered into his ear before kissing his cheek.

Alden groaned again, both in pleasure and frustration. He shook his head, gaining control, and withdrew her hand away from him. A lonely and absent cold replaced her warm touch. He missed it already.

"I will know," he said.

Mayli took a long inhale then blew it out, sending a lock of hair flying.

Taking the chance to relax, he released his hold of the princess. This time, she didn't stir. He let his hands rest upon her, then cursed inwardly as they had found the only comfortable spot—her waist. She, however, responded pleasantly with a gentle hum. *A beautiful sound*, he thought. He sighed and melted into the bed, allowing the much-needed rest from their adventure to take hold.

Startled by a loud shout, Mayli lifted from Alden's chest, waking him as well. The twinkle of morning sun silhouetted her form in the window as she stretched and yawned. Subconsciously, Alden reached out for her, grazing his fingers along her extended arm. She smiled curiously as their hands locked and he brought her back down to cuddle.

"I lost five shadows to just two men?" said a cool, calm and familiar voice passing by their room.

"Yes…" replied another.

Shadows? Alden shot up causing Mayli to tumble aside with frustrated whine.

"Come. Let's discuss this inside," said Pierz.

The Shadowens quietly passed by. A door clicked open and then slammed shut.

Alden scurried from bed, tripping as a blanket clung to his legs. He hopped and spun to unwind from it, then pressed his ear to the wall.

Though he wasn't in sight, Alden could hear Squirrel's young, adolescent voice. "Kira was arrested and brought to the castle! We have to help…"

"She's fine," Pierz interrupted. "I gave her orders to gather more information on King Olivar. And if not, it's not our priority to help a thief foolish enough to get caught. What have you learned of Alden's relation to Briar?"

Alden winced as his heart further broke over Kira's dedication to the guild.

"Nothing," said Trod.

"You never learn nothing," argued Pierz.

Squirrel piped up, "He hasn't sailed on *The Albatross* for several months and his office was a mess of useless papers. There was a letter of the princess's kidnapping casually tossed aside. I'm not sure he cares."

"Considering it was she who destroyed his life, I'm not entirely surprised," said Pierz. "Now, anyone have word on Reyn's troop? They should have been here."

Alden glanced at Mayli, who now stood by his side. She pinched her lips together.

"There was talk of thieves dressed as Hioreans found dead southwest of Basevein," said a husky voice.

"Do you have the count?"

"Three."

"Paige?" gasped Trod.

"Shot in the woods."

There was a deafening thud and the wall shook. Alden lifted his head from the wall then slowly pressed his ear back.

"Control yourself Trod. We've lost too many shadows to lose ourselves now. We need to focus on these renegades who nearly took out an entire troop just last night. Who were they?"

"One moved fast and kept to the shadows like a keenreaver. The other had dark skin and wore clean, white silk robes. He wielded dual scimitars."

Alden leaned close to Mayli. "Charli…" he whispered.

She nodded, having heard. Her once fearful face now beamed with hope. Alden took her hand and squeezed.

"Do you suspect it was a random attack or targeted?" asked Pierz.

"Ricky was telling the troop he was following a man in a brown cloak along with a black-haired woman with an orange scarf. Perhaps they heard and wanted in. The reward could make nobles blush."

Mayli tugged on Alden's arm. "Let's go…"

"May, we might find who is behind this…" Alden whispered.

She pulled him away, eyes wide in fear.

Alden looked to her, then the wall where the distant conversation continued. With a sigh, Alden hurried to strap on his armor then hoisted his packed bag to his back. Quietly, he eased the window open, then looked out. Below was a stack of crates.

"No way!" she protested, pointing at the door.

Alden looked at the door leading to the parlor. "Can't go out there, it's likely dark with Shadows. The jump isn't that far," he said in a reassuring tone.

Mayli whimpered as she climbed over the ledge and held on. Alden joined her but hopped down immediately. He looked back up and presented his arms. The princess took a deep breath then hopped down. She fell only momentarily before Alden caught her.

He set her down then jumped to the ground. Reaching up he offered Mayli his hand. She took it, but then pulled away, reeling with horror. Alden looked behind him—blade drawn and ready to fight. But nothing was there. He looked back to see Mayli reaching to grab her scarf which was snagged on the window above. She stood on her toes, trying her best to grab the garment.

Just as she was about to take it between her fingers, the bundle of silk broke free. It danced in a draft of wind, then swept out of view like a forgotten memory.

"That...that was my mother's..." Mayli said, staring in disbelief.

"I'm sorry," he offered sincerely. "Its not easy losing such a treasures, but we really need to run now...if they find it...*us.*"

She hopped down, wiping back tears. "I know..."

Alden squeezed her hand and together they ran from the inn.

DAMN GOODBYES

CHAPTER TWENTY-SIX

"Alden!" Mayli gasped, gripping his arm tightly.

Alden paused mid-bite of a sandwich wrapped in a thin bread. He looked up in concern, but she was beaming.

"Eee!" she squealed with a big grin.

"What?" Alden begged with a smile, curious what had excited her.

"It *was* my guard!" A piece of lettuce was flung out as she pointed with her wrap to a ship in the harbor. Mayli bounced about in a happy dance.

Alden's eyes narrowed at the small, worn sailboat. Its wood was raw and splintered. Barnacles grew on one side. Its sails were torn and weathered. Frayed ropes dangled aimlessly. This vessel made *The Lucky Fish* look like a royal cruiser. "You sure?"

"Yes! See the name? *Her Lady Damgard*. The Damgards have served my family for years! Charli *is* here!" She pulled at his arm.

Alden read the name on the ship. It was freshly painted in white and shadowed in orange. The swirling font was as elegant as any Ammosian calligraphy and clashed with the rest of the ship's aesthetic. "Okay, but before we get too rash, we have to wait and check that it's really him and not someone who knows the name of your guard and is trying to lure you out." He pointed. "That's not a castle-issued ship from Ammos."

The princess looked back at it, as if seeing it for the first time. She nodded. "Okay. But how can we know?"

"We watch." Alden took his last bite of the wrap and scanned the buildings, spying Sea Monster's Grinn. Alden bobbed his head. "Come on."

The tavern was mostly empty, still too early for most nocturnal hoodlums who frequented the pirate island, but it was full enough for them to blend in. Alden leaned heavily against the bar. The Barkeep smiled expectantly, waiting for him to order.

"Brim tea," Alden requested.

The barkeep raised his brow. "Whiskey?"

"Hot tea," Alden clarified. "With cream."

The man shrugged without judgement.

"And an ale," Mayli said, sitting beside him.

Alden looked down at the princess as a foaming stein was placed quickly in front of her. She grabbed it with both hands and took a long gulp, froth kissing her nose. He smiled. Mayli set it down, then noticed his gaze. Before he could tease her, she wiped her face with a playful laugh.

She offered the stein. "Want some?"

He shook his head. "Nah. Don't drink."

Mayli looked at her ale curiously, then back at him. She opened her mouth.

"Alters judgement. Can't think clear... Mistakes can be made," he said, watching the barkeep struggling to pour tea. "I won't risk it again."

She nodded as if understanding, shrugged, and sipped.

"*The Bosun Scraggs* rode a draclynn?" gasped a sailor as he walked in with another man.

Alden and Mayli exchanged humored looks as the two took a seat at the end of the bar.

"Aye! On his head! His leg got bit, but he ripped the tooth out and slayed the beast!"

Mayli brought her stein to cover her snickering mouth, while Alden sucked in his lips to silence his laugh.

The barkeep poured them each an ale. "It's true. He showed us the wound to prove it!" he said, then finally served Alden his tea.

Alden snatched it and pulled away from the bar before he could no longer contain his laugh.

He scanned the open seats and chose one with a view of the harbor and Charli Damgard's ship. Sitting, Alden sipped from his mug. He coughed and spat. He shook his head and snarled at his drink. *Whis-tea?* He rubbed his tongue on the roof of his mouth, trying to sooth the burn—both from the heat and the alcohol.

Mayli sat next to him with her half-drank stein. She tapped his mug. "I know someone who could fix a nice brew for you."

"Yeah. I shoulda just asked for hot water." He shoved it aside. "That is likely the most repulsive thing on this island…"

After an hour watching the ship's small crew mop the deck, secure knots, and carry on supplies, a dark-skinned man finally walked to *Her Lady Damgard*. Trailing behind was a long cape and a cream jacket that stretched down to his knees, hiding blood-stained silks. The tips of two curved swords peered out from the flared opening.

"It's him! Let's go!" Mayli flew from the table.

Alden scurried to follow. Hanging in the doorway, he looked over the flow of traffic. It was noon now, and crowds of people hurried by. Children called out, coaxing the newly arrived travelers to hire them as guides or to give a handout. Entrepreneurs offered baskets of fresh fruits, which were popular to those who had been stuck aboard a ship. A couple carrying planks of wood dropped their loads after a herd of rampaging sheep billowed past, followed by a barking dog and a frazzled man. Among the rush, dock workers hurried to bring crates of goods on and off of ships. Finally, he spotted her blue, linen cloak. She shifted from side to side, looking for a way to break through. Before she could, Alden pulled her into the alley.

"May…"

She frowned. "What?"

"I'm not going with you," he said, looking at the ground. He drew a labored breath and glanced back up. Tears were already dancing in her eyes. He held his own in. "And as far as this trip was concerned, you never met me or Briar."

"What? No! You saved me! You both did! What am I supposed to tell them?"

"You saved yourself after the Shadowens brought you here. You fought them off and escaped, finding Charli. You are smart and strong; they'll believe you. Besides, it's true," he said with an honest smile and lifted a falling tear from her cheek. He held her face with his palm. It beat hot against his skin.

"But why?"

"Because our involvement, even honest and true, will be discredited. So just be happy, May. You'll be home soon—around family and people who love and miss you. Cherish that." He turned from her. "And keep your guard close."

"Alden…" she said after a moment that felt like forever.

He continued to stare off over the shimmering sea. "Yeah?"

She touched his chin and led his face to look at her. "I'm sorry."

"What for?"

"Everything."

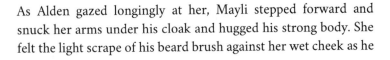

As Alden gazed longingly at her, Mayli stepped forward and snuck her arms under his cloak and hugged his strong body. She felt the light scrape of his beard brush against her wet cheek as he returned the embrace. He held tighter than he had before; more secure than when he was saving her from the Shadowens, or as she cared for him in Brimley, in the cabin, after he slayed the draclynn, or during their embrace last night... Mayli buried her face into the bend of his neck and breathed in his musty and masculine scent, catching a sweet undertone of lavender.

A light peck grazed her cheek as Alden stepped away. She put her hand up to where the thief had stolen a kiss. A deep sense of comfort, love, friendship, and then the loss of it all overwhelmed her in a way she'd never before experienced. She blinked, causing another warm tear to run down her face. Alden left it there and instead ran his hand through her hair.

"It's not goodbye. I promise," he said.

"Another promise? How good are thieves at keeping those?" she asked with a wavering breath.

"Terrible. But I'm not a thief," he reminded her with a wink.

"No, you're my rogue."

Alden smiled and pulled her in to kiss her forehead. As he drew away, Mayli gripped the sides of his hood. He jerked but she swiftly stood on her toes to touch her lips to his. As Mayli continued to press in, his lips parted, creating an opening for her to enter. Her tongue touched his, and at that, Alden caved.

Taking control, her rogue gripped her hair and drew her closer. Together they explored each other's mouths, unifying their love. After a moment that ended too soon, Alden faltered. Then dropped his head, breaking the seal.

Mayli reached to lift his face, but Alden stepped away. As he did, he pressed something cold into her hands. She looked to see his sheathed dagger sitting heavily in her palms. She turned it over, examining it, then looked up, but Alden had disappeared. She gripped the weapon and bit her lip. *He's gone!*

"Alle!" she called, stepping forward to scan the crowd.

The busy sounds of the street buzzed around her, but she heard none of it. She scanned each hooded figure swimming past in the swell of people, but none were him. She tried to call for him once more, but still, there was no response.

Her rogue was gone.

Realizing that had been the last she'd see of Alden, she shut her eyes and wept—flushing out all her pent-up feelings. Waves of emotions hit her with a pounding memory of everything she had experienced with him. He had saved her from the Shadowens. He was there to lift her up when she had fallen in the mud. He had kept her warm. He had fought for her—nearly died for her. Alden respected her and did everything he could to keep her safe. He asked for nothing in return—not even her body or her father's generous reward…

Mayli looked around, knowing he was likely watching her from some far-off and lonely shadow. She nodded and mouthed "thank you." Collecting herself, she focused on the task at hand. The task that he risked his life on completing: getting her home.

It took her a second to find Charli again. He had just finished talking to a man cloaked in black, and now stood at the slipway. He held onto its rail as if debating to step aboard the old ship.

Mayli looked behind her, checking to see if she could say one last goodbye, but all that remained were shadows. She latched Alden's dagger to her belt, took a breath, and merged into the flow of travelers.

A merchant bullied his way in front of her, encouraging her to buy his spiced bread. Although the toasted garlic and rosemary was alluring, Mayli waved her hands, smiled, and ducked under the tray. When she rose, she bumped into a burly man who wore a layering of belts across his waist, shoulders, and chest. Mayli stared in wonder, curious about what all were used for. She smiled innocently as the man began to growl. A hand grabbed her and she turned excitedly, expecting Alden, but it was a sly-looking woman with matted hair. A wild and pale eye scanned her body. As she raised a bony finger up to her, Mayli hopped away and quickly sidestepped to the other side.

Her guard still stood still at the ramp, head low in defeat. She heard him let out a defeated sigh before stepping forward.

"Charli."

He halted. Looked up—then down. He took another step, as if her voice was his own imagination. As he proceeded, Mayli pulled his right shoulder to turn him around.

Alden smiled as Charli greeted Mayli with an enthusiastic hug. The guard pulled away, looking her over, face wrinkled with joy. He then touched her wet cheek and then wrapped his arm protectively around her as he led her on board.

Mayli Drake, the Princess of Ammos was safe.

REVENGE

CHAPTER TWENTY-SEVEN

"*I*'m here for a dagger."

"You are indeed lacking. Might as well walk down the streets naked, my friend." The weapon dealer pulled out a long, triple-edged blade that tapered into a needle-like point. The cross guard was small as well as the handle. "Perhaps a stiletto?"

Alden shook his head.

The man grumbled and pulled it back. With a showy spin, he presented another blade. "More of the cut-and-tear type of fighter then? Might I interest you in this unique dagger from Gezmek? Its trace is unbelievable."

Alden's eyes widened. Besides The King's Blade he'd never seen another black weapon of quality. "If it is truly from Gezmek, it would be a worthy replacement." He humored the man, and himself, and extended his hand to view it.

The dealer tossed the dagger and Alden caught it with ease. It felt heavier than expected. He rubbed his thumb and soon realized why: crude iron. "Unbelievable indeed," he said, tossing it back.

Locked behind an iron-linked display box was a silver dagger. Its blade was straight and extended into a slender point. An arching feather design wound up the sheath and looked as though it continued up the metal handle. It was beautiful. Bold. Intimidating. Alden's lips curled. *Mayli.*

He pointed to it and the man pulled out a string of keys. He fussed with the mess until he found what he thought was the right one. It wasn't. Alden waited another moment as he dug through three more sets. *Even I could have picked the lock faster.*

Finally, the dealer presented the dagger.

Alden unsheathed it. The steel blade sang and winked in a beam of light piercing through a hole in the shop's tarp overhang. Alden spun it in the palm of his hand where it balanced perfectly.

He clamped his fist around the grip. "How much?"

"Two-hundred gold."

Reaching within his coin purse, Alden heard a yelp. Just as he turned to look, a dagger flew past. His eyes grew wide at the knife pierced in the wood beam inches from his face. Instinct kicked in and Alden rolled around behind the display as another whizzed by.

Carefully peering around the corner, Alden saw Trod parting the crowd with angry steps. A woman failed to move. The Shadowen shoved her aside and she collapsed to the ground, blood dripping from her gut. Dark shadows formed in the depths of Trod's eyes as he lowered his head.

Alden plucked Trod's thrown knife from the beam. Gripping the thin handle between his thumb and finger, he tossed it back. Following after, he leapt over the table, kicking a few crude weapons off.

Trod had dodged the blade and was now charging. With a kick, Alden thrust his boot into Trod's gut, sending him into a cabinet of weapons.

Knives flew into the air and glimmered like rain during a sun shower. They crashed to the tile floor, ringing like a dinner bell for thieves. A stranger snuck in and reached to steal a fallen blade. Before he could, Trod snatched the weapon and rolled to his feet. As he did, a spray of yellow powder burst from the Shadowen's hands.

Coughing, Alden waved to clear the air. His eyes watered as he squinted, trying to overcome the stinging cloud. A flash split through the plume and Alden ducked, dodging a blade's swipe.

Trod emerged out of the yellow haze and threw punch after punch—dagger in hand. Alden stepped back, pawing off the attacks. He then sidestepped and stabbed when an opening presented itself. His new blade sunk effortlessly into Trod's back and escaped just as smoothly as the man spun free.

Furious, Trod threw several more jabs in wild succession. Steel sparked as Alden brought his weapon up to defend. He smirked passed the kissing blades as Trod's blood dripped to the hilt. Trod used his other hand to unsheathe a stiletto that ran across his waist. Alden jerked his hips back just as the Shadowen stabbed. The blade struck his breastplate, bruising him, but it didn't pierce.

Their blades slipped apart and they began circling like wolves —growling. After a half turn around the shop, Alden suddenly released two throwing knives he'd stolen off the shop keep's table. One struck. Trod grunted but rushed forward.

As their weapons met once more, the steel of his new blade shifted oddly and he tumbled forward.

A hot sting burned across the brim of his nose. Trod struck again and Alden heard a tear across his chest. His shoulder guard slipped from a now disconnected strap. Pain grew.

Alden raised his knife as he backed towards the exit. He cocked his head to align it with his new blade which now sat crooked. *Broken?*

"You killed Paige!" Trod yelled, pointing his dripping red blade at him.

Alden lowered his knife and smirked. *I still may have a useful weapon after all.*

"Bitch deserved it," Alden lied with a pompous grin.

Trod's eyes grew large and round. His nostrils flared, and he bared stained teeth. With a yell, Trod charged.

Alden shifted his feet through the dirt and bent at the knees, preparing for Trod to pounce. As he came, Alden stepped into him, earning another heated cut across the arm. Using the man's forward momentum, Alden threw Trod over his back. The shadow hit the ground with an unhealthy thud and crack. Alden crept to escape through the door but suddenly Trod threw his legs into the air and spun, colliding into Alden's knees.

He fell to the ground beside the Shadowen. Trod mounted him. Alden blocked a swing then countered with his own stab. It struck, stunning Trod, and Alden pulled out to go for a killing blow. Trod grabbed Alden's wrist and twisted it toward his chest, leaning his full weight into it. The tip threatened Alden's neck, but he fought to keep it away. Trod then kneed him in the side.

Alden cringed as he relived the burn from Reyn all over again. Pain exploded in Alden's shoulder and he cried out. The Shadowen withdrew his wet blade and raised his knife to attack again. Using all of his remaining strength, Alden twisted his body, elbowing Trod in the face. The man skirted to the side, and Alden leapt to his feet and darted into the street, scattering a small crowd. He held his arm and searched for an escape. His eyes met with a boy's. *Squirrel.* A cream-filled pastry hung from his mouth.

Alden raised his crooked blade with his limp arm. He looked around, worried more thieves could reveal themselves.

Squirrel's jaw dropped and his snack fell to the dirt. Alden stared in disbelief as Squirrel dropped the bag of treats and swung his bow—the bow *he* had gifted the boy—off his back and tucked it between his legs to string. Squirrel notched an arrow, looked at him, then released.

Alden winced, expecting death.

"What are you doing?" screamed Trod.

Alden spun. Squirrel's arrow stuck in the ground inches from Trod's feet. *A warning shot?*

"Alden, run!" yelled Squirrel.

Trod rushed forward, snapping the arrow in his way.

Unable to run in time, Alden instead stepped in. He slashed but his blade yet again faltered, allowing Trod to cut through his defense. Alden cocked his head just as the man's knife tore through his hood. Alden saw a few tufts of hair fly out but felt no pain.

A wailing cry rang out as Squirrel charged. Alden hopped back, giving way for the boy to plow into Trod, sending him into a table of silks.

Squirrel sprang up and grabbed Alden's hand. "Run! Pierz is near!"

With the threat of the whole guild nipping at his heels, Alden fled with Squirrel down the road and disappeared into the thick crowd of Canopy Street. They pushed and prodded, but they met with resistance. Tapping his friend, Alden directed Squirrel into an alleyway.

As they rounded the end of the building, they found a dead end. Squirrel looked around nervously, bouncing on his toes. Without missing a beat, Alden jumped at the wall and caught a ledge. He grunted as blood dripped down his shoulder but managed to pull himself up. Alden looked down and held out his other hand. The boy leapt and caught his arm. Squirrel used his feet to help walk up the wall as Alden pulled. Once up, Squirrel put his hands together and boosted Alden to the next ledge. They crawled away from the edge on the roof and sat against a smoking chimney.

The heat warmed Alden's back and he eased into it. Parched from the fight, he took out his waterskin and drank, then offered some to his friend.

"Kira got captured in Dregs! We gotta save her!" Squirrel blurted out after taking a gulp.

Alden rolled his shoulder, testing his mobility and pain tolerance. Everything ached. "No, Squirrel, Kira told Reyn and Pierz about Briar. She's not loyal to me."

The boy shook his head. "But she's the one who knocked me out at the cave! She wanted you to escape... I would have helped too, ya know?"

"That was just a rock that fell."

"Yeah, she threw it on me! I was in a daze but when she crawled back down she checked on me...*apologizing*. She beat herself to look like there had been a fight."

"Beat herself?" Alden closed his eyes. "She's an actress. She likely did that to save herself the embarrassment for not stopping me."

"No! We all helped you save the princess! I saw your drawings at Prince Briar's. You drew every Shadowen except Kira and me. I left the folder, not telling Trod."

Alden looked down at his fingers. He smiled as he counted from four back up to five, accepting Squirrel a worthy friend. He pointed another finger out, then curled it back into a fist, still unsure about Kira. "If she truly was helping, then we shall do the same for her. And if not—" He blew out a breath. "—then she's locked where she belongs. Let's go."

"Wait, you came on this? *You* fought the draclynn?"

"Yep. Killed it myself," Alden said, stepping aboard *The Lucky Fish.*

"Talk is that Captain Scraggs killed it! Rode on its head a hundred feet above the water before stabbing it!" Squirrel picked up a white scale and examined it.

"That's Captain *Bosun* Scraggs!" corrected the man as he

walked to greet Alden, tipping his tricorn hat. "Don't ye be taking away me thunder now." He winked.

"Are you a pirate?" Squirrel asked with excitement. His eyes were big, absorbing every detail of the man.

"Aye lad…" Scraggs said then glanced at Alden. "See ya made a friend."

Alden nodded and glanced around *The Lucky Fish*. There were no longer planks of wood scattered about and the deck was mopped clean. Many parts had already been mended. *Being made a legend had perks.* He faced Scraggs. "What's the status?"

"The shipwrights quoted a week, but that's including a couple upgrades here and there. The rudder was twisted, hence our drunken approach, but that's fixed now too. I've got the boys installing a new mast this afternoon. There are still plenty of fractures in the wood, but we have mended the holes so she'll now stay afloat, just a matter of flushing out her belly of water."

"Great. Bring up the anchor. We have to go."

Captain Bosun Scraggs crossed his arms. "I can't take her out while she's wounded!"

"Eh, I'm wounded too." He rolled his shoulder back and touched it as more blood oozed out. The cut across his nose had stopped bleeding, but the sting still flared. Alden looked back to Scraggs. "Like her, I am alive and can move around regardless of the damage. If you help patch me up and set sail, I'll arrange for Briar to fix your ship up proper back in Dregs. Promise. But right now I need to leave this island."

The captain grinned at the idea. "That does sound nice not to have to use me own gold…" Scraggs rolled a sack of coins from one hand to the other along his fingers as if it were riding a wave. He looked around his crew. "Fine. OKAY, you dry fish! Let 'er loose! We're going for another swim!"

The crew, including Squirrel, responded in a roar of excitement.

A BRIGHT DISGUISE

CHAPTER TWENTY-EIGHT

*T*he room was wrong.

The leather chair, the mountain of papers, William's tack, and books above the mantel were all missing. Briar's coat rack—which was always draped in a collection of jerkins, cloaks, ropes and bridles—now stood naked. A fresh lemony scent lingered instead of horse. Alden could even see the wood from the desk as neat stacks of documents were sorted by date and urgency. A quill, whose feather was clean from stains and was as smooth as if it had been brushed, rested neatly in a silver dish alongside a jar of ink and a wax seal. He snatched the seal and looked at the emblem. It was not the royal crest of Brimley, but that of the guard captain; a snake coiled around a shield. He set it down and turned on his heel. Slow at first, he strolled down the hall, then ran up the staircase.

"Briar?"

A hot flash pulsed within his body, heart thundering in his chest. The bed, nightstand, clothes, weapon rack, extra saddles, chests, tapestries, and even his hideous painting were all missing.

Only a crude kitchenette, a small table, and a wardrobe remained.

As if he were a passenger in his body, Alden walked across the deserted floor of Briar's old home. He found himself looking out the window and could see the castle in the distance where high-strung banners flew in the wind. A jolly repetition of tunes carried along the breeze and tapped irritably on the glass.

As he and Squirrel traveled the back alleys, he had heard a distant voice of a herald. There was mention of a ceremony in a guard's promotion as well as one's funeral.

Briar?

Alden rolled away from the bright sky and joyous world. With eyes pressed firmly shut, he slid down the shiplap until he sat on the wood floor. He folded his arms around his legs and hugged them in, burrowing the depressions of his eyes into his knees. His body shook as he sucked in wavering breaths through the small gap between his legs and chest.

Damnit, Kira.

With a labored breath, Alden drew his head back and rested against the wall, staring into the empty room through a fog of tears. He wiped his eyes and adjusted his hood to hide his flushed face and tilted it to his friend. He cleared his throat. "We need to sneak into the castle somehow."

"That should be easy," said Squirrel as he approached.

"Not without Briar, and he is...gone." Giving up on his brave voice, Alden allowed it to crack, and continued: "And, Squirrel, you and I, we're all right shadows, but...we can't just walk into a guarded castle."

"We can with these!" He tossed a bundle onto Alden's lap and grinned from ear to ear.

The patter of water echoed throughout the plaza, competing with the roar of the crowd. In the fountain's center sat an array of twisted silver and gold snakes, representative of the Draclynn River, holding up an imposing white marble sea monster who spat water down into the basin below. The draclynn. Upon its head rested a tempting yellow sapphire. To any senseless thief, it would seem to be easy pickings. Alden looked to Squirrel, who, to his surprise, resisted the urge.

From the docks, a fisher carted her catch up the hill. Townsfolk outside Dregs were forbidden to cast a line during peak fishing hours, resulting in late night rendezvous. The sun hadn't quite set, and the time for them to fish wasn't legal yet. She spotted Alden staring and hurried away.

Alden tugged at his colorful tabard and grimaced. The bright yellow uniform commanded attention and authority. Squirrel, however, seemed to fit right in and played his role well. Unaware of the fishing curfew, he allowed the woman's passage along with her catch. He did, however, keep his attention on a rowdy group of kids.

They had been following closely behind a noble woman whose purse bobbed against her hip. It jingled with the sway of her hips and sang a song favored among thieves: coin. When one of the girls had reached for it, Squirrel called out in a strong, authoritative voice, unheard from the boy before. The thieves scattered into the closest alleyway.

"Thank the king for such fine guards!" the woman praised, handing Squirrel a silver piece.

Alden raised his eyebrows as Squirrel waved, trying to refuse her. "Just doing our jobs, ma'am!"

The woman insisted, cupping it in his hands, and continued towards the castle.

Squirrel beamed at Alden, teeth shining. Alden grinned too, reminded of his late younger brother, Dominick. Squirrel and he both shared the same goofy smile, tender heart, and rambunctious personality. Dominick also had tried his best to follow in

Alden's footsteps to make him proud. Alden nodded in approval and together they made their way to the gatehouse.

The stone fortress loomed over them like a daunting memory —heavy, stagnant, and unforgiving. Long yellow banners smacked against the wall with a hiss and a snap as if the draclynn stitched upon them was trying to break free of its tethers. Alden followed the flags' pointed direction to where guests showed off their tattoos before entering through the gates.

Squirrel nudged him. It was then that Alden realized he was locked in place, fidgeting. *Shit, without Squirrel I'd probably have found my way into the Binx & Drinx, become drunk for the first time in years, stirred up a fight, and likely gotten myself killed.*

Alden shook his head, and after a deep breath, began climbing the stairs, Squirrel close at his side. As they reached the top, two guards revealed themselves. Out of reflex Alden took a step back.

"What are a couple of Yellow-Coats doing here?" asked the Black-Coat. He spat on the ground and crossed his arms. Before Alden or Squirrel could provide an answer, the guard continued, "You were supposed to be here a turn ago!"

Alden smirked at his foolishness. "We, ah, were caught up protecting our guests from thievery." He gestured towards the noblewoman who waved graciously at them before entering.

"Oh yeah? You Yellows always try to be so honorable, but what's it get you? Late!"

A second guard gave the gruff man a sidelong glance, seething with annoyance. "Their valor also earns them promotions, as Lieutenant Carl's has." She looked back to Alden and Squirrel and calmly addressed them. "Thank you, see to it the event continues to go smoothly. Thomas is in the grand hall. You can meet him there for your assignment."

Alden nodded and stepped toward the gate. Turning from the inviting doorways inside, Alden instead led Squirrel around the castle to the dungeon. The guards looked at them only for a moment before they stepped aside without question.

Locked inside the cells were only a few rough folks. There was a smiley lady with missing teeth, two hoodlums, a merchant, and a group of young noblewomen. Kira was not among them.

Defeated, they left the dungeon. Alden stood in the inner bailey, watching the guests arrive. Lords and ladies entered the castle with cheerful expressions, none seeming to share remorse for Briar's death. *Why would they?*

He glanced to Squirrel, whose eyes shone brightly in awe. *He's probably never been inside a castle before*, Alden realized. Being the good big brother, Alden led him inside.

The grand foyer was marvelously decorated with vases overflowing with bouquets of calla lilies and black roses, tips sprinkled in gold powder.

Alden tipped his head to hide in his helmet as he saw Evelyn Allwell passed them by. Her red hair was held in a gaudy barrette and she wore a bright silver gown which lifted her breasts, drawing looks from each passing man.

She had been Briar's first, dare he say, lover. Alden had seen the way she manipulated him, using his gullibility to elevate herself to a higher status. She led him on to earn gems, dresses, and pretty horses. All things she didn't deserve as she repaid no favors back to the man. Alden glared, seeing a smile and glow across the woman's face as she entered the great hall.

Bitch.

Once she was out of sight, Alden followed, then all air escaped from his lungs.

Dressed in an asymmetrical sleeved jerkin, piped in gold, was a king. And it wasn't Olivar...

A long yellow silk cape draped across his left shoulder and flowed over the throne like rays of sun. The man scratched his head, releasing a wispy strand of blond hair to escape the weight of his grand crown. It had a ring of snakes reaching to the sky, each with an emerald on its head. The golden shine made his hair seem white with age and wisdom in comparison.

An orderly man in conservative attire took a step forward, licked his finger, and then combed the lock back into place. The king sighed and leaned casually against the arm of the throne. His gentleman-in-waiting tapped the new ruler's back so that he stood straight once again. Instead, the king leaned back into the comfort and isolation of his throne, crossing his leg over his knee.

More tears rose to Alden's eyes—no longer from fear and sadness that Briar had died, but joy that he lived...and that he was *king*. Upon his right arm was a fresh tattoo of a shield highlighting the royal crest of Brimley, proving it so.

Alden's cheeks pressed up against the cool steel of his helmet as he grinned. He looked around the grand hall with newfound appreciation of the work put into the celebration. No expense was spared to welcome King Briar to power. Full-roasted boars, tanned by hickory coals, sat seductively on each table. Each was decorated with well-seasoned vegetables and fresh fruits. Slabs of lean meat from assorted slain beasts were arranged platters, bathed in sauce. In the center was a mound of spiced yams, where a river of sweet gravy spilled over like the delta of Dregs. Each place setting had a set of gold dishes accompanied by black linen napkins stitched with the Dreggan coat of arms. Large bouquets of black roses hid candlelit chandeliers that warmed the room with a sweet scent.

A stunningly beautiful woman in a flowing blue dress wandered shyly across the room. Briar quickly stood and a boyish smile filled his once bored face. The king hopped down a step and met her at the base, eager to be by her side. Alden chuckled, happy to see the strings of love raise him off his feet again. The woman shied her head away and Alden gasped in recognition of a cute round nose, strong build, and scar hiding under bangs. *Kira.*

A protective rush of rage flowed through Alden and he found himself reaching for The King's Blade, but it wasn't there; it was now in Ammos. He cursed and looked down to Squirrel, but he was missing. Fearing he too was in on it, Alden scanned faces for Thomas.

A playful cheer rang in the hall and a few nobles clanged forks to their dishes. Alden looked back to Kira and Briar. His heart stopped. They were kissing.

He put his hand to his crooked and nearly useless dagger, watching helplessly as Briar foolishly held her. They concluded their kiss. Face flushed, Briar stepped back to his throne. The king now stood proudly with his back straight as he overlooked his subjects. Kira floated into the crowd as if she rode a cloud. Some applauded. *Damn actress.*

Music began to play. Guests found partners and lined up in the hall's center. Kira quickly stepped back, allowing the dancers space. She watched for a moment, then stole a pastry off a table. She bit into it before sneaking under an arch leading onto the balcony. Noting her leave, Evelyn and her friends followed.

Alden's face sank even lower. *It wouldn't be the first time Evelyn had used the Shadowens to conspire against Briar.*

Alden hurried to follow after the women.

As Alden lurked in the shadows, he watched the nobles position themselves around the thief. Kira smiled at them and a few brief unheard words were spoken.

Alden crept closer.

Suddenly, the nobles pounced, clawing at Kira's dress and pulling bows and ribbons off. Evelyn grabbed her hair and pulled down so that Kira's ear was level with her mouth. "Think you can come in here and assume queen? Briar is *mine!*"

Kira sprang to her instincts and her braid unraveled in the fury. Looking more like herself, she twisted and elbowed Evelyn square in the nose, making it bleed. The noblewoman yelped and fell backward in surprise. Kira's dress tore as she threw a back kick into the stomach of another woman. The thrust gave enough room for the thief to then throw a punch, but the noble was already scurrying toward Alden as he revealed himself.

Evelyn helped her friend up and also ran to him. "She attacked us!"

Kira took a nervous step back, then stopped.

"Yes! She's jealous of Lady Evelyn's past with Briar!" Her friend pointed to Kira.

"Throw her in the dungeon!" Evelyn said, elevating her chin.

As they continued to spew lies, Alden closed his eyes, drowning out their yapping.

"We all know Briar and I are meant to be," Evelyn said, matter-of-factly.

Alden chuckled with irritation, then threw a wicked grin. "Evelyn Allwell, after all of your lies growing up in court, do you really think for a second Briar would believe a siren like you?"

"Excuse me? I've never lied!" Evelyn defended as she took a hesitant step back.

"No? Are you forgetting the last Festival of Gezmek? If I recall, a certain lady hired Shadowens to rig the joust so that Sir Stridan won. Briar was not happy about being embarrassed like that. And what of Sir Stridan now? He tired of being with an unmuzzled bitch?"

"HOW DO YOU...?"

He smirked with satisfaction. "Yeah, so don't cha fucking think Briar would ever consider you! Even without your schemes, your stuck-up attitude strips your nobility to that of a street rat! Get outta here!" Alden barked, sending her and her companions scurrying down the stairs like vermin.

"ALDEN!"

Alden shifted to a defensive position just before Kira leapt at him. To his surprise, he was not greeted with daggers, punches or a fight. What hit him was a strong, friendly, and familiar hug. He couldn't help but return it, breathing in her peppery-scent. *Kira...*

After a tight, lung-crushing embrace, he stepped back and looked her over. "You okay?"

"Yeah, I was handling it. They were annoying but posed no real danger. You didn't need to step in, ya know."

"Yeah…but I've wanted to yell at her for years!" he said with a grin.

"I can see why," she said, rubbing her neck.

"Kira, what happened to you? Squirrel claimed you were locked up but Pierz said you were on a mission." He waited for an answer but she hid her face from him. Alden put his hand to her chin and lifted it gently. Still, she avoided his eyes. "…Kira? Are you?"

Kira shrugged him off, and touched her shoulder, then closed her eyes. "No. I… I'm a noble of Dregs now, Alden." Her voice quavered, as if guilty.

"Huh?" Alden asked while leaning in. He arched his brow, sure he had misheard.

She pulled off the blue lace that draped conservatively over her right shoulder and exposed the yellow and black draclynn that claimed her arm. Alden bent in to investigate. He rubbed it to determine if it was genuine. It was. Alden couldn't help but smile wide. *She's noble…*

Alden stepped around to face her. She was crestfallen—nearly in tears. *She can't be acting.*

She looked at him briefly. "I wasn't helping Pierz or the Shadowens, Alden. Always you. I turned myself in thinking I'd be safe until Briar's return. But Olivar's guards took me up to the others…"

"Others?"

"Women…"

Alden gulped. "The rumors were true? He had a har…" His jaw clenched, prohibiting him from saying the word.

"Harem," Kira finished for him and finally looked up. "Don't worry, he didn't touch me. Only branded me."

Alden began to growl. "If you hadn't already killed him, I'd be slitting his throat right now! King or not."

"*I* didn't kill him! I only gave the other women a means of escape. I promptly fled, but they became…" She bobbed her head back and forth. "Distracted."

"I see…"

There was a brief moment of silence. In it Kira sighed. Alden took off his helmet and looked around absently. Finally, with a soft voice, he found the courage to ask, "So, what's with you and Briar?"

"Hmm?" she hummed innocently.

"The kiss…" he reminded.

"…You saw?"

Alden nodded. He tried to find a smile, but there wasn't one to offer.

She snuck a peek into the hall.

He looked too, catching a glimpse of the new king who danced with an old woman. While Briar twirled, he scanned the crowd, as if searching for a missing face. Alden looked back to Kira, finding it. She smiled briefly before averting her gaze to the floor, then shuffled her feet.

Kira's cheeks flushed, unable to hide her ever-growing smile. *She is happy… She deserves it. Deserves a king who can provide.* Alden chuckled and leaned into her view. He raised his brow and presented a cocky smile, trying to overcome his own jealousy. "You've been sleeping together." It wasn't a question.

He hadn't thought her face could have glowed any redder, yet it had. Alden forced a wry smile. "Nice."

"Shut up." Kira pushed him. He acted with her and took a fumbling step back.

Alden smiled further and put his hands out. "Come on, he deserves a good Dreggan noble like you."

"Shut up!" Kira yelled again, stepping forward to beat a fist to his chest.

Alden endured the assault and frowned. *She wasn't being playful.* She kept her fists clenched and her jaw began to tremble as she glared at the emblem of Dregs stitched onto the yellow tabard he wore. *She really isn't acting.* Alden took a step forward and pulled her in. She wrapped her arms around his waist, burying her face into his chest.

"I'm sorry, Ki." Alden kissed her forehead before resting his chin comfortably on the top of her head.

She sniffled. "You always blame yourself for things that aren't your fault! It's okay… I'm only scared."

He nodded and hugged her tighter. "We'll keep you safe."

"Safe?" She chuckled. "No, I don't fear my safety, Alden." She stepped back.

"Then, what scares you?" he asked, holding her arms.

"Quite a few things. But one being is I…" She laughed, brushing an invisible hair from her face. "Nah, it's stupid."

"Nothing you do is stupid."

She peered up with huge brown eyes. "I, uh, don't know how to be noble. I'll ruin everything."

He chuckled. "I'm sure the actress can figure that out; it's easier than you think."

"Alden, everyone's seen us now and expect a dance, but I never have like that and now I look a mess!" She pulled off a loose thread. "I shouldn't have come. I can't go back in there!" She gestured toward the hall, frowning.

"If you are worried, let me show you how." Alden held out his hand.

"How what?"

"How to dance." Alden crossed his arm to his shoulder then bent at the waist. He peered up at her from his bow and offered his hand.

Alden's hand cupped Kira's tenderly as she took a step in. He placed his other respectfully on her tattooed shoulder. With a gentle squeeze, he pulled her nearer. His musty scent hugged her, calming every worry.

Kira stared at Alden in a daze. He smiled politely and averted his eyes. Embarrassed, she did too and focused on his movements. Alden stepped forward, leading her back. She stumbled slightly, not anticipating him to move to the right.

"Just mirror my feet and follow. Feel the rhythm. Don't think," he offered.

Kira nodded with a flushed face. "A bit different than teaching one how to fight..."

Alden smirked then started off again. This time she moved fluidly with him and completed several circles around the balcony in a whimsical trot. Alden moved perfectly, without missing a beat. It was fun—freeing. With each step they took, her heart lifted, just like every time she was beside this man.

Kira peered up at her handsome partner with a warm, glazed smile, but he was somber. She stopped. Alden looked down at her, brokenhearted.

Mayli...

"Is the princess safe now?" Kira asked.

He blinked, as if not expecting the question. With a nod, Alden took a step away. He rested his arms over the stone rail and looked out over the moonlit ocean. She watched as a long frown formed over his face and he closed his eyes with an unsteady sigh.

"You're doing it again."

He opened his eyes.

"Blaming yourself."

He gave a flat, tired smile.

Kira turned him from the sea. She then grabbed his chin through his overgrown beard and eyed him. "You're a hero."

Alden swept her hand away. "I'm nothing like that."

"Bullshit. You are to me! And now Mayli—she'll remember you for that."

Alden took in a deep breath and rolled his shoulders to stand proud.

There's the man I know.

"Thanks, Ki."

"You betcha!" she said, putting her hands to her hips. A bow fell to the ground.

"Here," he said, pulling his dagger free from its sheath.

She smiled at him as he brought the knife to a frayed ribbon. The blade shifted oddly and he struggled to use it. She glanced down. Her mouth opened in surprise. The blade wasn't the rare and expensive black ore from Gezmek.

"Where's your grandfather's blade?" she asked.

Alden froze.

Kira smiled wide, watching his eyes narrow as if trying to comprehend what she had just said. She began to snicker.

Alden's mouth gaped like a fish. Then he flattened his lips and shook his head. "Dunno what chu're talking about, Ki," he said with a nervous and thick Brimleyn accent. He focused on trimming her dress.

"*Your* black knife."

Alden laughed at her sheepishly. "Oh. That old blade was just crude iron… I never had enough to upgrade till now."

"You upgraded to a crooked weapon?" Kira rolled her eyes. "No, you kept that blade from me because it had been King Edune's knife." she said, poking his chest. "I'm your best friend, not an idiot, *Colin.*"

The cold steel of his new knife now threatened her neck. *One swipe and I could die* she realized, but Kira didn't flinch. She smiled instead.

Her king leaned in until he was an inch from her face, flames of panic burning within his eyes. "I know you gave my connection to Briar up to the guild! Reyn nearly killed me and you know what he would have done to May! Best friend? How can I trust you?"

"Yeah, I had to give them something so I didn't look guilty too! You didn't leave me much choice! Besides, I wanted to be tasked to Dregs so I could warn Briar! Ask him or Thomas!"

Alden growled and broke his gaze from hers. "Reyn said you willingly slept with him."

"I did."

"What!" He snapped his attention back to her, pained and furious.

"It was the only way he'd allow for you to be on the mission."

"Kira..."

"I had to! If the princess were to see the man you truly are, perhaps she would learn to reconsider her judgement, just as I had." She slipped her hand free and placed it to his shoulder where she knew the royal crest of Brimley hid. "I'd do anything for my king... For you."

Alden's eyes pained and his head fell, weighing heavily against hers.

She patted him. "*Alden*," Kira cooed. "I've kept your secret safe. Always will." Kira squeezed his shoulder tenderly.

He released the dagger from her neck and wrapped his arms around her. Her king held on tight, nearly suffocating her. She rested her face in the curve of Alden's neck, feeling his quick pulse as he took in wavering breaths.

After a long, heartfelt embrace, Kira didn't believe he'd ever let go, so she pulled away. As she passed by his cheek, she kissed it. "I love you."

"Kira..." he choked.

"Don't worry, not the way how lovers are, though I had once wished to see us like that once..." She blushed at the lie, having never lost that fantasy. She focused back on his puzzled face. "No, I don't love you romantically or even like family. I love you the way someone loves their name, their home, or their reason to live. I've loved you, Colin, because you are my king." She reached to touch his face once more, hesitated, and instead placed it back on her own shoulder. She bowed respectfully.

A commanding finger lifted her chin from her bow and their gazes met. Her king caressed her cheek with the back of his hand to brush a hair behind her ear. As he kept constant eye contact, he traced his hand slowly down her neck, sending shivers down her spine. Then, he squeezed her shoulder possessively. "I've loved you too."

Her mouth dried.

Alden's eyes trailed to her lips and his own parted slightly. As he leaned in to kiss, Kira nodded awkwardly and looked away in mock search. "So…" She patted her legs. "Where is it?"

"What?" He cleared his throat.

"The King's Blade. *Your* blade."

He stepped back. "Gave it to May."

Kira raised her brow and blinked in disbelief. Twice she had held his dagger, but she had stolen it both times. She hadn't known he was the heir of King Edune then. The weapon and the man each earned her respect once she had. For Alden to give up his most cherished belonging, especially to Mayli, shook her. The blade was one of the few things Alden had left of his past. "Why?"

"I owed her for something precious I think I took from her…"

"Virginity?" Kira kidded playfully.

"Ah hah! *No!*" He laughed as he cut another tattered bow off her dress and brushed her shoulder free from fibers. He frowned. "Her mother."

❦

"What's a Yella' doing over here?"

Briar stood up from his throne, breaking conversation with a tall and plump noblewoman to look. A young man—no more than fourteen, Briar guessed—was cornered near the dessert tables. He was dressed in a Yellow-Coat and was being hounded by several hard-faced Black-Coat guards. He chewed a stolen treat as he tried to explain himself, but the bits of crumbs falling out of his mouth did little to help his case.

An attractive face parting the crowd of onlookers pulled Briar's attention away from the arguing guards. After she ducked past a couple dancing, Briar saw her torn and tattered dress, frayed hair, and concerned frown.

"What's going on? What happened to you?" he said, reaching for Kira.

"I'm fine, but you need to help him." Kira pointed at the boy.

"He's not part of my guard."

"He's a friend," said a familiar voice.

Briar snapped his attention to the man in the yellow guard's uniform who had escorted Kira. His cousin.

"How'd you? Where's…?"

"She's home. And I had come here to save her," Alden nudged Kira, who grinned innocently. They smirked at each other as if sharing a secret.

"And him?" Briar looked at the boy.

"That's Squirrel," Kira answered with a squint of her eyes.

"Squirrel…" Briar grimaced at the name. *The stories Alden has told…*

"Yeah, do ya mind?" he pleaded, nodding to Squirrel who was now grabbed by the scruff.

Briar rubbed his face. "Yeah…"

"Earl," he said as he walked toward them. "You were assigned to the outer corridors. Have you forgotten your way around already?" Briar asked as he stepped within the ring of questioning. The boy's eyes grew huge and he stopped chewing—cheeks still stuffed. Briar held in a laugh. *He really does look like a squirrel.*

The boy shifted his eyes, seeing Alden beside him. Alden was smirking, just as amused. Finally Squirrel swallowed. "OH! Yes! Sorry, king! Sorry! I came in to ask uh, Thomas, when I got…

distracted." Squirrel pulled out a pocketed cookie and set it back on a table. It broke apart upon contact.

Briar shook his head. "You're new, so I'll forgive it this one time, but be warned, if you are unable to follow simple orders or keep focused, you won't last among the guards anymore." He turned to Alden. "Nick, would you escort him?"

Alden placed his hand on his shoulder and bent into a perfect bow. "Of course, Your Majesty," he said with an act of class, then turned to Squirrel. "Come, *Earl*, the outer corridor is this way."

The Black-Coats looked from their king, to Alden, and then to the young guard. They sneered but released the boy. Squirrel awkwardly bent at an attempt at a bow, crossing the wrong arm, and skirted against the wall so Alden could collect him.

"Continue the good work, lads," Briar told the Black-Coats before finding his way back to Kira.

He hooked his arm around her waist and smiled, but she looked away in shame. Several guests were staring at them with the same face he had been accustomed to seeing as guard captain: judgmental, ugly, and mean. He narrowed his eyes back at them and they turned away. Briar turned to Kira. The dress he had left out for her in hopes that she would join the party wearing it was in ruin. Bows were missing, threads hung loose, and the hem was splitting at her shoulder, boldly exposing the Dreggan crest. There was even a faint scratch on her face like a cat's whisker. *Training the thief to be noble will be harder than expected.*

She stepped away to follow Alden and Squirrel, but Briar kept hold on her hand, lightly tugging her back. She turned and looked shyly around the crowd, noting the whispering faces. Briar kept his gaze solely on her, then placed one hand on her shoulder.

"Will you dance with me?"

Kira shifted her big brown eyes to catch his confident gaze. She gulped, stepping in to boldly cover his royal tattoo. Briar smiled wide, cupping her other hand. He kissed it and she finally smiled.

Heart racing, Briar tapped his fingers to find the rhythm of the music. Having found it, he stepped her back. Together they glided around the room, uncaring that all eyes were judging them. Kira's dress twirled as he lifted her and bits of loose thread fell asunder, leaving the dance floor layered in gold and blue silk.

The series continues in

Book Two of The King's Renegade

BURDEN

GLOSSARY OF TERMS AND NAMES

ALDEN: A rogue loyal to Brimley; artist

ALLE: Nickname given to Alden by Mayli

AMBER: A shy, young, round woman in Olivar's harem

AMMOS: Large northern desert island kingdom that specializes in archery; colors are orange, white, and black

ARKELLO DENSEN: Claims to be from Gezmek as the true heir of King Edune

BAKHARI DRAKE: King of Ammos

BASEVEIN: Town built upon a series of bridges and islands crossing the huge sea-like lake at the base of Mount Hiore; ruled under Hiore

BLACK-COAT: High-ranking guard of Dregs

BOSUN SCRAGGS: Captain of *The Lucky Fish*

BRIAR DENSEN: Prince of Brimley; Captain of the guard in Dregs; Colin's cousin; son of Jamus and Trish Densen

BRIM NOSE: Insult given to Brimleyns

BRIM TEA: A black tea with lavender and vanilla that is served with cream; Alden adds orange peel to give it an Ammosian flare

BRIMLEY: Fallen kingdom in the western woods of Vatan; colors are blue, black, and gray

CAD ISLANDS: A cluster of islands in Zollner's Bay near the southwestern tip of Vatan where pirates, thieves, and rogues take refuge in the bohemian life

CANTWELL INN: Hub for the Shadowen Thieves Guild located in the center of Colville

CARL: Yellow-Coat Guard of Dregs who later is promoted to lieutenant

CHARLI DAMGARD: Mayli Drake's personal guard

COLE: Fake name Reyn gave himself

COLIN DENSEN: Outcast Prince of Brimley; accused of murdering Queen Margaret Drake of Ammos; Briar's cousin

COLVILLE: Mining and port town ruled under Hiore; north east tip of Vatan

CROWN MOUNTAINS: Span of large mountains in the north

DEAN WILKUS: Marshal of Brimley; miller after the war

DESERT OF GEZMEK: Huge desert spanning half of Vatan in the south; known for its traveling sand dunes

DOLO: Pirate on *The Lucky Fish;* fisherman

DOMINICK DENSEN: Colin's younger brother; passed from fever at age eight

DRACLYNN RIVER: River that flows from Lake Ironmere and runs south through northern Vatan, connecting to Zollner's Bay

DRACLYNN: Sea monster covered in thick white scales with a wolf-like head, wing-like fins, and a long snake-like body that ends with many tentacles

DREGS: Kingdom at the delta of the Draclynn River, consisting of many islands

DUNE ALE: An extremely potent liquor from Gezmek

EARL: Squirrel's new name, dubbed by Briar

EDUNE: King of Vatan when Gezmek fell

EMMA: Mayli's alias

EMORY: Colin's horse

ERYN WRIGHT: Blacksmith from Brimley; leader of Olivar's harem

EVELYN ALLWELL: Noblewoman; ex-lover to Briar Densen

EXTEN: One of Briar's royal knights

GALLIVANT: Name of Jamus Densen's saber

GAVIN HENMURY: Prince of Hiore; looking to wed Mayli Drake

GEZMEK: Lost kingdom buried underneath the traveling sand dunes in Ammos

GINA COLTE: King Olivar's sister

HAILEY: Youngest girl in Olivar's harem; Thomas's daughter

HER LADY DAMGARD: Small ship Charli Damgard used to search for Mayli

HIORE: Kingdom ruling around the Crown Mountains; the towns of Colville and Basevein are under its control; known for their quality steel; colors are purple, black, and gray

JAIR DRAKE: Mayli's younger brother

JAMUS DENSEN: Briar's Father; brother to King William; Prince of Brimley

JIM: Pirate on *The Lucky Fish;* cook

KANAVAUR: A large, ancient, crustacean-like creature with claws; has tentacle-like acidic jowls; lives in the sand; lays eggs; silk used for crafting

KEEGAN: Mayli's carriage guard

KEENREAVER: A fabled creature who hunts and steals at night

KIRA HARLOW: Shadowen thief; shadow seeker

LAKE IRONMERE: Lake under Mount Hiore; source of the Draclynn River

LIDIA: Mayli Drake's lady-in-waiting

LILY DENSEN: Late Queen of Brimley

LOST TREASURE OF GEZMEK: Fabled legend of great wealth buried with the city of Gezmek in the sand in Ammos

MARGARET DRAKE: Late Queen of Ammos

MARY WILKUS: Wife of Dean; baker

MAYLI DRAKE: Princess of Ammos; master archer; was on her way to meet Prince Gavin when ambushed by the Shadowens

MR. GREY: Old man who owns The Five Leaves tea shop in Colville

NICK: Alden's alias

NOBLE'S DICE: Betting game using a twenty-sided die

OLIVAR COLTE: King of Dregs; Briar's uncle

PAIGE: Shadowen thief; pathfinder

PIERZ: Leader of the Shadowen Thieves Guild

REK: Alden's one-eyed black cat with a white chin

REYNOLD: Shadowen Thieves Guild shadow commander; assassin; master of poisons; better known as Reyn (pronounced "Ren")

RICKY: Shadowen thief

SAMMIE: A thin, chipper girl in Olivar's harem

SAND STRIDER: Large bird-like creatures used for riding in the desert; their feathers are used for fletching

SHADOW COMMANDER: Second in command in the Shadowen Thieves Guild

SHADOW SEEKER: Position in the Shadowen Thieves Guild; individual gathers information

SHADOWEN THIEVES GUILD: Notorious thieves guild stationed at the Cantwell Inn in the center of Colville

SHADOWEN: Someone belonging to the Shadowen Thieves Guild

SICAN: Pirate on *The Lucky Fish*; barrelman

SIR STRIDAN: Winner of the Bahar Festival earning nobility; witness of Queen Margaret's murder

SQUIRREL: Shadowen ranger; archer; thief

TAREK: One of Briar's royal knights

TAVERN SEA: Eastern Sea

THE ALBATROSS: Large galley ship owned by Briar Densen

THE BINX & DRINX: Tavern in Dregs

THE BRIM WAR: War against Brimley after their prince, Colin Densen, was accused of murdering Queen Margaret Drake of Ammos

THE FESTIVAL OF GEZMEK: A celebration that honors unity across Vatan, hosted between Ammos, Brimley, Dregs, and Hiore every three years

THE FIVE LEAVES: Mr. Grey's tea shop where Alden lived while in the guild

THE LUCKY FISH: Captain Bosun Scragg's ship that has a narrow hull fitted with oars, an angled foremast, and red sails

THE SEA MONSTER'S GRINN: Inn along the docks in the Cad Islands

THIELEN'S LODGE: Inn in the Cad Islands

THOMAS: Lieutenant of the Guard in Dregs

TRISHA COLTE: Briar's late mother; married to Jamus Densen

TROD: Shadowen thief; traps specialist

VALOR: Name of Briar's saber

VATAN: The country composed of the five small kingdoms of Ammos, Brimley, Dregs, and Hiore

VERIDIA: Hiorean knight

WAYPOINT: Inn in Basevein

WILLIAM DENSEN: King of Brimley

WILLIAM: Briar's black warhorse; named after King Liam when he passed in the war

YELLOW-COAT: Common guard of Dregs

ZOLLNER'S BAY: Western Sea

ACKNOWLEDGMENTS

BETA AND ALPHA READERS

Amanda Johnson * Amanda Why * Aubry Carpenter * Caitlin Circk Vaga * Chris Holmes * Dorothee Ledermann * Jamie Kornahrens * Kelly Tamburello * Kirsten Lynn * Livi Sprick * Louise-Jayne * Haddaway * Lucy Summers * Nikaya Chausmer * Patricia Favreau * Renée Purdie * Stephanie Shields * Tia Nicole Pennells * Virginia Merrill * Will McDow * Ximone Willis

SPECIAL THANKS

200 Rogues * Aarika Deanna Copeland * Patty Earp * Amanda Johnson * Bakhari Burrell * Brian Lewis * Chris Holmes * Doug Turner * Erica Russikoff * Ethan McDaniel * Garrison Tyrone-Alexzander Garner II * Jamie Kornahrens * Kelly Tamburello * Kim Gibson * Kirsten Lynn * Lasse Suurmunne * Livi Sprick * Louise-Jayne Haddaway * Lucy Summers * Linn Tesli * Nikaya Chausmer * Patricia Favreau * Reika Hayashi * Stephanie Shields * Than Blood * Will McDow * Ximone Willis

DEDICATIONS

Pat Terry: Mum, you are the strongest person I know. Thank you for your continued strength, courage, and creativity! You are my hero. I am overjoyed to be able to share this with you.

Chris Holmes: My beloved. You are my world. With you, my true love fantasy story has come to life, as well as the one in this book. Thank you for your patience, support, friendship, and love.

Virginia Merrill: Nana, although we do not have everything in common, we can share the joy of art, passion, and perseverance to achieve anything. Thank you for your unconditional support and for encouraging me to share my work with you and now the world.

Matt Colville: Without seeing you write your books, discuss your process, and get tips as to move forward, I'm not sure I could have had the confidence to take that first step and pursue my dream. In my copy of your first novel *Priest*, you wrote: *Writers crave readers, but we like friends better.* Thank you for being mine.

Jamin Mitchelle aka The Bosun Scraggs: Thank you for lending me your knowledge of seafaring, and of course, your name.

Fran Nardone: My Mayli. Thank you so much for allowing me to paint your likeness to represent the beautiful Princess of Ammos. You made a dream come alive.

Thank you for reading Asunder, Book One of The King's Renegade. Any and all feedback on this debut novel is encouraged, so please take a moment to review on Amazon, Goodreads, Facebook, and blogs.

Keep updated on social media!

www.theartofliz.com
www.instagram.com/theartofliz
www.facebook.com/AuthorLsteinworth
www.twitter.com/Liz_Steinworth

37222730R00187

Made in the USA
Middletown, DE
23 February 2019